At the height of the Sp....... by the name of Bishop Promane tortures a fellow priest, Father Sanchez, for information about the whereabouts of a relic known as the Judas Robe, rumored to be the only piece of physical evidence of God on earth. Promane succeeds in recovering the robe only to lose it to Sanchez's saviors, knights belonging to The Order of Christ.

In the Present Day, Joel Gardiner, a pre-med student, is attacked by a group of religious zealots after leaving a campus pub. A young woman calling herself Sophia rescues Joel and reveals that he is descended from of the Order of Christ who still has the Judas Robe in their possession. Joel dismisses it as a hoax or farce, but zealots renew their efforts to seize the robe. Joel and Sophia embark on a quest to verify the existence of the so-called relic while trying to elude the murderous cabal.

Praise for Larry Rodness' new novel The Judas Robe

"If you had a chance for proof-positive of God's existence on earth, would you go for it?... The author's med-student protagonist, Joel Gardiner, finds himself suddenly faced with just that dilemma...Here's a novel for those looking for an unusual plot-line with lots of action and adventure." — *William Maltese: Amen's Boy; A slip to Die For; Thai Died; A Conspiracy of Ravens*

"In the spirit of a Dan Brown thriller, *The Judas Robe* cleverly fulfills the promise of its thought-provoking subject. Like the fine weave of a robe, Rodness intertwines his inspired premise with theology, mystery, action and suspense to engage the reader in the timeless battle between science and religion, which couldn't be more relevant today."—*Stephen Witkin, Screenwriter, Los Angeles*

"...a ride of mystery and suspense. The pacing and character development are exactly on point. It is a book you will not want to put down. No matter what side of God versus science you are on, this book is for you."—*Carol Itoh, Itoh Press*

"...historical drama and traverses through time, bringing the mysteries of the past into modern day. But what is this relic and why the desperate need to obtain it?...*Judas Robe* will keep you turning page after page, wanting more."—*Lisa Maine, editor*

"Larry Rodness weaves together Biblical interpretation, Crusades-era lore and modern-day pulp fiction into a single, smart and gritty timeline..."—*Alex Shifrin, writer for Playboy Russia, The eXile and Afisha, President LP/AD*

Excerpt

Mother Natalie entered the room wearing a standard white blouse and navy skirt. That was the only thing standard about her. Standing five foot seven, she had sparse feather-like hair. Her skin was almost translucent, and her slight-build made her look like she would tip over at the slightest breeze.

"Joel, isn't this a nice surprise," the nun said.

"Someone in my dorm was murdered last night. Do you know anything about it?"

"No, of course not. How would I?"

"A couple of nights ago, I was jumped by two men."

"Oh my, you weren't hurt, were you?"

"I'm all right. Mostly, because this girl intervened."

"What girl?"

"Goes by the name of Sofia. She said the thugs who attacked me were after something called the Judas Robe."

Natalie emitted a tiny gasp as the look of concern on her face turned to fear. "What did you tell her?"

"I told her I had no idea what she was talking about.

But I'm here because my mother and her wacked-out family have been part of some religious cult for years."

THE JUDAS ROBE
Larry Rodness

Moonshine Cove Publishing, LLC

Abbeville, South Carolina U.S.A.
First Moonshine Cove Edition Sep 2020

ISBN: 978-1-945181-931
Library of Congress PCN: 2020918345
© Copyright 2020 by Larry Rodness

This book is a work of fiction. Names, characters, places and incidents are products of the author's imagination or are used fictitiously. Any resemblance to actual events, locales or persons, living or dead, is entirely coincidental.

All rights reserved. No part of this book may be reproduced in whole or in part without written permission from the publisher except by reviewers who may quote brief excerpts in connection with a review in a newspaper, magazine or electronic publication; nor may any part of this book be reproduced, stored in a retrieval system or transmitted in any form or by any means electronic, mechanical, photocopying, recording or any other means, without written permission from the publisher.

Cover image by Miki de Goodaboom, Cover design by Erin Rodness, interior design by Moonshine Cove staff.

To Sophie and Stella who are much too young to read this.

About the Author

Larry Rodness began his entertainment career as a professional singer at the age of 19 in Toronto, Canada and continued in the business for over 40 years. In the 80's Larry studied writing in various disciplines which led him to compose music and lyrics for theatre, screenplays, and novels. In the past 10 years Larry has published the following novels,

"Today I Am A Man" – 2010 – Savant Publishing

"Perverse" 2012 – Itoh Press

"October 32nd" – 2105 – Deer Hawk Publications

"Crystal Vision" – to be published 2020 – Deer Hawk Publications

"The Judas Robe" to be published Oct, 2020 – Moonshine Cover Publishers

"Urban Myths" is his current project.

https://www.larryrodness.com

Acknowledgment

To my Writers' Block group including Reva, Herb, Deedee and especially my loving wife, Jodi.

The Judas Robe

CHAPTER 1

"Bishop, scripture teaches that God is beyond the physical reach of this world," Father Sanchez said. "The only way to the Eternal is through faith and prayer. No golden calves, no magic, no potions. To seek him by any other means is blasphemy, a sin."

"And what is sin, Father, but the single most important quality that engenders us to God," replied Bishop Promane. "We are born of sin, made from the very essence of sin. If there was no sin, there would be no need for God to save us from it. How many souls have been converted to the faith through fear of eternal damnation? Thousands? Millions? Sin is what keeps us forever tethered to the church. It is its greatest ally. Without sin, religion would crumble." The bishop took a moment for his words to sink in and then came to the point of his discourse. "The robe."

"I know nothing of a robe, Bishop." Father Sanchez said as rivulets of sweat ran down his bald pate and along the creases in his neck.

Instead of replying the bishop let the silence hang in the air like a weapon. It was one of many he'd cultivated over the years. His imposing physicality was another. The bishop was a solidly built man with a ruddy complexion and aquiline nose. His dark hair fell about his shoulders framing coal colored eyes that gleamed when his ire was up. It was up now. He swept his robe back and hovered over the priest so that they were almost nose to nose.

"Now you are guilty of the sin of lying! We found the scroll in your apartments."

"I do not deny having the scroll. But it is written in Aramaic. I have no idea what it says."

Bishop Promane sighed deeply. This was not going well. He did not enjoy these 'examinations,' especially that of a fellow priest. But his duty was to the church first and foremost. There was a hiss of hot metal being dipped into water and it made Father Sanchez's heart race.

"Have no fear, father. I'm sure your faith will sustain you."

Bishop Promane nodded to one of his guards who brought a searing, hot iron over to the rack Father Sanchez was strapped to. The guard stood over the trembling, half naked man. The bishop gestured to a spot on the priest's body and without hesitation the guard pressed the iron into the priest's ribs, making his flesh sizzle.

"Ahhhhhh!" screamed Sanchez.

"My apologies, Father. So?"

Sanchez feared pain as much as any man. But he feared the consequence of acquiescing to the bishop's request even more. The cleric's body quivered. He raised his tear-filled eyes to the ceiling and began to pray. It would all be over in a matter of minutes. Bishop Promane nodded to the guard who tightened the ropes on the rack another notch. 'Pop' went the priest's left shoulder as it separated from its socket. Sanchez screamed again but remained resolute. The bishop was impressed, not just by how well the priest withstood pain, but that his obstinate nature confirmed that he must have the knowledge the bishop was seeking. The poor man only needed the proper incentive.

"I do admire your tenacity, Father, but time is a weighing factor and the Pope is an impatient fellow."

"Please..." cried Father Sanchez, "I cannot tell you what I do not know."

The inquisitor shook his head and then nodded to another guard who stood at the top of the stone staircase by a door, high above the dimly lit chamber. The sentry exited the dank room and returned a moment later with a confused and terrified maiden who looked to be in her late teens. The slim brunette was forced down the steps, faltering every so often on the granite stone, slick with moss and blood. At the bottom of the chamber she was led past various torture devices that included the iron maiden, the breaking wheel, the knee splitter, and strappado. The sight of them sent her stomach into spasms. Even more bewildering was the sight of Father Sanchez bound to the rack with his limbs stretched beyond their natural limits. The priest sensed the girl's presence and turned to find his young charge standing over him.

"Dear God," he said as a new dread gripped him.

"I have failed and only have myself to blame," said Bishop Promane. "You are free to go."

The guard untied Father Sanchez's ropes. His long, angular body slid to the ground as his joints buckled with pain. One of the guards helped him to his feet while another other forced Sofia to take his place.

"Father?" cried the distraught maiden.

"No! Please..." said Sanchez.

Bishop Promane ripped the girl's dress from her body and exposed her nakedness to the guards' lascivious gaze. The guards began to lash her arms and legs to the device with blood-soaked ropes. Steeling herself, she looked defiantly into Bishop Promane's eyes, "You might take my body but never my soul."

The Bishop returned her defiant stare with an admiring look. "Brave words, Sofia. I am told you also have a younger sister, Belle?"

Father Sanchez, who was bracing himself against one of the machines, began to whimper. Sensing victory, Bishop Promane leaned into the priest again.

"Whisper to me where the robe is and I promise this sweet child and her sister will never endure a moment's pain."

With labored breaths, the priest whispered the words his provocateur was so anxious to hear. Bishop Promane smiled and ascended the staircase. Then he stopped and turned back.

"Come, Father, you'll accompany me."

Sanchez looked worriedly at the bishop's hostage.

"She will remain here until the robe has been recovered." Turning to his guards, he said, "No one is to touch her."

Two guards bolstered Father Sanchez under his arms and escorted him up the staircase.

"Place your trust in the Lord," Father Sanchez called out to Sofia. "He will not abandon you."

After Promane led Sanchez out of the chamber, the heavy wooden door slammed shut, leaving the girl trembling on the rack.

* * *

The monastery stood in the midst of a large, barren field. The sky above it was murky and cloud-filled. A stiff breeze blew across the pampas as if warning all God's creatures to take cover. There were no high walls, moats, or parapets to protect the structure, for this was a sanctuary open to all those seeking the shelter and comfort of the Lord. Bishop Promane and his guard stood a hundred paces away, at the edge of a forest. He turned to Sanchez who lay propped up in a donkey cart.

"In there," Father Sanchez said. "Where, exactly, I do not know, and that is the truth."

Bishop Promane took the donkey by the reins and pulled the cart across the grassy loam to the monastery door.

"Father Ignatius?" called the bishop.

There was no reply from within. Nor was one expected. Promane withdrew his sword and hammered its hilt against the door.

"Father Ignatius, I am Bishop Promane, here by order of Pope Sixtus 111 who demands that you hand over the relic known as Judas's Robe." His request was met again with silence. "You are surrounded, there is no way out. Father Sanchez's immortal soul and many others rest in your hands. Know that your silence condemns them."

Within the walls of the monastery, a small group of priests stared out at the threatening forces. The abbot, Father Ignatius, turned to his brethren.

"This is the moment we have dreaded. None of us would stand up very long to this inquisitor."

With resolved looks the priests nodded in agreement. "We understand," replied Father Grappelli on behalf of the others.

Bishop Promane did not actually expect the priests to fling open the doors and embrace him. But after five minutes there had been no response and he was an impatient man. Satisfied in the knowledge that he acted in a lawful manner, he turned to his second in command who ordered his soldiers to advance on the door with a battering ram. After several blows, it splintered and gave way. The soldiers rushed in with weapons drawn but they were not prepared for the sight that met them. Laying there on the ground were over a dozen dead priests. Promane could see knife wounds at the backs of their necks. They had all allowed themselves to be slain. A quick movement off to his left caught Promane's eye. Father Ignatious came into view at the top of the steps that led to the main hall. He sneered at Promane and lifted his eyes to the heavens.

"Forgive me, father," Ignatious said.

Then he dragged a knife across his own neck. Blood spurted from his artery and he fell where he stood. Bishop Promane rushed to his side and pressed his hand against the wound to try to stem the flow of blood.

"Father, suicide is a sin against God. I can save your immortal soul. Tell me, where is the robe?"

Father Ignatious could not speak, nor would he if he had the chance. A calm came over him, he closed his eyes, and allowed his spirit to take flight.

"Burn in hell for all I care," said the Bishop. Composing himself, Promane turned to his second, "Release them."

The lieutenant ran to the gates and repeated the orders given to him. Promane called out, "Stand back or perish!"

A large, heavy cart was wheeled to the doorway. Inside was a gruesome pair of malevolent canines.

"Find me the robe," the bishop said to the animals, "And I'll make you a feast fit to burst those hungry bellies of yours."

The animals snarled in response. The soldiers stepped back fearfully as the door of the cage was lifted. The dogs charged up the steps, past the dead Abbot, and into the hall. Bishop Promane pressed his reluctant soldiers to follow. The canines raced through passageways and sniffed out alcoves in search of their prize. They continued into the bowels of the monastery until they came upon a crypt filled with wooden coffins in various stages of decay. Here, they stopped and barked. A moment later, a clattering of man and metal announced the arrival of Promane and his soldiers.

"Thank you, my pets," he said.

Wary of these unpredictable animals, the Bishop signalled his men to slay the dogs with arrows. The dogs yelped in pain and fell dying. Then he said to his soldiers,

"Open them!"

One by one, his men began prying open the coffins, holding their breath against the stench of rotting corpses. But the prize they sought was not there. One of the soldiers turned questioningly to his master who then grabbed a torch and crept deeper into the back of the chamber. There were inscriptions on the wall. One stood out to the bishop, a single letter Y.

"There! Break it down!" said Promane.

His lieutenant asked, "You are looking for the robe of Judas but this is marked with a Y."

Promane answered as if he was addressing an imbecile. "There was no letter J in those times. Jesus was known as 'Yeshua,' Jerusalem was pronounced 'Yerushaliyim.'"

The Soldiers nodded and used both axes and the hilts of their swords to break through the mortar which yielded with little difficulty. Inside they found an alcove. Sitting on the shelf sat a small wooden box or ossuary. One of the soldiers reached in and pulled it out. It too had the letter Y inscribed on it. When he handed the box to the bishop he stepped back and one of the dying dogs clamped its jaws onto his leg. The soldier yelped in excruciating pain. His comrade lopped off the dog's head with his sword but the dog's jaw would not release. Two more men used their blades to pry the jaws off the soldier's leg as he screamed in agony.

"Silence! More light," said the bishop.

Soldiers brought torches close enough so that the Bishop could examine the wooden box and the inscriptions engrained in it. He felt along the seams as if familiar with its construction and then he unfastened the top. He peeked inside, careful not to let anyone else see the contents. All this time the soldier moaned in agony. The dog had bitten clean to the bone.

"Your mewling could wake the dead," said Promane.

The bishop glanced once more at the contents and closed the box. Then he turned and left the room. The soldiers picked up their comrade who cried out in pain.

"Enough! Leave him!" said the bishop.

Reluctantly, the soldiers let their comrade down on the ground and followed the bishop out of the crypt.

"No, Bishop Promane, please!" cried the terrified man.

The Inquisitor did not look back. To him, second guessing his judgment was a weakness, the trait of an indecisive man. The prelate led his soldiers out of the monastery and back into the open field. There, he opened the box again to take a closer look at his prize. The clouds in the night sky parted. The moon shone down on the cloth, yellowed and stained with age.

"Hello, old friend," Promane whispered.

He lifted the robe out carefully and placed the box on the ground. The relic seemed to glow. The superstitious soldiers stepped back fearfully. The bishop wrapped the cloth around his shoulders and felt what could only be described as rapture. A moment later, the robe's luminescence faded and the bishop returned to his senses. That's when he noticed it. The field around him had fallen still, no sounds of animals or birds. A moment later the silence was broken by the whistling of dozens of arrows flying through the air. Several of his soldiers cried out and dropped to the ground. Promane hastily placed the robe back in its box and ran for the cover of the forest. A coterie of knights charged into the field, their shields and white tunics emblazoned with a large red cross.

Promane's soldiers battled back but were outnumbered and soon fell. The Bishop had almost made it to the edge of the forest when one of the knights overtook him and attacked. The bishop, an able-bodied soldier in his own right, defended himself with a sword in one hand and the box in the other. After several blows, the bishop was slashed on his hand and was forced to drop the ossuary onto the ground. Fortunately for him, one of his guards came to his rescue, ran his attacker through, and dragged the bishop toward the woods. The bishop, who should have been thankful, turned on the soldier and ordered him to go back for the box. Reluctantly, the soldier did as he was told. But that only led the knights in the white tunics straight to the ossuary. The soldier defending it was slain on the spot and the box was brought to the leader of the coterie, Captain Domingos. The captain opened the wooden container and gazed at the robe inside.

"This must be destroyed," he said.

One of his knights threw the garment onto the ground and put a torch to it, but the robe would not burn. Next, he tried to run it through with his sword but it would not tear.

"Captain," said the confounded knight. "It must be made of the very fabric of evil."

"Place it back in the box, bring it here," said Captain Domingos.

Father Sanchez, who had been sequestered away before the assault, crawled out from under his cart and shouted, "Captain, whatever its nature, it has been protected by the church for hundreds of years and..."

The captain turned to the unfortunate priest. "Father, be thankful for your rescue and don't presume to tell me what to do."

"Of course not, Captain. It's just that—"

One of the scouts galloped up to the officer with the fateful news. "Sir, all the priests inside the monastery, they're dead."

"Take three men. Give them a proper burial, burn these defilers. Then—"

"Captain!" called Sanchez again, "They gave their lives for this robe. I beg of you, put it back in its place of rest."

"I'm not sure what the nature of this cloth is," declared the Captain, "but from this day forward it will become the property of the Order of Christ."

"Captain," implored Father Sanchez a third time.

The captain shook his head in frustration as the priest continued.

"Forgive me, I am thankful of your efforts. But there is one in my charge who needs your protection more urgently than I. She is being held against her will back at the fortress along with a great many other innocents."

The Captain laughed. "Father, you are more trouble than you're worth."

The knight placed the robe back in its box. The soldiers saddled up and made their way back to town followed by Sanchez in his donkey cart.

On his way, Father Sanchez searched his memory for everything he knew about the Order of Christ. He recalled it grew out of the famous Knights Templar, a Catholic military order instituted in 1139. Their chief mission was to protect European travellers heading to the Holy Land. Over time they became so powerful that Pope Clement grew jealous and systematically discredited them with false charges of heresy. Many were put to death and the order was disbanded in 1312. King Dinis of Portugal saved the surviving knights and created a new faction called the Order of Christ. Thus, the similar clothing and insignias. Sanchez wasn't sure how much the Order knew about the robe, so at his first opportunity, he waved the Captain over.

"Grateful as I am, Captain, I am curious as to how you came to be here at this time, on this night."

"You have friends, Father. Informants in Promane's castle who sent us information about your detention. We watched and waited and when the bishop brought you here, we followed."

Father Sanchez nodded and replied, "And none too soon. I owe you my life. Again, many thanks. So, did you come here for me, or for the robe or for Promane? Because..."

Impatient with the priest's incessant questions, the Captain spurred his horse and galloped to the front of the line.

*　*　*

Two hours later, the Knights of the Order of Christ were at the gates of Promane's fortress. When they approached, the doors were flung open and surprisingly, they were invited in by the villagers. Most of the servants and much of the guard had no love for the bishop. The townspeople led them directly to the bowels of the citadel where many of their loved ones were imprisoned. The knights slew Promane's remaining guard and hurried down the fetid steps of the torture chamber to find a number of victims. Sofia was still strapped to the rack, now with several branding wounds on her thighs. The soldiers freed her and all the other captives. Minutes later, the contingent emerged to the cheers of the villagers. With his quest completed, Captain Domingos announced he would return to his homeland, making no mention of the robe. Father Sanchez and Sofia were asked to join them but decided to remain. These people needed their priest and Sofia needed to tend to her younger sister, Belle.

The Spanish Inquisition wasn't the only one of its kind. The original inquisition was instituted in 12th century France to combat public heresy and spread to other European nations. From there it migrated and was taken up by King Ferdinand and Queen Isabella in 1478 in order to purify Spain. The original decree required that all other faiths either convert to Catholicism or be expelled from the territories. But it was really a thin excuse to drive out the Jews, Muslims, Protestants and other 'non-believers.' Amongst them was a faction known as crypto-Jews who practiced as Catholics in order to hide their true identity. The church employed many nefarious means to 'out' such heretics including the bribing of children to betray their own parents.

Communication between provinces and countries were slow. As a consequence, it took days for word of the attack on Bishop Promane to reach the highest offices of the church. The Judas Robe was an obscure relic few were aware of. These factors combined allowed the knights of the Order of Christ the time needed to return to Portugal with their prize. Sanchez and his confederates were not as fortunate.

Sofia Almanza and her younger sister, Belle, were orphaned years ago by a father who ran off when his wife died in childbirth. The children were brought up in the church under Father Sanchez and the nuns. At eighteen and sixteen respectively Sofia and Belle were grateful to the church and were preparing to join the nunnery, until Bishop Promane arrested Father Sanchez. After the rescue, the Father returned to his apartments where he and Sofia were tended to by Belle. She, the youngest, had become the 'mother'. On the third night Belle was preparing dinner, grateful to have her loved ones back.

"Bless the people of our church, Father, for this offering of food," prayed Belle as she dropped the vegetables into the boiling pot of water that sat over the fire.

"Did I not tell you to trust in the lord?" said Father Sanchez to Sofia.

"It was you who saved me, Father."

"Well, sometimes even God needs a helping hand."

At that moment there was a knock on the door. Everyone froze, wondering whether it could be fellow parishioners or the military. Belle looked at the priest who gestured for her to approach the door cautiously. Belle put down the soup ladle and opened the door to find Bishop Promane lying outside, half-dead. His left hand, wrapped in bandages and bleeding profusely.

CHAPTER 2, Present Day

It was 9:30 in the evening when Joel Gardiner finally left the Biopharm labs. He drew his collar up against the brisk October wind that streamed through the downtown corridor. The young med student was tired but happy. He had scored a part time job over the summer with a renowned facility by suggesting two promising research projects. The job not only gave him a foothold in the company but helped pay for his tuition. However, now that he was deep into the school semester, he found his research cutting into his study time. After a full day of classes and three hours at Biopharm all he wanted to do was to get back to his dorm and crawl into bed with his girlfriend, Lisa.

As he made his way to the bus stop, he passed two dark-clad figures spray-painting a statue, probably a prank initiated by one of the local fraternities. Some said it built character and formed life-long friendships. But Joel had no patience with that aspect of university life. The youngest of three, he was too driven to waste his time drinking, partying, and being at the beck and call of his seniors. As he shuffled along, he heard footsteps following behind him. By the time he sensed trouble it was too late. One of the figures pushed him. When he turned around, he was slugged in the jaw.

"What the fuck!" Joel yelled.

Joel fell back a few steps but righted himself and took a defensive stance. He threw a punch at the closest thug but his opponent was too fast. He sidestepped Joel's fist and cut his arm with a knife. Luckily his jacket took the brunt of the assault.

There was no provocation, no argument, just the attack. Even though Joel was fit he knew he was no match for the both of them. He reached for his wallet and offered them cash.

"Twenty bucks. It's all I have. Take it, walk away, I won't report this."

They smiled viciously. Twenty bucks was not going to cut it. Joel steeled himself for a beating. And then he noticed a third figure approach his assailants from behind. Before either could make another move the stranger zapped one of the thugs with a taser. When the second thug turned around the stranger drop-kicked him and drove him to the pavement, unconscious.

"Wow," was all Joel could manage to say.

"Are you okay?" asked his rescuer.

"I guess," replied Joel, holding onto his arm.

"You're cut," she said.

To Joel's surprise, his rescuer was a woman. She stepped over her victims and examined his wound. She looked to be in her early twenties and wore tight-fitting clothing that accentuated her slender, muscular build. A knitted cap worn over her wispy, brunette hair kept the bangs out of her eyes. Beneath the hair sat a hauntingly attractive face.

"Does it hurt?" she asked.

"It'll hurt worse tomorrow. Who are you, Neighborhood Watch, Charlie's Angels?"

The young woman did not reply. Curious, he figured a little conversation might prod her.

"I saw them back there tagging a statue and took 'em for a couple of pledges. Then the next thing I know..."

"We should go," replied the girl. "They'll come to in a minute."

Joel took a few unsteady steps. Apparently, he had lost more blood than he thought.

"Come. I have a car," she said.

She led Joel around the block to a Corolla sedan. After opening the door, she helped him inside, and climbed into the driver's seat with clean, precise movements. Only when they were safely on their way did she bother to strap on her seatbelt.

"Lucky for me, I guess, you came along," he said.

Or was it, he wondered. Strange that he was mugged in a relatively safe part of town. Stranger still that she was there just at the moment he needed her. The girl monitored her rear-view mirror to make sure they weren't being followed. Satisfied, she turned to Joel.

"They're part of an extremist group."

"What do they want from me? I'm not political. I didn't even vote in the last election."

"Not political. Religious."

"Everybody kills in the name of God these days."

"They're after a relic."

"What kind of..."

Joel's head began to loll back and forth. The girl pulled up to a drug store and got out.

"It's a flesh wound, nowhere near an artery."

"You still might be experiencing shock. Wait here," she said.

Joel's first reaction was to get out of the car and run. But between the dizziness and the shock he knew he wouldn't get very far. And if his attackers were still looking for him he wouldn't stand a chance. Blood was pooling in his sleeve. He pressed his hand to the wound to stem the flow. The last thing he needed was to black out. How had he been pulled into this Penny Dreadful melodrama? Four minutes later his rescuer exited the pharmacy with her purchase. She climbed back into the car and dumped the items onto the console - gauze bandage, alcohol, scissors, Q tips.

"Good thing you were wearing a jacket. Take it off and pull up your sleeve."

"What are you, some kind of ninja nurse?"

Joel was having some difficulty taking off his jacket in the cramped car so she grabbed his sleeve, yanked it down, and then ripped his shirt sleeve up to the elbow. The cut had produced a good amount of blood but it didn't appear too deep. She cleaned the wound while Joel tried to make sense of his predicament.

"You know these guys, don't you? You've been tracking them," he said.

The girl nodded.

"Do they have a name?"

"Jimmy, Max," she said with a smile. "Press your hand over the bandage."

"I don't think we've been properly introduced. My name is Joel. But I have a feeling you already know that." Still no reply. "So, this relic, what's it supposed to do?"

"They believe it will give them access to great wealth and power."

"Like the chalice or something?"

"It's called the Judas Robe."

"Never heard of it."

The girl gave him a skeptical glance. "It's the one true physical proof of God on earth."

"Isn't Judas like the biggest villain in the bible?"

The woman finished the dressing and placed the items back in the bag. Then she started the car and drove off.

"To some Judas was a sacrificial lamb, maybe even a hero."

"Are you kidding me?"

"'Have I not chosen you, the Twelve?" the girl recited. "'Yet one of you is a devil!' John 6:70.' Jesus knew his fate all along. Judas was just a pawn, a scapegoat."

The girl drove on a few more minutes and pulled to a stop in front of Joel's dorm apartment.

"So, thanks again," he said as he got out of the car.

"I still didn't get your name."

"It's Sofia. "

Joel exited the car. "Sofia. Is that French?"

"Spanish. You know, anyone else would have asked, 'why me?' Joel, you can't ignore this any longer."

With that she drove off leaving him with a lot of questions, chiefly, 'ignore what, and how did she know he lived here?

Reeling from fatigue and pain, Joel stumbled up the steps of his building. Entering the foyer, he felt assaulted again, this time by the loud rock music that thrummed through the walls day and night. He grabbed the banister and yanked himself slowly up the stairs to the second floor. A fellow student exited one of the dorm rooms and sneered at him as he shuffled past with a look on her face that said, 'nothing worse than a frat boy who can't hold his liquor.' Joel fumbled for his key and entered his apartment. Without turning on a light he stripped off his clothes, lurched into his bedroom and dropped onto the mattress next to his girlfriend.

The next words he heard were, "Get up you drunken pig."

Joel pulled the covers over his head and his girlfriend, Lisa, pulled them down again.

"C'mon, Joel, you can't afford to be late for class again."

The twenty-two-year-old was about five foot five, short blonde hair, and muscularly built from all the years spent on the swim team.

"Not drunk," he said sleepily.

"You stumbled into bed last night, didn't bother to wash or brush, and your clothes are all over the floor."

Joel grabbed his sheets again at which point she noticed the bandage on his lower arm.

"What happened?"

"Not drunk. Mugged."

"Mugged?"

"Last night...couple of jerks."

"And they cut you? Baby!" She sat at the edge of the bed and tried to examine it. "Is it deep? Has it been treated? Let me see."

"I'm okay, Lisa. I cleaned it, it's fine, no infection. I'm a med student too you know."

"Doesn't stop me from worrying about you. Can I see it?"

Lisa tried to examine the bandage but Joel pulled his arm away.

"I'm okay, honest. Lemme sleep and I'll tell you all about it later."

"What do I tell Professor Brown?"

"Nothing. I'll be there, promise."

Lisa shrugged, tucked the covers tenderly up around his shoulders, and left the tiny bedroom. She padded to the bathroom and climbed into the shower. After her shower she dried her hair, pulled a sweatshirt over her shoulders, and slipped into her jeans. Then she looked in on her boyfriend once more before leaving. The two had been a couple since their second year in university. She admired Joel for being so independent but that same quality also made him distant. After six months together he had softened and opened up but he rarely spoke about his family or his home life. As she headed out for classes she knew she liked him well enough but wasn't sure if they had a future.

Joel tried to fall back to sleep but the trauma the night before gave his mind no reprieve. He was right; the pain would be worse in the morning. Ten minutes later he crawled out of bed feeling as if his entire body had been pounded by a sledgehammer. He showered as best he could and got himself together while he tried to place the pieces of last night's nightmare into some kind of coherent form. How much was real, how much was imagined? The bruises on his face and the wound on his arm were real enough. What about Sofia? And the Judas Robe? And that's when the thought hit him; was Sofia following the two thugs last night or was she following him? Joel got dressed and headed to his first class of the morning.

CHAPTER 3

Wellington University was built in the center of a modern, mid-sized town. It was bounded on the north, east, and west by farm land. Its southern boundary was a major highway that stretched for hundreds of miles connecting other major cities across the province. Wellington U. had a decent scholastic reputation but it was mostly known as a party campus and that aspect of its reputation was what drew undergrads from all across the country.

The air this morning was both crisp and life-affirming and to Joel it acted like a dose of smelling salts, making the strange events of the previous night seem like a fantasy born out of a drug-induced binge. As he made his way to the lecture halls his cell phone beeped with a message. "Where are you?" He fumbled back with a reply to Lisa, saying, 'Almost there,' and quickened his step. Everything would be better when he got back to his normal routine.

Professor Paul Brown was a tall, lanky man in his forties with curly hair and a goatee, a look akin to Alexander Dumas's fictional musketeer, D'Artagnan. He had been teaching at the university for seven years and hoping soon to make tenure. He was a good prof, open and accessible, especially to the pretty, young coeds. He liked to encourage free thought in class but sometimes, like this morning, the lecture had broken down into a heated, tangential discussion. As usual Lisa was leading the charge.

"My point is," she said, "the scientist is amoral by virtue of having to defend his discovery no matter what its ramifications."

"Yeah, like a parent defending his child who got caught plagiarizing," agreed her friend, Morgan Nedelco. "It's her kid so she's got to defend him whether little Johnny stole it or not."

Morgan was the darker version of her friend. The two came from opposite ends of the socio-economic divide. Lisa was attending school on her parents' dime, with tuition and boarding all paid for. Morgan was on a partial scholarship paid through a university mandate to give lower income families equal opportunity at a higher education. There were rumors that Morgan was making extra money by hooking on the side but Lisa never believed them. And even if they were true, she respected Morgan for doing whatever it took to get there.

"Anyone else?" asked Brown.

A few other students chimed in, "I mean, new drugs are created every day to sustain life even after the mind stops functioning."

"Does that mean it's right to prolong life just because we can?"

Professor Brown tried to appear interested in this well-worn discussion, but more intriguing for him was his student, Morgan. Joel, who had listened to the dialogue at the door, tip-toed down the stairs wearing a baseball cap and sunglasses to hide the bruising on his face.

"What news from the dugout, Mister Gardiner?" the prof said.

Joel ignored the titters around the room and took a seat next to Lisa, trying to make himself look invisible. Not a chance. The professor had nothing against the bright lad except that Joel was in that sweet spot of life where everything was possible and within his grasp. Brown had passed that point long ago. Being a professor carried a certain measure of authority but fading youth and declining vigor was a never-ending source of worry for the 'prof,' to the point of self loathing.

"Someone to play devil's advocate? Mister Gardiner?"

Joel had only caught the last few words of the argument and was not prepared for a proper response.

"Are you for or against?" asked Professor Brown.

"Well I guess..." replied Joel. "ever since Jerry Lewis invented the love drug in the "Nutty Professor," I've been a big fan of science."

As soon as the words left his mouth, Joel regretted it.

"Such an intelligent, well thought-out rebuttal, Mister Gardiner."

Lisa winced and gave her boyfriend the stink eye.

Morgan saw her opportunity and jumped in. "What about stem cell research touted as a cure-all for everything from migraines to Alzheimer's?"

The students began a free-for-all.

"But who owns the rights to the cells? The donor or the company cultivating them?"

"And what about cloning organs from those cells? Who owns those and shouldn't they be available to anyone who needs them?"

The professor continued to guide the argument, "And who's to stop Mister Gardiner here from using that same technology to create the next master race or weed out all the Blacks, Jews, Vegans, and left-handed sub-humans? Hence, in this case, science, not society ends up defining the new morality."

"So where is God in all of this?" asked another student. "I mean, if you're talking ethics, doesn't God come into the equation?"

The professor put the question to the class. "If you had to make a decision between putting your trust in God or science..."

"That's a bullshit proposition," said Joel.

"Because?" said Brown.

"Because no matter how you argue it, it's human nature to go where no man has gone before. You can't stop research, you can't stop the creative force, you can't stop—"

The bell rang.

"Apparently we can," said Professor Brown. "What have we concluded? To be a research scientist is to be revered and reviled at the same time. As for God, he is later to this class than even you, Mister Gardiner."

The session broke and the study hall emptied as students hustled to their next class. As Morgan passed her professor, "I pick science every time," she whispered. Professor Brown took it as a personal compliment.

Joel and Lisa strode through the campus under the cloudy morning skies.

"Jerry Lewis, huh?"

"Beats the Eddie Murphy remake any day."

"Are you ever serious? And how's your arm?"

"Fine. And I'm sick of defending our profession. The day Doctor Frankenstein breathed life into that stinking corpse, the witch hunt began."

"That was fiction, you know."

"Yeah, but today the medical community is branded the monster."

"Sure. You need to fill me in about last night."

"I will, later. Got Anatomy."

"Will you be home for dinner?"

"As soon as I leave Biopharm."

"Again? What are you're doing up in your castle, Herr Doctor?"

"Actually, we're working on a theory that's been haunting man for centuries; are women sexier with their clothes on or off?"

"And your position?"

Joel gave her a squeeze. "Needs more research. Promise when I get home we'll investigate."

"Don't bet on it."

As Joel started to make his way, Lisa shouted after him. "You are going to report the mugging, aren't you?"

Joel was pretty sure those people were not after anyone else but him. But to placate her, he replied, "Tomorrow for sure."

Joel ran back to kiss his girlfriend on the lips and strode off. Lisa turned to go to her next class and noticed a brunette wearing a wool cap watching her boyfriend from afar.

CHAPTER 4

The town of Wellington had grown from being a mainly agricultural center to a metropolis. The university attracted the housing industry which attracted all the other feeder businesses including restaurants, clothing and furniture companies. It also attracted a number of hi-tech organizations that employed many students upon graduation. One of the most prestigious was Biopharm, a pharmaceutical company ensconced in a large granite and glass edifice in the center of the downtown core.

It was after 5:00 p.m. when Joel arrived and slid his badge into the security slot. Phil, the head security guard, lifted his eyes from the monitor and buzzed him in.

"Hey, Phil, who's winning? Jays or Leafs?" asked Joel.

Phil always had one eye on the door and the other watching whatever televised sport was in season.

"Don't worry your pointy, little head about it. You just keep your fingers away from the Bunsen burners and leave the important stuff to us."

Standard repartee between the two. Joel didn't have the first clue as to who was playing who, or whether the games were ruled by innings, periods or downs. Phil just shook his head as if Joel and all the other Poindexters in the building came from a different planet.

Joel proceeded to the elevator, slid his card into the next security slot, and pressed 'Sub-level Six.' This was a restricted area for which only Joel and a select few others had special clearance. It was also one of the reasons he couldn't be entirely truthful with Lisa. Joel had devised a protocol to develop a universal blood type. To a company like Biopharm, this was pure gold. And a top-secret project of this nature had to be protected from electronic hacking, corporate espionage, and loose lips. After Joel made his proposal and outlined the procedures, he was given clearance at the top levels and assigned a lab. But he agreed with one condition. He also wanted the opportunity to investigate a second project — to isolate the gene responsible for a rare condition that only affected a miniscule portion of the population. Joel's boss, Marie Champlain, was not keen on anything that didn't turn a profit. But Joel was insistent that the two projects be tied together. In the end Marie acquiesced, chiefly because the universal blood type research would make the company a fortune.

The elevator doors opened to a series of corridors that required Joel to use his badge at every juncture. They loved their security here. Down the hallway he saw a familiar figure.

"Hey, Emile," said Joel.

Emile was one of the few caretakers assigned to the lab level. He stood about 5'9" and looked to be well into his 60's. He was partially bald and walked with a slight limp as if he was in need of a knee or hip replacement. Joel watched him gather waste baskets from the various labs with slow, measured steps.

"Hello, Mr. Gardiner, nice weather the past few days," replied the janitor in a European accent. He was a man of few words and generally kept to his own business. But he always had a pleasant air about him, like a man grateful for the work and the wage.

After passing through three more security doors Joel reached his lab. He opened the door and was greeted by the sounds of grand symphonic music, a welcome change to the hard rock that always permeated Joel's dorm. The music belonged to Joel's senior lab colleague, Roger Naiman. In his mid forties, Roger looked more like a lumberjack than a scientist with a prominent beer belly, a head of bushy hair, and a large mustache. And his lab coat was always stained with whatever food he was constantly snacking on. Roger liked to play classical music because of its grandiose themes and it served to remind Joel and everyone else that the lab was his territory. As far as Roger was concerned the student was just passing through. Roger was at the far end of the room hovering over a computer when the intern entered.

"Hey, Rog,' had a chance to look at any of the results? Rog'?"

Roger would only acknowledge Joel after he repeated his name at least twice. Having been with the company for over 12 years he resented the fact that he had been saddled with babysitting some kid's project.

"I have my own work to do, you know," he said.

A researcher's worth was tied to the value they provided their company. Some were innovators who inspired vision and others were technicians who were there to advance those visions. Roger had been a dutiful employee but never had the vision. Joel came on board like a fireball nine months ago and Roger resented him for it.

"I know, I know, Rog.' Not trying to be—"

"I get the research for a universal blood type. But this ectodermal dysplasia," he said. "What the fuck is that about? It only affects 7,000 people, maybe."

"The condition can cause a whole host of problems for those who carry the gene. Cleft palate, translucent complexion, shrinkage of the bone, heat exhaustion. If we identify the mutant gene before a child is born maybe we can eradicate it."

"Sure, but how's the company supposed to make money from that?"

The health sciences field could be as treacherous as a bet in a casino and just as reliable. Companies like Biopharm spent millions on the development of drugs and waited years for them to be passed by government watchdogs before they could be sold on the market. And even then, they had to promote the drug for as long as it took to catch on fire. Not all did. Those that did, helped to pay for the cost of research for the next 'phenom.' Pharmaceutical companies took as few chances as possible with their dollars but still, it could be a crapshoot.

"Marie Champlain says every once in a while Biopharm will fund a project for humanitarian reasons."

Roger doubted it. More likely, the kid was banging the boss.

After checking the results of his previous day's work and getting no results Joel set up the next experiment. It was common knowledge that Type O, the universal blood type, was compatible with all the other major types. But you could not donate type A to a subject with AB blood, O to A, etc. What was needed was a way to strip away the antigens from all the major blood types to make them compatible to each other. Joel came up with the idea that the antigens which break down food in the gut would be most efficient. But which one? There were thousands.

It was 10:30 p.m. by the time he set up his next experiment and left. That's when he remembered about dinner with Lisa. When he reached for his cell phone, he saw three messages she'd left. Damn! All during the course of his bus ride home he cursed himself for forgetting. He entered their apartment quietly, took off his clothes, and crawled into bed. When he caressed her thigh to see if she might be in a forgiving mood, she swatted his hand away. Not tonight.

* * *

Mother Natalie had just completed her Daily Examen, a reflection she and her sisters partook of at the end of each day that included recalling God's presence, feeling gratitude, expressing thankfulness, asking for forgiveness, and resolving to grow. She had lived in St. James Convent along with her sisters for the past few years and enjoyed this part of her bed time routine. While this completed the daily rituals for her sisters, Natalie had more to do. The slightly built woman removed her cowl and tunic to reveal a head of sparse, feather-like, hair. She sat at her night stand, dipped a pad into a bowl of lukewarm water, and began removing the makeup from her face to reveal a skin that was almost translucent. Next, she took out her false teeth and placed them in a jar. Lastly, she applied a balm to her elbows where the dermatitis was the worst.

The image in the mirror stared back mockingly and asked, 'Why bother? Pride, ego?' She smiled and answered her own question, 'Because it diminishes the questions and stares and it gives me the opportunity to serve you better, lord.' Natalie turned off the light and crawled under the covers, content.

It was late that night when they broke into St. James. The convent was an adjunct to a hospital that had stood for 120 years. It was initially built as a religious retreat but with diminishing funds over the years it had to find new ways to increase revenue. So, it sectioned off one portion as a middle school and another for palliative care for the elderly. There were no alarms on the doors or the windows. The cost of security was exorbitant and this particular order was not swimming in cash. Nor was there anything of great value on the premises to protect, no golden crucifixes or bejewelled goblets. The three intruders had little trouble prying open a window and gaining access without detection. Two of them were the same young thugs who attacked Joel the night before. The third was their leader, a young woman with short, red hair. The room they found themselves in was a classroom filled with desks, a blackboard, and a row of text books. Quietly, one of them began turning the desks upside down. The second began ripping the pages from the books and throwing the leaves all over the floor. The third went to the blackboard and wrote 'when the true king is anointed" in fierce, capital letters. Their goal was not to destroy property as much as to instill fear and chaos. It took less than a minute to accomplish their task before they went in search of more mischief.

Dressed in black clothes and rubber-soled shoes, they tread silently down the hallway until they came to a sanctuary. There, they entered and overturned everything they could get their hands on. There were no alarms in the building but what they did not count on was Rasmus.

A year ago there was a great debate amongst the nuns whether or not to take in an animal, not because they couldn't afford to feed it but because they didn't want to make a decision about the needs of a pet over the needs of their parishioners. In the end the shared agreement and responsibility of all the members enabled the order to handle parishioners, students, and the dog.

Rasmus, a cocker spaniel, had the freedom of the building and would roam wherever he liked, although he generally took to bed in the laundry room next to his bowls of food and water. It didn't take long for the dog to sense the intruders and make a bee-line for the disturbance. In the midst of their mayhem the intruders were confronted by the animal and giggled. This was no attack dog. The three ran at the animal with the intent to scare it off. Rasmus didn't have deadly fangs but he did have a voice. The animal ran back the way he came, barking as loudly as he could. Between the sounds of the dog, the opening of doors, and the shuffling of feet, everyone in the building was alerted. By then enough damage had been done. The leader told her comrades to retreat the way they came as a host of nuns scurried down the hallway giving chase. Rasmus nipped one of the intruders and got a swift boot in the head for his trouble. Mother Natalie and the other nuns found the dog walking in circles. One of the sisters tended to the animal while another called 911. Natalie forged on until she found the window in the classroom where the perpetrators entered. By that time they had fled into the night.

Fifteen minutes later three squad cars filled with police officers arrived to assess the damage. Because nothing was stolen the patrolmen assumed the perpetrators may have been kids looking to let off some steam. Or it could have been an initiation into a gang or a fraternity. They requested any video that might be available but the convent had not invested in any such security measures. They suggested now would be a good time to do so. There was however footage from the CCTV cameras mounted on the street corners outside. But when viewed they saw that the intruders wore hoods and dark clothing and couldn't be identified. Since nothing was stolen the break-in was listed as a low priority for the police.

Mother Natalie, however, knew this was more than an act of vandalism. It was a warning

CHAPTER 5

Joel and Lisa woke the next morning after a restless night. He apologized again for forgetting about their date but his apologies were beginning to grow stale. After half a year together their romance was maturing but day to day life was beginning to exert its pressures on them. Lisa, an only child, had always done well in school and her Presbyterian upbringing had kept her on an even keel from an early age. Joel was the youngest of three from a broken family and lacked motivation throughout his youth. His parents were generally on the same page about faith and lifestyle expectations but there was always an underlying current of unrest. Joel's mother could be domineering and unbending. His father wore a constant scowl as if he'd lived a life of regret, where promises were rarely fulfilled. It was only after Joel left home that he began to thrive by immersing himself in his studies. The better his grades got, the more he pushed himself and the more he succeeded. However, the extra-curricular research projects at Biopharm were taking its toll on his studies and his relationship. An air of tension hovered above the two from the time they woke that morning and followed them to class, through Professor Brown's opening anecdote.

"True story," said the professor to his student, Morgan. "A friend of mine, a vet, had a client whose dog swallowed a box of razor blades and the blades became lodged in the stomach cavity."

"OhmyGod. Did they have to operate?" she asked.

Professor Brown smiled and said, "Vaseline sandwich."

"Beg your pardon?"

"They gave the dog a sandwich coated with Vaseline which when digested, coated the stomach and intestines. Next day, the dog passed the blades unharmed."

"No shit."

Professor Brown laughed at the unintended pun. "Some things by the book, others, for the book. As a physician one day, it'll be up to you to distinguish between the two."

The class continued discussions over morals and ethics until the hour was up. Lisa and Joel sat in silence, wrapped up in their own angry world. At the end of the class the two made their way out and Professor Brown caught Morgan's eye.

"Another fun fact, Morgan; did you know that humans and dolphins are the only species that have sex for fun?"

She giggled as she exited the lecture hall and then caught up to Joel and Lisa down the hall.

"Lisa, you guys coming to the kegger tonight?"

"Maybe," she answered in a tone meant to inform Joel that he needed to pay her some extra special attention. Joel remained non-committal.

"And maybe I'll bring the professor." Morgan laughed lasciviously before going on her way.

Generally, Joel and Lisa would have traded comments about Morgan's behaviour. But today little else was said between them. Shortly after, they swapped frosty goodbyes and headed their separate ways without any further mention of the coming evening. Joel was going to bus over to Biopharm after classes. But the mugging the other night was weighing heavy on his mind and he decided to make a detour to St. James' Convent. Sofia's warning had unsettled him and he had the gnawing feeling that the reason for the attack lay hidden inside those walls. It took him twenty minutes to get to the convent. As he approached, his phone vibrated.

'Where are you?' texted Lisa.

He paused to answer. 'Visiting my Mom."

Joel noticed a young woman exit the convent escorted by a middle-aged nun. He stepped out of sight and watched the two walk down the block together. Neither of them said a word but it was evident through their solemn faces that there was some serious business going on between them.

Visiting his mother, thought Lisa? That was odd. Joel rarely spoke about his family. All he told her was that his father had walked out on them when he was sixteen and his mother was in a mental institution. Joel also had two other siblings whom he was estranged to. In any case Lisa was the type of person unable to let an argument fester. She needed resolution as soon as possible and was not above taking the first step. The first text message was a soft opening. She followed it up with, 'Hope you have a nice visit.' Then she closed with, 'Coming to the kegger tonight? See you there.' Lisa, the caretaker in the relationship, knew how hard Joel pushed himself and thought a night out with friends might loosen him up, be good for the both of them. Joel tapped back, saying he'd try to make it and then shoved the phone into his pocket. When he lifted his eyes from his cell, he noticed the two women climb into a cab and drive off. His window of opportunity had closed. Joel checked his watch and headed back to the bus stop to continue on to Biopharm. The visit with his mother and the answers he sought would have to wait. As he jumped onto the bus he was unaware of two sketchy figures boarding behind him. He was also unaware of Sofia climbing on last.

Every rush hour seemed worse than the previous — the crush of humanity filling vehicles to bursting with exhausted, anxious people eager to get home and shake off their frustrating day. Sofia looked like every other harried commuter except that she had some very unique anxieties to deal with. The attack on Joel the other night signalled the beginning of an incursion, an initiative of sorts that would have serious consequences to both their lives. It was Sofia's job to keep him out of harm's way until the enemy could be derailed. Slowly, she inched down the aisle of the bus until she found Joel standing about three quarters of the way back. His two stalkers were wedged in the crowd, trying to look inconspicuous. Sofia wasn't sure whether they were there to monitor his movements or do him harm but she wasn't going to allow either. She edged her way further until she got between them and Joel. Then she discreetly caught his eye and whispered, 'get off.' By the time the words registered, she'd gone into action.

"Take your hands off my ass!" Sofia shouted at the stalkers, which got the attention of the entire busload. Then she pressed the emergency strip which resulted in the vehicle coming to a sudden stop.

Sofia levelled her eyes at the two offenders, "Jeez, you'd think that after 'MeToo' you perverts would've learned something. But Noo!"

The two lurkers were broadsided by the accusation. Every eye on the bus was trained on them. And if that wasn't enough, the bus driver was on his way back.

Sofia began to chant "MeToo, MeToo, MeToo!" The intonation gathered steam until everyone joined in.

"Calm down here, calm down," said the driver. "What's going on?"

"Those two assholes were taking turns grabbing my ass," said Sofia. "Like I was their own private sex toy."

"We didn't touch her, I swear! Not a finger," said one of them.

"One more pass and you'd lose those fingers," shouted Sofia.

As people began to argue and takes sides, Sofia nodded to Joel who slowly made his way toward the middle doors. The two befuddled characters, blocked by the incensed crowd, could only watch haplessly as Joel stepped down the stairs and climbed off the bus. Jogging away, he glanced at Sofia through the window where she gave him a discreet smile.

* * *

"Hey, Rog.' Roger?" Joel called out as he entered the lab.

Joel arrived fifteen minutes after the bus incident. Roger answered in his patented monosyllabic grunt. As he did every evening, Joel checked the results from the previous day's experiments by placing slides containing the blood samples from various enzymes under the microscope. This time something looked different and he stared at the results for a long moment.

"Roger, would you take a look at this for me?"

"What? Did the boy wonder find the cure for cancer?"

"Maybe."

It wasn't the cure to cancer but it was 'something' and Joel needed a more experienced eye to confirm what he suspected. Joel knew his lab partner could be a curmudgeon but everyone in the scientific community needed allies. Roger pulled himself away from his computer and meandered over as if he was doing Joel a favour. The intern stepped aside reverentially to let the senior researcher take a look.

"These were type A blood cells," said Joel. "See how they're behaving now?"

Roger studied the slide before making a comment. "You're sure you didn't mix up your samples?"

"Nope. Do we call Marie?" Joel's voice bubbled with excitement.

"What you need to do is check your work before you say a word to anyone."

"But—"

"Listen, kid, if you can't back up your claim with notes and explanations of every step in the process you'll get blown out of the water and never get another chance."

"Gotcha, Rog.'"

"You recorded the enzyme you used in this particular procedure?"

"I think so."

"You think so? Do it and then get back to me, young Einstein."

Both understood the implications of such a find and the need for absolute proof. Too many claims had been made without doing a proper proof through the scientific method. Whenever that happened, heads rolled and companies went bankrupt. Joel hurried over to his table and opened his computer where he had documented each procedure and every enzyme that he'd tested. But when he turned to the page, he noticed an entry in his notes that was written in someone else's handwriting. Nervously, he went through the entries on his computer where he backed up all his work. Nothing was mentioned there about this particular enzyme. Someone had supplied the correct one and noted it in long form for him to find. It had to have occurred within the past twenty-four hours. Joel decided to keep it to himself and repeat his experiments based on the revised notes.

After three intense days of repetition, it was undeniable; the enzyme that someone substituted had actually changed the other blood cells to Type O!

*　*　*

"You're sure?" asked Marie Champlain.

At thirty-nine years old Marie had risen through the ranks to become the C.E.O. of Biopharm Pharmaceuticals. As befitting a corporate C.E.O., the offices were appointed with sleek furniture. The desk was burnt mahogany. Two captain's chairs sat in front of it for guests. There was a grand view of the city from the office that stood twenty floors above ground. Numerous signed paintings adorned the walls. Roger and Joel were not sitting in those chairs, they were standing next to them. As the senior researcher Roger suggested he make the presentation and Joel had no quarrel about it because it only added credence to his discovery.

"You know me, Ms. Champlain," replied Roger, "I wouldn't be bringing this to you if I hadn't done my homework. I had Joel test and re-test for three days straight. Same conclusion every time."

Joel noted the spin Roger put on the discovery but was smart enough not to challenge it in front of their boss. Marie got up from her desk and took the papers in Rogers' hands. Two minutes later the trio were down in the lab.

"You notated the enzyme, you've documented each procedure, and you've verified it a hundred times just like Roger said, because in this business there is no room for error. Am I right?" asked Marie.

"To be clear," replied Joel. "We located the enzyme somewhere in the gut."

"But you haven't tagged the actual little bugger? Identified it?"

Roger stepped up. "We, uh, have, we will, we're really close. We just need a little more time."

"How soon until you've—"

"Soon," Roger said. He looked at Joel for corroboration but there was hesitancy in his eyes. Joel didn't want to jump the gun but Roger was hungry for a win. "Like I said, we're pretty close."

"When in fact you can confirm, I promise I will pull out all the stops. But until that time—"

"Understood," replied Joel. "Roger can take charge and I can put time into my other project."

Roger grinned, knowing that this project would make his career. But Marie had other plans.

"Joel, this work could be a huge benefit to all of us here at Biopharm. Until we discover the enzyme, you're both on the project full time."

Joel rubbed his forehead from the pressure that built over his brow. This was not how he envisioned the process. Of course, he knew Biopharm would never have agreed to working on a project as insignificant as ectodermal dysplasia unless there was some kind of payoff. That's why he led first with the concept of a universal blood type. Once he discovered the enzyme for that he believed he could hand off the main project and be free to work on the secondary one which was much closer to his heart.

"But you said—"

"*But you said, you said?* I am not your mother, young man, I am your boss. You don't seem to realize that we stand at the threshold of a discovery that will change science, benefit mankind, and most likely make you famous. It will also give us the resources we need to fund your other research. Because if we don't have the money... Anyway, first things first; You and Roger go back to work and finish this little treasure hunt."

Roger almost licked his lips. "You know what kind of potential this could mean?"

"Let me worry about that."

That said, Marie exited the room. Joel shook his head and turned to Roger.

"Rog' I thought we were gonna wait...there are thousands of enzymes in the gut. How are we—"

"You found it once, you'll find it again."

Roger grinned widely, imagining dollar signs in his head. There was no arguing with him. Joel would just have to play along.

After the meeting, Joel headed home. He should have been elated about the discovery but he was torn between the importance of bringing a universal blood type to the world and allegiance to his own project. His other concern was that he had no idea who discovered the correct enzyme and jotted it in his notes. How in good conscience could he claim it as his own? He said goodnight to the security officer and stepped out onto the sidewalk. Just then a car whizzed by and he was reminded of the incident on the bus. Who were those guys and what did they want? And then Lisa's face came into his mind. The kegger. He forgot again! He took to his heels and ran to the nearest bus stop.

CHAPTER 6

The Ramada on Wellington Avenue was one of the more popular hotels with businessmen and work crews. The cost was just over $100.00 a night, breakfast included. All that was needed was a credit card. The three youngish travellers had booked a room for five nights. They wore jeans and tees like all the other students, and claimed they were in town scouting the university before enrolling next semester. Two were male and the third was female. The clerk was concerned the men might be pimps trafficking the girl from one city to the next along the 401-highway corridor. But in fact it looked like the girl was running the show. She was the one who enquired about the room and offered her credit card. 'Belle Almanza,' it read. The clerk's job was to take the money, rent the room, and mind his own business. But he was new and wanted to make his mark with the company. So, he made a note to keep an eye on the trio to see if a parade of random men came and left the room. If the other two were pimping out the girl he'd report it and hopefully get a promotion. It was early evening when the clerk noticed the two young men return to meet the female in the lobby.

"She's been on him like a mother hen," said one of the males quietly. "There's no way to get to him."

The girl thought for a moment and replied. "We may not be able to get to him but we can get to one close to him."

With that, all three got up and left.

* * *

By end of day, Lisa had become concerned about Joel's safety, especially in light of the mugging the previous night. She knew how stubborn he was, that he would not report the incident to the police. He tended to compartmentalize his uncomfortable feelings in order to avoid dealing with them. Toss them in a box, and shut the lid. As Lisa stood in front of the mirror getting dressed, she drifted back to the time they met, attending the same classes, running into each other at pubs. It didn't take long until they were dating exclusively. Yet the couple was a study in opposites. Where Lisa was idealistic, Joel had an inbred distrust of people. She was an extrovert; he could be moody. However, what Joel did bring to the relationship was an intensity and commitment to everything he set his mind to and Lisa admired that. But now, between pre-med studies and the Biopharm project (which he would not speak of) she felt she was losing him. She didn't want to give her boyfriend an ultimatum but she felt he did need to sort out his priorities. And she was one of them. Lisa checked her cell one more time and made a call.

"Morgan, got a minute? I dunno what to do. Joel's been so wrapped up in his work at Biopharm that he's missing classes and he's not eating right and I'm scared. I'd hate for him to get kicked out of school but he doesn't see what he's doing and I don't want to give him an ultimatum but I don't know what else to--"

"Lisa, I'm kinda in the middle of something," replied Morgan.

Morgan was lying on her stomach wearing panties. Professor Brown was straddling her, applying massage lotion to the smooth curves of her lower back.

"Okay, I won't keep ya but I just need some advice."

"Look, no matter what you say, Lis', he's gonna do what he wants."

"Lemme ask you, do you think this is more about me? That I come off too needy?" There was a pause and a sigh. "You do!"

"Lisa," Morgan said, "I think with a guy like Joel, his work is his mistress."

A male voice was heard saying, "Boy, is he missing out."

Lisa recognized her professor's voice, "So busted!" she shouted into the phone, then hung up.

Morgan turned her head around and said, "You're all pigs." To which Brown slapped her ass playfully, making her laugh.

Lisa got off the phone feeling even more upset and confused. She glanced at herself in the mirror and decided she was not going to be a victim. She was a hot chick with a brain. She could get any guy she wanted. If Joel wasn't interested in her she'd be all right. All she needed to decide at this moment was whether to tuck the sweater in or leave it out. She tucked in, shot herself a winning smile in the mirror, and stormed out of her dorm room toward the blaring music down the hall, and quite possibly, a bright new future.

At that very minute Belle and her cohorts entered the dorm building. When they arrived at Lisa's door they stopped and leaned in. They detected no light or sound from inside. But as if picking up on her scent, they continued down the hallway.

It was a typical beer-fueled mixer, music cranked up to the max. Students were either drinking, undulating to the music, or spaced out on drugs. Lisa entered and grimaced. She thought, this was not a great idea. Too late. Andy, the inebriated host, spotted her and dug into a cooler for a cold beer. "Lisa, glad you could make it. Dark or light?"

Well, she was already here. And she told Joel to meet her. "Decidedly dark tonight, Andy."

"Love the sound of that. Where's Joel? Lemme guess. Working late again?"

"What can I say, he's motivated."

It wasn't a lie but it was better than admitting that her boyfriend was too busy for her. It was also obvious to Andy who handed her the beer.

"Let's get wrecked!" he said.

Another couple, Jack and Diane, started the chant, and soon the whole room joined in.

"Poor Lisa,'" said Dianne to Jack. "A widow before she's even married."

"If you're like, looking for someone to get back at him with," whispered Andy, "I'm here for ya."

Andy leered suggestively at Lisa, anxious to hear how she'd respond. "Fuck off, Andy."

Andy laughed and clinked beer bottles with her.

* * *

Joel sat on the bus, willing it to go faster. He needed something or someone to soothe him, stabilize him. Too much was happening too quickly. He'd made an incredible medical breakthrough but couldn't share it with anyone. In addition to that, he was being terrorized by some kind of group or cult for no clear reason. And then there was the mystery of Sofia. Who was she and how did she fit into all of this? *Stop thinking about Sofia!* Lisa was the one. Even when they fought, she was the one who made the effort to mend fences, she was the one who put all his problems into perspective. She was the one and he was the asshole. He reminded himself to tell her that when he saw her at the party.

* * *

After fifteen minutes, Lisa was already tired of the sophomore drinking games and Andy's obnoxious behaviour. Coming here was a mistake. She was about to leave when Darlene came over with a worried look.

"Lisa, are you caught up in Biochem 'cause I'm having a helluva time."

Lisa smiled and began to chat with the girl in an effort to calm her nerves. Then the door opened and three people entered, none of whom anyone knew. Andy, the host, took one look at Belle and went into his routine.

"Welcome weary travellers. Pray, enter our humble abode. Find some space, sample our hops, and make a friend or two. You dudes in the med program? Haven't seen you around."

"We're checking out the campus for next semester," replied Belle. "Word was, this was *the* dorm."

"Abso-fuckinlutely," said Andy.

Jack nodded in agreement. "I'm Jack and this is Diane, like the song. You want a tour?"

Belle smiled suggestively at both Jack and Andy while her two male friends took seats opposite Lisa. Diane gave Jack a sharp elbow in the ribs. "Don't start with that 'threesome' crap," she said.

Andy jumped back into the conversation, "Methinks our new friends could use a cold respite."

"You are so boring everyone with that medieval silly-speak," said Jack.

"Methinks it would please this saucy wench," Belle replied, encouraging Andy.

Andy gave Jack a wide grin. He stepped over to get Belle and her friends a beer while the two males discreetly kept an eye on Lisa. Andy handed Belle the beer can. She smiled and instead of opening the tab on the top, she turned it on its side. Then she punctured the can with a single stab of her fingernail. She put her lips to the hole in the can and then opened the tab. The liquid shot out of the can and directly into her hungry mouth.

"Shotgun!" exclaimed Andy.

Belle grinned back and licked her lips.

"Can you teach me that?"

"Sure."

"Maybe if we go into the bathroom," he replied, "only 'cause I don't wanna mess up the carpet."

Belle glanced at the carpet which was already sopping wet with beer and filled with food crumbs. She smiled, stood up and followed Andy down the hall. Lisa, who had overheard the conversation, shook her head and concluded that the girl was either naive or stupid or a slut. Jack scowled at Andy as he passed and muttered, "I saw her first."

"You are so cut off!" replied Diane.

As soon as the two entered the bathroom Andy's friends grinned at the prospect of what was about to go down. Lisa glanced at the two males Belle left behind. Oddly, they didn't seem to mind at all. As soon as the door closed Andy put his hands all over Belle. She laughed, enjoying herself.

"Mmmm, you're full of life, aren't you?" she said.

"You bring it out in me, lady," he said as he slipped his hands inside her shirt and pawed her breasts. Then he unbuttoned Belle's top and began to lick every inch of her chest.

"Go for it, baby, while you can," she whispered in his ear.

Andy was so filled with drunken lust that her strange comment barely registered, "Huh?" was all he said.

Andy unzipped Belle's jeans and started tugging them clumsily down her legs. Then she stepped back to pause.

"You wanted to know how I did that trick with the beer?" she asked.

"Yeah, sure," he said. "I got a condom here somewhere, I think."

Belle held up the finger she used to pierce the side of the beer can. At the end was a long, sharp fingernail which she then used to slice Andy's throat open. Blood spurted from his carotid artery and he grabbed his neck. His eyes opened wide as if seeing the true nature of this murderess for the first time. What he wanted to say was, 'Why did you do that? I gave you a beer.' But all he could do was gurgle through his mouth which was awash in blood.

"Sorry, what was that, Andy?"

In the adjacent room. the drinking and the dancing was getting wilder. Lisa was becoming frustrated with the small talk she'd been forced into with Darlene and Joel had not yet arrived. She glanced over at Belle's two friends and wondered why they didn't seem upset about her going into the bathroom with a drunken slob she didn't even know. In fact, they looked somewhat amused. As a shudder ran through Lisa, she looked at her cell phone as if she'd just gotten a text message.

"Sorry, Darlene, that's Joel. He asked me to meet him back at the dorm."

"Sure, sure. See ya around, thanks."

Lisa stood up to leave and noticed both of the strangers becoming alert to the fact.

"Lis,' where ya going?" asked Jack.

Before Lisa could answer Belle exited the bathroom with a satisfied grin on her face.

Jack shouted, "Hey, Speedy Gonzales, that musta bin' a record."

When his friend, Andy, didn't reply, Jack got up to investigate. He passed Belle and opened the bathroom door to find Andy sprawled out on the floor with blood pooling from this throat and mouth. Diane followed her boyfriend in and screamed when she came upon the sight.

Chaos erupted. Lisa bolted out of the room with the three intruders following. Dozens of students poured into the hallway at the same time, some from the party, others from their dorm rooms. As Lisa tried to make her way down the crowded hall, she turned to find the three strangers coming toward her. In that same moment someone pulled the fire alarm and panic engulfed the entire building. People bolted in every direction. In the chaos Lisa found herself surrounded by the three intruders.

CHAPTER 7

Joel was strolling toward the university when a police cruiser sped past. It was followed by another and two fire trucks, their sirens blaring. Curiously, all the vehicles were headed in the direction of the campus. Joel's spidey-sense told him it might have to do with him and he broke into a run. By the time he arrived he could see that all the action centred on his dorm building. When he got close enough he saw that the police had cordoned off the area with yellow tape so Joel could only watch the flood of students pouring out of the exits. Desperately, he searched the crowd of panicked faces for Lisa and when he didn't see her, he fought his way up to the police tape.

"Nobody past the tape," said a cop.

"What's going on?" asked Joel.

"You're going to have to stand back," replied the officer as he blocked his way.

"I live here! My girlfriend's in there!"

"Then the best thing is to let us do our job and wait until we give the all-clear."

"All clear for what? Is there a fire? What if she's trapped and can't get out?"

"She have a cell phone?"

It was a remarkably salient question. Joel took out his phone and made the call. After five rings she answered. "Jen, you all right?"

"It's crazy in here! There're some sketchy people...where are you?"

"Outside in front. Can you get out? Hello?"

The line went dead. Joel made a move to get by the cop again but the officer pushed him back. "You wanna get arrested, son?"

Before Joel knew it, two more cops rushed over to back up their partner. Frustrated, Joel waited for what felt like an eternity before Lisa finally emerged from the building and ran down the front steps into his arms.

"You okay?" he asked.

Lisa's sobs were a mix of fear and shock. After a moment she calmed down and then pounded on his chest. "Where were you? Where were you? You promised to be here!"

He was dying to tell her about the discovery but his priority was his girlfriend's safety. This time his being late might have cost her life.

"Sorry. There was a problem at the lab and from where we work there's no signal. Couldn't call out. What happened in there?"

"Andy's dead."

"Dead?"

Lisa began to hyperventilate. "Three scumbags crashed the party—"

One of the officers overheard and cut in. "Slow down, Miss. Take a breath and tell me what happened."

Lisa did as she was told and tried to explain, "There was this kegger upstairs...I mean, 'party' on the second floor. These three kids, two guys and a girl, crashed. Andy, whose apartment it was, went into his macho act and took the girl into the bathroom. Next thing we know, there's blood everywhere and Andy is lying on the floor, dead, his throat slashed."

There was a pause and then both Joel and the cop asked the same question at the same time, "What did these people look like?"

"In their twenties, I guess," she said, trying to pull together all the images at once. "Guys were under six feet tall, lanky. One had stringy, long hair, the other was balding. The girl was about my height. Red hair, cropped short."

"Not brunette?" asked Joel.

"If you're talking about the skank who was scoping you out the other day, it wasn't her."

The cop gave Joel a sideways glance as if to say, 'If I were you, I wouldn't be fucking around on my girl.'

"It's not what you think, officer," Joel said.

"It never is."

Lisa's nerves were about to snap. "Joel, this is freaking me out. What's going on?"

"I wish I knew. But at least you're safe. Okay if we go now, officer?"

"No. Your girlfriend is a witness to a crime. We're going to need her to speak to one of the detectives. Wait here."

While the cop went searching for a detective Joel took Lisa by the arm and the two melted into the crowd.

"Joel, we can't just go."

"You can drop into the police station tomorrow. In fact, it will be better then because your head will've cleared. Right now, I need to take care of you."

They walked a little further until they felt they were a safe distance away and Lisa said, "Stop, I have to talk about it. There's more."

"More what?"

Lisa gathered her thoughts and recounted the events of the past hour. "After they hurt Andy, they followed me into the hall. Somebody pulled the fire alarm and the three of them surrounded me."

"Did they say anything? Do anything?"

"No. That's just it. The girl just kind of smiled at me, like a warning or something. And then she led the other two away. What is this all about, Joel? Are they the ones who mugged you the other night?"

"Maybe, I dunno."

"What do they want?"

"I'm just guessing, but it might have to do with my work at Biopharm. 'Corporate espionage' is what they call it. I'm thinking they went after you to scare me."

"But the girl killed Andy. *Killed* him. That's more than a scare. What the fuck are you doing up there in Castle Frankenstein?"

"The police are on these guys so they're not going to bother us. Tomorrow, you're going to give a statement and I'm going to report this to my boss."

"Joel, I'm afraid."

"I know. Look, they're probably a million miles away by now. But we're not going back to the dorm tonight. We'll go to a hotel."

It was all a lie. Joel had a sense of what this might be about but he was not ready to drag Lisa into the abyss that was his family history. As he escorted Lisa down the block, they were both unaware of being watched. Not by Sofia or by Belle, but by Emile, the janitor who worked at Biopharm.

Joel and Lisa hopped on a bus that drove them away from the campus, to the far side of town. When they passed a small, non descript motel they exited the vehicle and registered for the night. Joel picked up some food and drink from a nearby donut shop while Lisa took a hot shower. Then the two hunkered down in front of the T.V. The 11:00 news spooled out the same stories they'd been reporting on for months, the latest terrorist attack, school shooting, U.S. sanctions against one foreign country or another.

"Is it my imagination or is there more crap going on in the world than ever?" Lisa said.

"Part of it is your nerves are raw and you're sensitized to it all right now. But news organizations thrive on fear. And with the internet and social media, that kind of shit travels faster than ever. Sometimes it can feel like end-times."

A fresh, new story popped up on the newscast about a murder that occurred on a local university campus just hours ago. Details were sketchy but there was video of emergency vehicles arriving at the couples' dorm.

"Joel, earlier I asked you what was going on where you work that these people would be acting so desperately."

"It was research on a condition called ectodermal dysplasia."

"What's that?"

"A rare condition, affects facial features mostly. Cleft palate, sparse body hair. Sometimes people are born without teeth."

"I hadn't heard of it. That's awful."

"Well, it's rare but...anyway..."

Joel thought about the lie he'd just told. It was a habit he'd developed over the years for self preservation. Well, part of it was true, meant to shield her from a more serious threat. This time, though, he felt he owed her a little more honesty.

"There's something else. This is going to sound stupid but it's top secret."

Lisa gave him a dubious look.

"We found an enzyme that stripped certain antigens from A and AB blood cells which enabled them to become compatible to the others."

"Are you shitting me? That would mean—"

"A universal blood type, yes, a solution every pharmaceutical company in the world would kill to get its hands on."

"You think that might have something to do with Andy's murder?"

"I don't know. I've just been ordered to go full tilt on developing the process. Also, I've been sworn to secrecy by the company and that's why it's important not to say anything about it."

"But those three assholes at the party, they didn't look like corporate spies to me. And why kill Andy? What did he have to do with it?"

"I don't know. It's late. Have a Ding Dong. Try to get some rest."

Joel fed Lisa a bite of the pastry and turned off the television. A few minutes later her head dropped onto the pillow and she drifted off to sleep. Joel remained fixed on the real problem and denied himself rest until he'd decided to how proceed tomorrow. That would include a meeting with his mother.

Next morning the couple woke and dressed. Joel offered his girlfriend some reassuring words and escorted her back to classes. Then he told her he was going to speak to his superiors at BioPharm. Instead, he returned to St. James Convent. Joel entered the foyer and stepped up to the lady at reception.

"I'm here to speak to Mother Natalie."

"She's busy right now, teaching. Can I—"

"Tell her it's Joel Gardiner and it's important."

The receptionist did not like being challenged. But Joel met her eye to eye and stood his ground. Reluctantly she picked up the phone and dialed.

"Sorry to bother. I know Mother Natalie is in class but there's a Joel Gardiner at reception to see her." With a glare, she added, "And he's insistent."

The receptionist waited for a reply and then hung up. "I cannot confirm whether or not she'll step out of class to see you. Perhaps if you leave your name and number we can set an appoint—" The phone rang and the receptionist answered. After she acknowledged, she put down the phone and addressed Joel, "Library, down the hall, to the left."

"Thanks," he replied curtly and walked in the direction he was told. It was a large library for a building of this size. Most convents had the requisite books on religion and social sciences. But this was more of a reference library and the shelves were packed from floor to ceiling. As well, a number of religious paintings hung on the walls, many which appeared to be hundreds of years old. Joel let his eyes wander through the book titles until he came to a section that had always fascinated him, the Spanish Inquisition and the Knights Templar.

The Knights Templar had been romanticised in history and literature for years. They were instituted in 1139 A.D and originally known as the 'Poor Fellow-Soldiers of Christ.' Their mission was to protect pilgrims on their journey to visit the holy places in Jerusalem. The order began with eight members and grew from there. Over the years they became known throughout Europe as fierce warrior monks who defended the church with their hearts and swords. In time they became so famous and strong that their notoriety threatened the monarchy. Under orders of King Philip IV, Pope Clement initiated a purge and by 1312 they were hunted down as heretics, burned at the stake, and disbanded.

There were a number of inquisitions across Europe but the Spanish Inquisition was the most infamous. In 1478 King Ferdinand and Queen Isabella instituted it to purify Spain and make it an entirely Catholic country. They obtained a papal bull, an edict from Pope Sixtus IV, to defend the faith by identifying those in the flock who strayed. Local priests were encouraged to bring the lost souls back into the fold. But the mandate quickly became corrupted. The hierarchy in the church, bishops included, began to view all other sects as perversions of the faith. Protestants, Muslims and Jews were persecuted with vigor. People were encouraged to inform on their enemies. Children were even recruited to inform on their parents and relatives. From there the list quickly grew to encompass anyone suspected of practicing sorcery, sodomy, polygamy, blasphemy, and usury. The most notorious offender of this practice was Grand Inquisitor Tomas Torquemada. Under his command, people were expelled over the slightest of accusations. It was worse for others. Those imprisoned were often strangled. They were considered the lucky ones. The less fortunate were tortured to death or burned at the stake.

Joel reflected on the radical Muslim attacks on the U.S., and on Christians in other parts of the world. Some extremists assigned themselves the role of becoming defenders of their faith. Was this a cyclical phenomenon? Did every major religion feel the need to take a shot at ruling the world in the name of God? Why was somebody else's interpretation of the almighty the only right one? Joel was deep in thought when a nun in her 50s entered, the same woman he watched get into a cab with a younger woman the other day. Mother Natalie stood about five foot seven. Her skin was on the pale side and she had a delicate frame. She entered the room in a calm, reassuring manner.

"Joel, I'm surprised but glad you came to call—"

"Last night someone in my building was killed."

Joel's state was anything but calm and the statement felt like a stinging accusation. Natalie's back stiffened. During the past few years the two had seen each other infrequently. Joel was never one for pleasantries and it seemed the only thing that had changed over time was that he had become more direct and caustic than ever.

"You say that as if accusing me."

"Well? Do you know anything about it?"

"No. How would I? And keep your voice down."

"The night before that, I was mugged by two men."

"You weren't hurt, were you?"

"I'm okay, thanks for asking. Mostly, because a young woman intervened."

"What woman?"

"Goes by the name of Sofia. You don't know her either?"

"No, and I don't understand what all this has to do with me."

"She said the two who attacked me were after something called the Judas Robe."

That tidbit of information changed the whole dynamic and Natalie's face turned grave. "What did you tell her?"

"What do you think? I told her I had no idea what she was talking about. And I'm pretty sure those two were the same ones involved in the murder on campus."

'Shit!" It was the kind of reply that could be heard anywhere in the city, a thousand times a day. But in this house, it hung in the air like an evil spell. "And in spite of everything you know, you came here?"

"Everything I know? Here's what I know; my mother is a religious fanatic. That you and your wacked-out friends are part of a cult that worships this legendary robe that is supposed to have some kind of magical powers. If that's what you want to believe, fine with me. But last night my girlfriend was threatened and I won't have her involved."

Natalie found a thread on her blouse and began pulling on it.

"Something has triggered this attack."

"I don't care what triggered it. Put the word out to your devil worshippers that me and my friends are off limits. We know nothing, we believe in nothing, I want no part of this. In fact, tell them I left the country because this is the last time you'll ever see me."

"Please, Joel, wait, don't leave. There's more we need to..."

But Joel had already turned on his heel and stomped out of the library fueled by his burning rage. He'd divorced himself from this nonsense years ago. He stopped going to church at 16 and left home when he was 18. His only regret was that he wasn't able to leave sooner along with his siblings and his father. Unfortunately, at that time he was ill and everyone concerned felt it was best that he remain in the care of his mother until he got better. Joel remembered the day he left. It was etched in his psyche like a wound. He had received a scholarship and was moving out to live on the university campus. His bags were packed and waiting at the door. He found his mother in the kitchen drying dishes, standing with his back to him, tears streaming down her face.

"Well, I'm going," he said.

There was no response. She didn't turn to say goodbye or wish him well. She just stared out the window. Joel assumed she was angry at him for leaving because now there was no one around to listen to her crazy stories about her faith and her family legacy. Natalie, however, was wise enough to know that every child had to leave the nest someday. Tears streamed down her face, not because she was angry, but because she had failed him. The legacy would all catch up to her son one day and she had not properly prepared him. Joel walked out of the kitchen, grabbed his things, and left. That was two years ago. Now all those concerns were coming home to roost.

Natalie rubbed her jaw. The ache in her face was beginning to throb again. She left the library and shuffled back to her quarters. She reached for the pain pills in her drawer and swallowed them with a glass of water. Then she picked up her cell phone and made a call.

"Rosemary, please tell the sisters to take over my class. Yes, another one of my spells."

After she hung up, she made a second call.

"We need to speak. Same place. Tomorrow, noon."

She put down the receiver, took out her false teeth, put them in the glass of water by her bed, and removed her wig, cradling it in her lap. The sparse hair and eyebrows and her pale complexion made her look almost ethereal. Her body slumped as if she carried the weight of the world.

Perhaps she did.

***

The precinct office was a maze of desks, phones and half-filled coffee cups. Officers in uniform and plain clothes lounged around and consulted with each other on various cases. No one seemed to be in any particular hurry. Lisa was cloistered in a small room sitting opposite a middle-aged detective who was making notes during the interview.

"Tell me again."

"I've already told you twice. Why do you officers always ask to repeat?"

"Because there may be a detail or two you've forgotten that may help."

"Or you think you might catch me in a lie."

"You're not a suspect, Miss Palmatiere. You're a witness and we need all the help we can get. Too many witnesses these days refuse to speak to police and then we get blamed when we can't bring the right people to justice. You want us to catch Andy's murderer? Right?"

Lisa fidgeted nervously before she gathered her thoughts and recounted her story a third time. "It was around nine when I got there, the party had already started, there were a couple of dozen kids. I was standing, talking to Andy when they walked in, the three of them."

"Strangers? Anybody else recognize them?"

"No one. That's why Andy asked them how they found out about the party. They didn't really answer. But Andy was already drunk. After he hit on me and I turned him down—"

"You turned him down, why?"

"Because I have a boyfriend. I guess he figured this girl was Plan B."

The cop looked questioningly so she replied, "He was a drunken frat boy looking to get laid. Jeez! It's in their DNA."

"Did any of the three do or say anything that might give you any information about them? Indicate where they were from, what they wanted, where they were going? Anything odd?"

Lisa thought a moment and then answered. "The two guys said absolutely nothing. There was one thing; the girl opened a can of beer with her fingernail."

"How'd she do that, exactly?"

Lisa used her own finger to illustrate as she described the action. "She pointed her baby finger, took aim and pierced it one thrust. The beer poured out into her mouth like a fountain."

"Not easy to do with a metal can," noted the cop. "Then?"

"Andy invited her into the bathroom to show him how to do it."

"Any other discussion or anything else you heard?"

"Nothing until the girl came out."

"What were the two other guys doing all this time?"

"Again, just sitting there, watching everybody."

"They let their girl friend go into the bathroom with a random stranger?"

"Yeah. Fucked up, right?" Lisa looked away. "Excuse the language."

"S' alright. Then the girl comes out and—"

"And Jack finds Andy bleeding on the floor and the place goes nuts. We all ran out into the hall; someone pulled the fire alarm."

"What did the girl and her friends do?"

Lisa hesitated. She did not want to tell him about the silent threat in the hallway because she did not want to implicate Joel. "I dunno. Everyone was everywhere, it was chaos, I didn't see. After I ran into the hallway, I lost track. Joel called me on my cell and I ran out."

The cop rubbed his wrist and looked over his notes. "What else can you remember?"

Lisa giggled nervously.

"What?"

"You remind me of those people at the donut shops or the movies who always ask, 'Will that be all? Anything else'?"

"Yeah, I guess. So, anything else?"

"No," she replied firmly.

The officer handed her his card. "Here, Miss Palmatiere. You get ten percent off your next order of donuts when you do."

Lisa smiled at the joke and for the first time she thought he wasn't such a bad guy.

***

The Biopharm board room was as opulent a place as could be found in corporate America. The lighting was seductively soft. Twelve Ethan Allen leather chairs circled the boat-shaped conference table. On the table were six crystal glasses and a matching water pitcher. Six executives sat around the table grumbling to each other over the abrupt call to this hastily called meeting. Marie Champlain strode confidently into the room and addressed everyone including her boss, Arnon Biltmore.

"I hope this was worth getting us together in such short notice," said Arnon.

Marie took the file she had under her arm and placed it on the table. With a flourish she said, "Gentleman, the enzyme has been found."

"You're serious, Marie?"

One of the execs asked, "What enzyme?"

"We have found the enzyme catalyst that makes all blood types compatible with each other."

Every suit in the room straightened in his seat. "You mean a universal blood type?"

Marie nodded. "I don't have to tell you impact this will have on Biopharm."

She paused waiting for the flurry of questions that would follow.

"Is there a copyright on this enzyme? Can the process be patent-protected? How do we protect ourselves and keep it from our competition? When would it be ready for market? How much could we charge per litre?"

Marie smiled and waited for the buzz to settle before answering. "In front of each of you is a non-disclosure agreement. There will be no further discussion until they're signed."

"Are you fucking kidding me?" asked one of the suits. "We're the ones paying your salary. You'll tell us what we want to know, when we want to know it, or..."

Arnon Biltmore shifted in his chair and brought himself up to his full measure.

"Gentlemen," said Arnon in his most commanding tone. "This is for your own protection. A find like this is a seismic shift in medicine. Each one of you is in line to make more money than you've dreamed of and I don't believe you want to risk your future to any corporate leaks."

To show his sincerity Arnon scribbled his signature on the non-disclosure letter in front of him. The others followed. When each was signed Marie collected them.

"Now then, moving on," she continued. "Full patent protection has already begun as have licenses. New 'Class B' shares are being drawn up. Call those blood-sucking lawyers of yours and tell them they can kiss their trophy wives goodbye until all the "Is" are dotted, and the "ts" are crossed. And if anyone is contemplating divorce, I suggest you start proceedings now to mitigate your settlements in the future because you're all going to be richer than King Midas."

CHAPTER 8

Mother Natalie applied her makeup, fitted her dentures, placed the wig on her head, and slipped on a grey skirt. After donning a simple, white blouse, gray stockings and black shoes she admired herself in the mirror. Now she was as invisible as any other middle-aged matron in the city. Natalie was good at hiding things. It had become part of the fabric of her life. Clothing was the simplest aspect of the deception. The makeup and various appliances to cover her sparse hair, conceal her sallow complexion, stunted teeth, and nails, took a little more effort, even after the operations. But none of these could compare to the biggest secret she kept.

The nun notified the school that morning of a last-minute medical appointment, something not uncommon for her, and took the bus across town to the museum just after 11:00 a.m. when she arrived, she paid for her ticket and entered. She loved the museum and its meditative atmosphere which often reminded her of church. She would roam freely amongst the tourists and children through the many exhibits unencumbered, her mind free to drift away from her constant concerns. The cooler air was its best feature. Designed to protect the delicate artifacts housed in the building, it was also a godsend to a woman like Natalie who was born without sweat glands.

The nun took the elevator to the third floor. Today was not a day to leave her concerns at the door. Today, she brought them here to deal with. She made her way purposefully through the hallways until she came to a large room filled with relics from ancient Jerusalem. She'd visited this exhibit many times and was familiar with its layout, its entrances and exits. She wandered around admiring the glass cases filled with displays of earthenware, bracelets and ancient coins. A few minutes later, a middle-aged gentleman with dark hair and a short-cropped beard entered the hall. He was tall and muscular looking for his age, dressed in such a way that he could easily have been taken for a scholar or professor. The only noticeable thing about him – and you had to look hard - was that he was missing the pinky finger on his left hand. Like spies in a James Bond movie neither acknowledged the other until they'd confirmed no one was paying them any attention.

Then the gentleman ambled over and casually remarked,

"Keeps us humble, doesn't it, to think some of these insignificant relics may have been witness to the greatest moments in history. That pitcher could have been the very one Mary used to carry the water that washed Jesus' feet. That goblet might've been present at the last supper."

"Somebody attacked my son and his girlfriend the other night," Natalie replied curtly.

The gentleman digested the sobering information and spoke. "Were either hurt?"

"Not them, thank God. But one of their class mates was murdered in a separate incident."

"And you believe it has something to do with the robe?"

"What else?" She scowled at him briefly to make her sobering point. "They're innocent students at university, and before you dismiss this as a random attack..."

Natalie sneezed. She took out a small bottle and applied a saline spray to her nose, a necessity to keep it free of infection.

"I don't know how much you know of its history..." the gentleman said.

"It's called the Judas Robe because it belonged to the traitor himself." The nun spat out the words as if expelling a rancid taste in her mouth. "For generations my family has had the task of keeping it hidden from fanatics. My parents told me little else. But as you well know it's been an enormous weight to carry."

The gentleman nodded slightly as a gesture that he appreciated the burden she was carrying. A narrow grin drew across his weathered face. "Funny how little has been written about Judas beyond his role in the passion."

"We're getting off topic," she said.

"Take 'Iscariot,' for example;" he continued. "How many know that refers to the town he was born in, a region in Judea."

Mother Natalie paused, knowing how exasperating this man could be. She studied the room, monitoring the crowd that ebbed and flowed and realized it would be better to go along with him for now.

"But," said Mother Natalie, "the big question about this man has always been, why?"

"Why did he betray our lord, you mean? Therein lies the conundrum. A number of theories have been floated, one of the most popular having to do with the 30 pieces of silver paid by the Romans. In today's parlance that would translate into anywhere between $100.00 and $325.00. A sufficient price to betray such a friend, you think?"

"He had a wife and children to feed."

"Yes, but he was also the disciple chosen to collect the money his brethren raised to help the poor. If he had the mind to, he could easily have pilfered that and more without turning on his brother. And if Jesus was such a money-maker, why kill the golden goose?"

"You have another theory?"

"Scholars have suggested that Judas was disappointed in Jesus for failing to implement his revolution against the Romans. Judas realized his error and gave back the silver but the damage was already done. His sense of guilt led him to hang himself at Aceldama. A few hours later Jesus died on the cross."

A gaggle of students made their way past the couple so the two waited until they were alone before resuming their conversation.

"That may be an explanation of the practical," said Mother Natalie. "I'm speaking of the existential."

The gentleman acknowledged and replied, "Judas was simply playing the part ordained to him by God. If not for him there would have been no betrayal, thus Jesus would not have risen to become the savior we know him as today. Ergo, to some, Judas is considered a saint in his own right."

"And you believe the fanatics who attacked my son are part of this cult of Judas worshippers?"

The gentleman nodded. The gaggle of students exited the hall leaving three young people, Belle and her two cohorts. A chill ran through the gentleman and the nun when they saw the trio staring at them. There was no mistake as to the menace they presented. Belle pulled a metal pipe from the back of her leather pants. The other two revealed similar weapons. The elders steeled themselves for an assault.

"What do you want?" said Mother Natalie. "We're clergy. We have no money."

"You know what we want," said Belle.

The gentleman turned accusingly at Natalie. "Is this a trap, Natalie?"

"Not of my making."

Belle smashed one of the glass cases with the pipe. Her comrades did likewise, setting off alarms throughout the building.

"Guards will be on their way," the gentleman shouted. "You should run while you have the chance."

But the three intruders remained where they stood. A moment later four guards appeared at the two entrances. Unfortunately, they were not police officers which meant they were not carrying fire arms.

"On the ground now!" shouted the senior guard. "Sit on your hands!"

Belle and her cohorts laughed in his face. The nun and her companion watched the first guard and his partner attempt to wrestle Belle to the ground and cuff her. She broke free and executed kicks to her assailants strong enough to floor both large men. The elders watched, helpless to prevent the assault. Then Belle's comrades advanced on the remaining guards. The attack didn't last very long. The guards ended up on the floor within sixty seconds, suffering multiple contusions and broken limbs. Belle turned to Mother Natalie. "This is a warning." As soon as the intruders exited the two elders hurried over to the injured guards to assess their wounds.

Natalie reached for her cell phone and called 911. After requesting medical aid for the guards, she ended the call without giving her name.

She turned to her friend and, in an anxious voice said, "These must have been the same ones who attacked Joel."

The gentleman spoke compassionately to the fallen guards. "The medics are on their way; we're going to get you help." Then he turned to the nun and whispered, "Best we leave, to avoid any further explanation."

The two stood up and exited the hall leaving the injured guards sprawled on the floor. Then they made their way casually down the stairwell so as not to cause any attention to themselves.

"Why is this happening now?" Natalie asked.

"I don't know."

"How did they know the robe even exists? Only my family—"

"And anyone they might have told. This robe is priceless for a variety of reasons. For your safety, Natalie, and that of your family, move the relic from where it is hidden."

The two arrived at the bottom of the stairwell. They emerged into the foyer to find the front doors locked and a squad of security guards preventing anyone from leaving. The couple offered their identification. The officer in charge asked,

"Did you see anything?"

The bishop and the nun shook their heads in tandem.

"We were actually leaving the floor," said the bishop, "...when we heard something behind us."

"What did you do then?"

"We ran."

Natalie explained in a nervous voice. "I am not a well woman, officer. As soon as we heard the ruckus the bishop ushered me out."

The head guard nodded and opened the door to allow them to leave. They took several paces down the steps toward the street, and then Natalie paused.

"One more question; do you know anything about the robe having...'powers'?"

"Nothing." The sound of footsteps was heard approaching. "I'll do whatever I can to help you and Joel but you must sequester the robe elsewhere before it is found."

"I will, I promise."

Bishop Newman held out his hand to Natalie who grasped it for comfort and reassurance. His touch was familiar and unmistakable, defined by the space where his pinky finger should have been. He had also been her family's priest for as long as she could remember. He was there before she was born and been witness to the severe physical abnormalities they first noticed at her birth. The doctors did a number of tests that led to a diagnosis of a rare condition known as ectodermal dysplasia. As Natalie grew up the neighborhood children shunned her on sight. But the bishop helped dispel their ignorance by including her and her family in as many social functions as possible. Personable and disarming, the man had the ability to interpret the bible to each individual's level, making God accessible to all. And in turn they came to accept Natalie in the same light. She particularly enjoyed his interpretation of scripture in terms of heroes and villains, how good triumphed over evil and love prevailed. Beyond that the bishop managed to arrange several operations to help normalize Natalie's appearance. And for that the family was eternally grateful.

When Natalie was 15 years old her mother, Rebecca, revealed a family secret to her daughter - that their heritage could be traced all the way back to the Knights Templar. She told a story filled with heroes and villains that had far-reaching implications into the present day. Natalie's father, Albert, liked to drink and would brag that the family came from royalty of a sort, even lay claim to being guardians of a precious, religious relic. Most excused his loose talk on the alcoholism. Rebecca was always chastising him for it because it garnered more attention than the family was comfortable with. One night Albert and Rebecca got into a fight. In a drunken fit he fell down the stairs at home and broke his neck. Natalie blamed her mother. Bishop Newman sat young Natalie down and explained that her father had a drinking problem and her mother could not be blamed. During the investigation of her father's death Natalie admitted to the bishop about overhearing the argument involving the family heritage and the relic, which if sold, would bring a fortune to the family. The bishop did disclose to the girl that there was some truth regarding the relic known as the Judas Robe. Few details were known about it except that it had been under the protection of the Gardiner family for centuries. Natalie asked her mother about the story but she claimed the priest was telling tales and there was nothing more to discuss. Then, on Natalie's twenty-first birthday, Rebecca revealed to her daughter that the Judas Robe was indeed real.

That statement vindicated her father in Natalie's eyes though it did not negate the fact that he was a drunk guilty of revealing a deeply personal family secret. Natalie pressed her mother; if this relic did in fact exist, then what was its place in history, and what kind of impact would it have today? All Rebecca would tell her daughter was that the robe's power, if placed in the wrong hands, could bring on a cataclysm of biblical proportions. Natalie took that melodramatic warning with a grain of salt and agreed to speak no more of it. In fact, she was happy to avoid the subject altogether. It was difficult enough trying to fit into society with her physical deformities. And the addition gossip about the family's growing reputation as drunks and religious fanatics only made life more difficult for the girl. Still, through it all, the bishop took great pains to defend mother and daughter.

Eventually, Natalie married and as luck would have it, had three children of her own. Joel being the youngest. When he was 12 years old, his grandmother, Rebecca, died of cancer. Natalie leaned on the bishop and in time, revealed what she knew about the robe to him. The priest never questioned or prodded her for information and she respected him for that. Now, with this new threat, she needed him more than ever.

The two strode down the block under the brilliant October sunshine. Natalie looked at each passing stranger and worried. Every face was a mask, every person felt like a threat.

"I don't think I'm up to this," said.

"Natalie, this robe has been entrusted to you for a reason. You are stronger than you know."

After a brisk walk they reached the convent where Mother Natalie resided. "Ironic isn't it that the single-most important proof of God on earth lies in a relic belonging to his son's greatest foe."

"Call me whenever you need me. And Natalie, do not procrastinate. Find the robe and secure it."

"Thank you, bishop."

CHAPTER 9

Lisa left the police station with her brain on overload. Death and murder were things best scrutinized at arm's length from behind a newspaper or viewed through a T.V. screen where victims were strangers, not fellow students. The fact that she was strolling down a street under the mid-day sun knowing her friend Andy was lying under a sheet in some morgue made everything seem all too real. Thinking about it made her eyes tear up which caused her to trip over a crack in the pavement and lose her balance. As she righted herself, she had the feeling something was wrong, that she was being watched. Lisa picked up her pace and entered the first building on campus she came to. She turned down several corridors listening for any footfalls that dogged her and finally ducked into an empty study room. She closed the door and shrunk behind a desk hoping to evade her stalker. A moment later the door opened.

"Lisa?" said the female voice. "I'm not here to hurt you."

With nowhere to run Lisa sucked in her breath and stood up to face the woman. Upon seeing the formidable looking stranger, she unloosened her belt and brandished it like a weapon.

"You won't need that."

"I know you," Lisa said. "You were following Joel the other day. I saw you so don't—"

"My name is Sofia."

"What do you want?"

"I want to talk to you about the other night at your dorm."

"Oh, Jesus. Are you one of them?"

"No. Don't panic." She waited for Lisa to catch her breath before she continued. "You're familiar with the name, The Knights Templar?"

"The stuff of T.V. shows and B movies."

Sofia let the slur pass and waited for Lisa to offer a more educated response.

"A group of soldiers in the Middle Ages whose job it was to defend pilgrims going to the holy land. That's about it. What the fuck do they have to do with Joel?"

"In the beginning, yes, they were proud warriors. Then, they were politically vilified and branded as traitors of the church. In 1312 they were officially disbanded by Pope Clement. But seven years later they were reconstituted in Portugal under the name, The Order of Christ. Joel's mother, Natalie, is a descendant of that order. Part of their mission was to protect a relic called The Judas Robe. There is currently a faction bent on acquiring the robe for their own purposes."

"You're talking about the people who murdered Andy?" The image of Andy sitting on the bathroom floor in a pool of blood engulfed Lisa's mind. "What did he have to do with anything?"

"His murder was meant as a warning. There will be more warnings, more collateral damage unless—"

Lisa's fists clenched and her cheeks grew red with frustration and anger.

"What do you want?" she asked.

"To protect the robe from getting into the wrong hands. And I want to save Joel and his family. But I need your help. Right now Joel and his mother are at war with each other. You need to convince him to trust her if you want to prevent any more havoc."

Lisa's defiant stare turned to bewilderment.

"Me? I don't even know her."

Sofia shook her head, gesturing that Lisa was on the wrong track. She relaxed her stance and changed her posture from aggressor to somewhat more of a confidant. "Joel believes this is all a myth. It's not. He won't listen to his mother; he won't listen to me. He needs proof and he needs to hear it from someone he trusts, you."

"What can I—?"

"It centers on a priest, Bishop Roberto Promane. Do your research and the truth will reveal itself."

"If you know so much about it, why don't you tell them and save us all a lot of trouble?"

"Do you believe me? No, you think I'm some kind of nut or fanatic. People will only believe when they see the truth with their own eyes."

"Yeah, well, what's this robe all about, anyway?"

"Among other things it's the single piece of physical evidence that proves the existence of God."

Lisa stared at Sofia, slack-jawed. It was the most absurd statement she had ever heard.

"The wheels are in motion, Lisa. You can ignore them or you can deal with them. The choice is yours."

"You forgot to say, the fate of the world rests in your hands."

"I thought that would have been obvious. After Promane, you'll want to look into another priest by the name of Emilio Sanchez."

With that, Sofia offered an assuring smile and left the room. Lisa took a moment to absorb the information and gather her thoughts. 'Fate of the world'? How cheesy can you get? *Girl, you're the crazy one.* Then again this Sofia could have hurt her if she wanted to. Which meant she probably wasn't in league with the maniacs who murdered Andy. After her stalker left, Lisa threaded her belt back in her loops. Curious, she pulled out her cell phone and Googled 'Bishop Roberto Promane.' What she read startled her. He was listed as one of the leading interrogators of the Spanish Inquisition back in the late 1400s. Lisa checked the time, an hour and a half before classes. A lot of historical material was loaded on the internet but much of it was condensed into a brief Wikipedia version which could be unreliable. The library in her university had much more extensive resources. She could have called Joel, but her instinct was to verify Sofia's claim before she confronted her boyfriend with it. Lisa peeked outside the room to make sure the girl was still not skulking about, and then hurried out.

All the way to the library her head buzzed with thoughts of Sofia and the robe and how they related to her own religious beliefs. Lisa was brought up in a Protestant home and attended a parochial school for most of her young life. At the age of 17, her parents allowed her to decide whether she wanted to continue in the same academic environment. She was a good girl who never questioned her parents but her strict schooling always felt like a yoke around her neck. So, when given the choice, she happily put it aside. Now, this revelation, if it were true, had her questioning everything.

When Lisa arrived at the library a half hour later, she headed directly to the reference books to research Bishop Roberto Promane. They confirmed he not only served with the Catholic Church during the Spanish Inquisition but had been one of its most active proponents. He was charged with rooting out those who strayed from the faith and bringing them back into the fold. That was a sham and she knew it. Even her clergy confessed years ago that the original reason for the inquisition was to purge Spain of the Jews. Lisa cross-referenced some of the material she found and the more she read, the worse it got. Innocent people were arrested at all times of the day and night and accused of heresy. Those who denied it were often tortured to death. Those who admitted their sins were killed as well.

There were no photos of Bishop Promane but there were portraits. Having read enough to turn her stomach, Lisa began a search for the second name, Emilio Sanchez, Sofia mentioned. He was also a priest who lived in the same era. But the records stated that he was one of Promane's victims. One priest torturing another? Why? Lisa checked her watch. An hour had flown by. The answers would have to wait. She put the books back on the shelves and hurried to her classes.

* * *

The color yellow was often associated with things bright and cheerful; the warmth of the noonday sun, the ripeness of a banana peel, and the promise of its sweet fruit. But the yellow police tape surrounding the dorm building had the effect of making the area look isolated and sinister. The school authorities recommended students take two days off to process their feelings. There were no candlelight vigils or flowers or teddy bears piled up on its doorstep.

The murder of the student was not perpetrated by some deranged shooter bent on causing as much hell as possible before turning the gun on himself. As far as anyone knew it didn't seem particularly religious or politically motivated. It was just a senseless murder. As a result, many students went home while others stayed with friends off campus. The few students who did remain in school were terrified they might be next. When the door to the study hall opened that day Professor Brown was a little surprised.

"Joel, didn't expect to see you today. Or ever again for that matter."

"Hey, Professor. Terrible thing about Andy. The whole campus looks like it's in lock-down."

Brown turned his eyes back to his notes on the lectern, barely acknowledging Joel.

"Look, I know I've missed some classes. I've, uh, got a part time job that has been eating up all my extra time. Anyway, I swear from now on I'll be at every one of your lectures."

Without raising his head, Brown replied, "I'm afraid you're way too far behind to catch up, son."

Joel took a few steps closer in order to grab his teacher's attention and affirm his commitment. "I swear, Professor Brown, I will bring my grade average back up to where it was. And more."

Brown squeezed his tired eyes and gazed back at his student with a lackadaisical look. "Have you considered practical medicine may not be your path? You've already got a foothold at Biopharm — yes, I know about that. Why not stay there and build your future?"

Joel raised his voice to show his earnestness. "Because I need...I've sorted out my priorities." My studies are the most—"

"Don't tell me what you think I want to hear."

Joel paused and rethought his approach. He placed his hands in his pockets to appear less volatile and more in control of his emotions. "It's my mother."

"What? She spent every last dime on your education and now you think you owe her?"

Joel could have argued with his prof,' but decided to let him think whatever he wanted. "Please, Professor, I'll do whatever it takes."

"Joel, if I allow you back in, what're you going to do about your part time job? It's obvious to both of us you can't handle both."

"The work is at a stage where they don't need me anymore. I've already spoken to them about it. It's being handled as we speak."

Professor Brown looked Joel in the eye and tried to gauge whether or not his motives were genuine. Then he gave out an exasperated breath.

"One more chance, Gardiner. And only because I don't want to see you waste your life. Or Lisa's. Yes, I know about that too. Pick a path and stick to it, whether it's medicine, or research, or the next bitcoin scam."

"Thanks, professor." Joel smiled gratefully and left the room pleased that the road ahead was clear. Brown shook his head, not believing a word that came out of the student's mouth. He'd been there himself in his younger days.

When Lisa arrived a few moments later she saw Joel exit. Instead of greeting him she retreated into an alcove. She had been through a lot in the past twenty-four hours and needed some advice before making a decision as to how to proceed academically and personally. She waited until Joel left the building and entered the lecture hall.

"Not much of a turnout today, huh?" she said to Brown as she shuffled down the steps toward him.

He smiled and responded, "Just missed your boyfriend."

"Actually, I was hoping to speak to you alone."

Oh shit. He knew how close she and Morgan were. Lisa was going to shake him down, blackmail him for a better grade or money or both. When would he learn the meaning of the word, discretion?

"I wanted to ask you some questions that aren't on the curriculum."

Brown lifted his hooded eyes. "Such as?"

"Do you believe in God?"

A religious fanatic. Even worse. There was no reasoning with them. Professor Brown decided to play it smart by playing dumb. "Huh?"

She continued, "When I was a girl, my parish priest would say, 'All you have to do is look around you to see the wonder of God.'"

"Mmm."

Lisa guessed what his reticence was about and wanted to make it clear she was not gunning for him. "Professor, everything else that's gone on or is going on recently, this is not about that."

Brown's shoulders relaxed and his expression softened. "Okay. Then my response to your priest would be, 'Excuse me father, but you're trying to qualify a metaphysical entity using physical properties. Doesn't that seem a little incongruous?'"

Lisa nodded. "And he might answer with, 'We can't see sound but we know it's there, don't we? We can quantify it. So maybe there is a God and we just haven't found the right tools to prove he exists.'"

"I'll buy that. But I have a feeling that's not what you're really asking. I know the death of that student the other night bummed out a lot of you people. If you want to speak to a grief counsellor—"

"No, no. I'm not...I'm literally asking how a scientist can believe in God."

A small grin crept across his lips. "It's a common trap people fall into."

"What do you mean?"

"Well, everybody thinks that science and religion are at odds, that an academic like myself cannot abide religion. That's bullshit. There is no conflict."

"Why?"

"Because science is all about proving, and religion is all about believing. No one can prove a belief, therefore a belief is as valid in its universe as science is in its."

"But here's the thing. What if there was something, some kind of object that could prove definitively that God exists?"

Brown raised his arms in an all-encompassing gesture. "You mean, besides 'the wonder of the universe'? That's where you run into trouble. Because for a scientist, the only way to prove a theory is through the scientific method, meaning you start with a question, form a hypothesis, make observations or conduct an experiment, analyse the data, and draw a conclusion. And that's where most people screw up;

they assume scripture is proof enough. But you're not going to find your proof in the Bible or the Torah or the Koran. They weren't meant to be taken literally. They're parables, ways to teach people of that particular time right from wrong, to provide them with a moral compass."

Lisa nodded and the excitement of the discussion made her hands become more animated. "But Jesus was an actual person. He walked the earth, he wore clothes. And a lot of things were documented, the last supper, the disciples."

"Documented? You mean like finding Jesus's fingerprints or his DNA on the holy grail?"

Lisa mused, "Or a robe? Jesus wore a robe, his disciples wore a robe, even Judas wore a robe."

Brown sighed at having to explain the phenomenon for the umpteenth time. "Stop right there. The Shroud of Turin was carbon-dated back to the Middle Ages. It did not belong to Jesus." Brown came around from his lectern and took a few thoughtful paces as he laced his fingers like a priest summing up his sermon. "For thousands of years people have been stymied at the intersection of religion and science. If you want to prove God exists, go right ahead. People smarter than you and I have tried and failed. You can't *prove* God or the existence of aliens, you can't define good art from bad. You can't even prove love. All these things belong to the realm of *belief*. If you want my advice, trust in what you can see in front of you."

"Thanks for the talk, professor."

Lisa smiled and turned toward the door.

"Lisa, are we cool?" he asked, referring to his tryst with Morgan.

"We are."

She left feeling more confident — if not about God, then about having something on Brown if he ever hurt Morgan. Continuing down the hall she considered that if the robe was genuine it would have to be proven like anything else, from a scientific point of view. Religion had lost its lustre for her years ago. But this question had re-energized her.

* * *

"Hey Rich, here are all the notes, the hard copies, and my USB stick. Anything else you need, just ask."

Back at the Biopharm lab Joel handed over his work to his partner who looked confused but delighted.

"You're sure about this?"

"The blood thing wasn't the path I was really on. It was more like a means to an end. Maybe after I've finished school I'll come back to it."

"You know Marie is going full tilt on this so you can kiss any ownership to the solution goodbye. But if that's the way you feel."

Joel smiled as he held out his hand and shook Roger's, then turned and exited the lab. Upon closing the door behind him Joel heard a yelp of joy and smiled to himself. Roger was a good guy. He'd put in his time and deserved some success to come his way. As Joel strolled down through the corridor to the elevator, he noticed the janitor. Another good soul.

"Emile, I just wanted to say goodbye."

"You're leaving?"

"Decided my schooling comes first."

"Well, we all have our own paths to follow."

Joel acknowledged the cryptic reply with a nod and waved goodbye. A smile crossed his lips as he thought, *One more goodbye and I'm outa here.*

"Not on your life!" Marie Champlain said. Joel had marched straight from the lab to his boss's office to hand in his resignation. "Ms. Champlain, you don't need me. I've given Roger all my notes. He's monitored the procedures from the beginning, he helped me with the proof. It's all mapped out. I need to finish school or I have no future."

"Your future? Your future is here right with us. Students would give their right lung to get an internship with this company. Out of the 50 or so interns that do, maybe three get full time jobs."

Marie could see she wasn't getting through to him so she softened her approach and drew seductively closer to the lean, young man.

"Some people put in their time and do the minimum. They walk through life blind to the riches all around them. Others like you," she purred, "when they see an opportunity, they rise to the occasion."

Marie placed her manicured fingernail on the zipper of his jacket and toyed with it. Joel had not seen this side of her before and was caught totally off-guard. He was so startled by the innuendo that he froze.

"You're on the crest of something great, Joel, surfing a wave of promise few are offered; money, status, everything. Yours for the taking."

Marie leaned in and gave Joel a soft kiss on the lips.

"I guess I'm a little old fashioned," he said, pulling back.

Marie was not used to rejection, business-wise or romantically. Her eyes grew reptilian, and she withdrew her hand.

"You want fashion, design a dress," her voice crackled. "This is the real world. Here, we have investors and stockholders. As an employee you have a duty to Biopharm. Not just us but to every man, woman and child lying in a hospital waiting for a blood transfusion. Do you know what a universal blood type could mean to mankind?"

"When I came to you, I told you I had a different project in mind."

"Yes, yes, a secondary project - ectodermal dysplasia. How many people are affected, a few thousand at most? This discovery, virtually within our hands, would affect millions, maybe billions."

Marie could see the indecision in his eyes so she decided it was time to turn the screws. She walked back to her desk and stood behind it as if she was a master of the universe.

"Let me put it to you this way; science does not exist as a welfare system. Everybody pulls their own weight. You can't come here sucking on the corporate teat without producing the milk. To be even more blunt; you walk out now and I'll make sure you're blacklisted throughout the entire scientific community for the rest of your life. Not only will you never see your pet project come to fruition but I'll guarantee you won't even be able to sell your swimmers to a sperm bank."

The doubt and fear in Joel's face made it clear that Marie's threat had sunk in. Now it was time to put some honey on the wound.

"I'm throwing a party for some of our investors tomorrow night and I'd like you to attend. Bring that little girlfriend of yours." Joel's eyebrows rose over the knowledge that Marie was so aware of his personal life. "Yes, we do our due diligence here. I'm sure Lisa would love to get a glimpse of your future, and hers."

Joel wasn't sure if that was a promise, a warning, or a threat. But the 'invitation' was clear enough.

CHAPTER 10

"We don't have time for this," Lisa said.

She slapped Joel's hands away as she raced around their tiny apartment dressed in her bra and panties. She found her little black dress in the closet and shimmied into it as Joel watched. They'd been living together for less than a year, and watching her scurry around barely dressed still aroused him.

Joel stuffed his white oxford shirt into his pants and finished zipping up his dress slacks. "So, maybe later, after the party?" Joel put on the hound's tooth sports jacket Lisa helped him purchase, the only one he owned.

"I know you. You won't have the energy."

"You don't know me *that* well," he replied with a glimmer in his eye.

The truth was, she did. Between classes and research, he'd been run off his feet. In fact, neither had much time for romance, sex or anything more than a peck and a hug. Lisa crossed to the corner where her mirror and makeup table sat, and put her gold earrings on.

"Tell you what. When you're introducing me to your lady-boss tonight, why don't you think about bending me over this chair right here and having your way with me."

"I like that." Joel came up from behind and pressed his body against hers. "How about a dress rehearsal?" he whispered in her ear.

Lisa giggled, pressed into him just enough to tease, and then scooted out of his grasp. Putting on her high heels, she changed the subject. "I thought you said you were quitting the internship at Biopharm."

"I am."

Joel watched his girlfriend step over to the full-length mirror that hung on the bathroom door and appraise herself. She still had a swimmer's slim, lithe body.

"I'm doing this for you, you know. Don't make us late."

Joel nodded and went to the cupboard to select a tie. Lisa twisted a few strands of her hair into place until she was satisfied. Then she turned around to Joel who was waiting with two ties for her to choose from.

"I don't get it. Why are we going to their party if—?"

"Haven't actually handed in my resignation yet. I wanted to wait until I passed my work over to Roger and I could leave with a clean conscience, do the right thing."

Lisa grabbed the red checked tie she preferred and hung the other one back in the cupboard.

"What about Brown?" she asked.

"I saw him today," he said as he wrapped the tie around his neck and fixed the knot.

"You did?"

Lisa wasn't going to mention she saw him leaving Brown's lecture hall. Neither was she going to admit she'd been to see him after. She also withheld the information about her run-in with Sofia earlier that day. She wanted to gather the facts about Bishop Promane and the Judas Robe before she jumped to any conclusions. This was the first time either had lied to each other. Both justified it in the name of protecting the other. Lisa gazed at herself in the mirror, wondering if not telling the whole truth was the same as lying. Another philosophical discussion meant for another time.

"He's allowing you to stay?" she asked. "You need to give your shoes a polish."

Joel went to a shelf in the closet, took out a kit, and sat on the bed to buff up his black oxfords.

"Yep. Told him I was quitting the lab and devoting myself to studying medicine."

"I called my folks and told them what happened to Andy," she said while grooming herself in the mirror. "I mean it was all over the news, I couldn't not. They wanted me to come home, but I said I'd be fine, that you were taking care of me." She turned around and ran her fingers through his hair. "You are, aren't you?"

Joel stopped buffing his shoes and turned up to gaze lovingly at her. "Yes, babe, I am."

Lisa rubbed his head playfully and continued dressing. "Does your mother know?"

"I haven't had much time to—"

"When was the last time you spoke to her?"

"A while." Joel dropped the shoe he finished and picked up the other.

Joel's cell phone rang. He shoved the shoe under his armpit while he pulled his phone from his pocket. When he saw the name, he grimaced.

"Who is it?" Lisa asked.

"My brother."

"Your brother? You haven't heard from him in years."

"I'll get back to him later."

"You sure? Maybe it's important."

"It's okay."

Joel put the phone back in his pocket, and crossed over to give Lisa a big hug.

"That's a coincidence, isn't it? We're talking about your mother and your brother calls, neither of whom you've spoken to in how long?"

"You are the most important person to me right now."

"So sweet."

They kissed fully, the passion rising in both of them, until Lisa pulled away.

"Later, promise." Then she brought out her cell phone and punched in some information. "Uber in four," she said. "This was your idea, remember?"

Joel put on his shoes and they left the apartment. He checked the door twice to make sure it was properly locked, and escorted Lisa down the stairwell to the lobby, keeping conversation to a minimum. Both were feeling guilty over the subterfuge they engaged in earlier.

The full October moon hung over the Westin Park Hotel like an ornament. The young couple climbed out of the Uber at 7:30 p.m. and climbed the granite steps, awkwardly aware that they did not fit in with the moneyed crowd that surrounded them.

"Good evening. Names please?" asked the security guard at the door.

"Joel Gardiner and guest," replied Joel.

The guard checked their names on his I Pad, smiled, and let them through. Joel and Lisa strolled through the expansive lobby toward the gilded doors of the convention hall. Over a hundred guests filled the ballroom inside. Dimmed lights and soft jazz underscored the polite chatter.

Lisa whispered into Joel's ear, "Maybe think twice about leaving this company. I could get used to this."

The youthful wait staff circulated with all manner of hors oeuvres and drinks. One of them approached the young couple from behind with a tray of drinks.

"Red wine? Cocktails? Meth, amphetamines?"

Lisa and Joel turned around and chuckled with surprise. "Morgan?"

"Sorry, we're out of speed," she said. For a giant pharma company, the party favors are pretty dismal."

"What are you doing here?" Joel asked.

"Girl's gotta make a living."

"You don't have to justify anything to us," said Lisa.

She turned and gestured to the room. "I'm not. It's a good gig. Pays well, and it's a great place to shop for a sugar daddy," she added glancing over the crowd with the eye of a connoisseur.

Lisa and Joel each took a glass of wine. Morgan made a little curtsey and continued meandering through the crowd. Joel whispered to Lisa, "I thought she was banging Brown."

"Guess a girl's gotta keep her options open."

Joel gazed across the room, surveying the crowd.

"Any familiar faces?" she asked.

"Thought Roger, my lab partner, might be here. Guess not. Actually, besides you and Morgan, I don't know anyone."

The ballroom doors opened and Marie Champlain entered. He felt a sudden giddy-up in his heart, knowing that he'd have to introduce Lisa to the woman who tried to seduce him less than 24 hours ago. And if that wasn't enough to churn the acid in his stomach, he noticed her two companions. The first one was a tallish woman in her twenties. He didn't know her, although her features were familiar. She was slim, balding, with a pale complexion, a cleft palate and an awkward smile, an appearance similar to his mother. The second person, a gentleman, was more disturbing.

* * *

On the other side of town, the Biopharm offices were virtually deserted because many of the executives were attending the festivities at the Westin Hotel. Phil, the security guard, was sitting at his desk, watching a hockey game on his laptop, when he heard a thud accompanied by a startling cry at the front doors.

"Help! Help me! Pleeease!" She shouted.

Phil looked up to see a woman with her blouse partially torn, screaming hysterically. Her voice barely penetrated the inch-thick tempered glass. She flailed her arms in a desperate attempt to convey that she had been attacked and that her assailants were coming for her. Phil remained transfixed for the moment, unsure whether or not to leave his post or call the police. Then he saw a pack of four aggressive males racing toward the defenceless young woman from down the block. He knew that within ten seconds they'd be on her so he made a decision and ran to the front door, unlocked it, and let the girl inside. Then he locked the door just in time to prevent the attackers from getting inside. They hammered their fists against the glass like drug-crazed fanatics.

"Leave! Get out of here!" Phil shouted. "I'm calling 911!"

As soon as Phil reached for his cell phone the men growled and retreated. Relaxing, Phil turned back to the girl. "They're gone now, it's okay, take a breath."

Belle covered up, aware that the guard's eyes were all over her."

"Wait right here. I have to call it in," he said, regaining his composure.

Phil walked back to the phone on his desk as his hands shook.

"This is 911. What's your emergency?"

While he was busy on the phone, Belle detached part of her necklace. She withdrew a small dart hidden in her hair and inserted it into a mechanism which functioned as a tiny crossbow. Before Phil knew what happened, she shot him in the neck. Startled, he felt a pinch and reached for the wound but it was too late. He didn't even have time to turn around to see what hit him before he dropped to the ground unconscious. Belle marched over and clicked off his phone. Then she ripped the security card from his belt and dragged him by his heels to a nearby closet.

***

Lisa noticed the disconcerting look on her boyfriend, slipped her hand inside his coat, and tickled his ribs to get his attention.

"You going to tell me who they are?" she asked.

"The bottle blonde is my boss, Marie Champlain. The other woman, I don't know."

"And the older, distinguished-looking gentleman?"

"A priest, actually a bishop," he said in a sobering tone.

The couple watched as Marie paraded her guests through the room and greeted the affluent crowd. When the palm pressing was over, Marie took to the podium flanked by her guests, and addressed the room using the microphone that had already been standing there waiting for her.

"Ladies and gentlemen, thanks for coming out tonight. It sure beats drinking alone."

The remark was followed by a wave of polite laughter. "Before we begin the festivities, I wanted you to meet two dear friends of mine. On my left is a gentleman many of you already know, Bishop Newman. The bishop has been one of our board members for a number of years and we have benefited greatly from his moral and spiritual guidance here at Biopharm."

Lisa felt Joel's body stiffen. "How well do you know him?" she asked.

"He's the family priest, my mother's priest," he replied as if the drink he was sipping suddenly soured.

***

After hiding the guard from sight, Belle hurried to the front door of the Biopharm labs and let her four comrades in. One of the males stripped off his shirt and went to the closet where Belle left the guard. A minute later he returned, dressed in the guard's uniform. He took a seat at the control panel while Belle led the other three to an elevator. When the door opened, they advance with military-like precision. Belle slipped the guard's security card into the slot and pressed Sub Level Six. The door closed and the elevator hummed to life. When the doors opened the intruders exited the car and marched down the corridor with menace in their eyes.

***

Marie was in the midst of her introduction. "My other guest is Amelia Masursky. Amelia was introduced to me by the bishop. She's a very accomplished musician as well as a media personality with her own You-Tube channel where she educates the public about a condition she has, called ectodermal dysplasia, which is the reason we're all here tonight."

"Sonofabitch!" Joel muttered, taken totally by surprise.

"What?" asked Lisa. She had not seen Joel this disconcerted in a long time.

Joel never liked the bishop. He felt the priest was too embedded in his family's personal business. From a young age he and his siblings were forced to attend services regularly at his church. On occasion, his mother would invite him over to dinner. Whenever Natalie had a crisis, it was him she ran to. Joel began to fear that he had too much control over her and his family. But there was a positive aspect to their relationship. The priest had used his influence over the years to get Natalie expert medical help which included surgeries to normalize her looks and help regulate her breathing. When Joel's parents' marriage fell apart, the bishop found his mother a safe haven at St. James'. And now, it seemed, he was advocating for others who had the same debilitating condition. The man was an enigma.

***

Roger was at his computer station in the lab scrolling through a site entitled, 'Ukrainian Brides,' women eager to meet eligible American men for marriage. He admired all the lovely faces and figures and dreamed of the waterfront condo he'd be sharing with one lucky lady the minute Joel's project paid off. Everything changed when the door opened and Belle and her cohorts strode in.

Roger looked up and slammed his laptop closed. "Who the hell are you and how'd you get in here?" he shouted.

Neither questions were answered. Instead, Belle gestured to her comrades who began breaking every piece of equipment they could get their hands on. Roger's eyes darted back and forth, looking for an escape. There was only one and it was blocked.

* * *

"This is not a single disorder," Marie said, "but a group of syndromes derived from abnormalities of the ectodermal structures. Despite some of the syndromes having different genetic causes...I hope you don't mind, Amelia?" Amelia nodded affirmatively to indicate that it was okay with Marie to continue. "It affects the hair, teeth, nails, sweat glands, salivary glands, cranial-facial structure, digits, and other parts of the body. Diagnosis is generally made through clinical observation and can help determine whether transmission is autosomal, dominant or recessive. Worldwide, around 7,000 people have been diagnosed with this condition. Now some of you may think this a miniscule number for a pharmaceutical company of our size to bother with."

She never glanced his way but Joel heard her every word and she knew it. "The bitch is blackmailing me," Joel whispered to his girlfriend.

"What?"

Marie continued, "But money is not always the defining factor here at Biopharm. Seven thousand people might be an insignificant number until someone you know suffers from the condition." This is where Marie made eye contact with Joel before she returned to her speech. "We have made a commitment to find and isolate the gene that carries this condition so that one day no child will have to suffer any further pain or discomfort. Tonight I am declaring that our mission is to eradicate it completely."

Generous applause erupted from the crowd. Joel clapped too, but there was suspicion in his eyes.

* * *

"Stopppp!" Roger yelled at the top of his voice like an enraged bear. Frustrated, he charged the nearest intruder who easily pushed the out-of-shape lug aside, and sent him head first into a steel countertop. As big and formidable as Roger looked, he hadn't seen the inside of a gym in over ten years. His head bounced off the solid surface, the impact of which opened a gash on his forehead. Through the blood that dripped into his eye he spotted a nearby phone and stumbled toward it. But Belle got there sooner and wrestled the receiver out of his hand. Then she back-handed him and sent him flying against the opposite wall. Roger ricochet off it and dropped to the floor.

"What the fuck do you want?!" He cried.

Belle did not reply. The other three continued trashing every piece of machinery in sight.

* * *

Marie accepted the accolades from her guests and nodded once again to Joel. Reluctantly, he nodded back. He was right. The woman had found his Achilles heel and was exploiting it. He knew if he quit his work on the development of the blood project, she would pull the plug on the research closest to his heart. Her point made, she continued to cajole her audience.

"I want you all to relax and enjoy yourselves and be generous. By the way, the entertainment will be supplied by Amelia herself."

Two technicians pushed a grand piano out of the wings and onto the middle of the platform. The crowd applauded again as Amelia sat down and began to play selections by Irving Berlin. Marie left the podium to mingle with her guests.

"What do you mean, she's blackmailing you?" asked Lisa.

"Ectodermal dysplasia. It's what my mother has."

Joel and stood listening dumbly to the musician play 'Cheek to Cheek' as a few couples took to the dance floor. He thought he'd been so clever by attaching his pet project to the big money-maker. He also assumed that after he initiated the project he could hand it over to his associate, Roger, whenever it suited him. But his boss was much savvier, and used his own machinations against him.

"This is going to complicate your exit, isn't it?" Lisa asked.

Before Joel could answer he heard his name called.

"Joel," said Bishop Newman, greeting him with a warm handshake.

The bishop had been working his way through the crowd until he reached Joel.

"Bishop," Joel answered coldly.

"Wonderful to see you here tonight." The priest leaned in and spoke more intimately. "I don't know how you did it exactly, but it appears that you inspired a major pharmaceutical company to pursue a project on a purely charitable and altruistic basis. No mean feat. And who is this?" the priest asked, turning to Joel's companion.

"Bishop Newman, this is my girlfriend, Lisa."

"Lovely to meet you, Lisa."

Bishop Newman offered his hand to Lisa who took it graciously. When she shook it, he saw the question in her eyes.

"Oh, the pinky. I lost it as a child, playing cops and robbers."

"Sorry."

"That's alright. The bad guys got what they deserved. Are you in medicine too?"

"Yes. Pre-med."

"Well, we'll be sure to watch out for you too. You should be very proud of this young man," turning to Joel and clapping him on the shoulder. "He's a David who took on a Goliath and won."

"Oh, I am proud, everyday," Lisa replied, and then squeezed her boyfriend's arm affectionately. Joel smiled back at her, trying to mask the agitation in his eyes.

* * *

Roger lay on the floor, gasping for air as blood poured from the gash on his head and pooled around him. A few feet away, Belle studied Roger's laptop and smirked at the page featuring Ukrainian women. She shut the site down and clicked on 'Documents.' Her cohorts were still laying waste to the lab when the door opened and Emile, the janitor, entered. The thugs laughed when they saw the old man in the custodial uniform. But the smirk on Belle's face vanished. Without hesitation, the janitor charged the nearest intruder and swung his fists with surprising effectiveness, knocking him to the floor.

* * *

How is your mother, Joel?" asked Bishop Newman.

"Fine. So, what's the deal with you and the girl?" he asked, pointing to the pianist.

The priest cocked his head as if not comprehending the question. "I beg your pardon?"

"Did you bring her to Marie after I told her I wanted to quit? Do you have a stable of people with various afflictions you trot out whenever it serves you?"

"Joel!" Lisa turned to her boyfriend; her face turned red with embarrassment.

Bishop Newman bristled for a moment and then regained his composure. "Joel, you may not approve of my methods but you and I both know this condition is not popular enough or financially attractive enough to warrant the millions of dollars of research it will take to isolate the gene and find a way to conquer it. Amelia was brought to my attention several years ago after it became known that I helped your mother." The bishop turned his head to the pianist who was now performing, 'Puttin' on The Ritz.' "This talented lady deserves as much support and assistance as your mother, do you not agree?"

Joel gave the bishop the slightest begrudging nod.

"You would be well advised to open your heart with the same humility and charity. Trust me, it will serve you both in the now and the hereafter."

Lisa squeezed Joel's hand hoping that might temper his anger and ease her own discomfort. Joel remained tense, but held his tongue. A bell rang out in the hall. Amelia concluded her song and stepped to the microphone as she pointed to the kitchen doors. "Ladies and Gentlemen, I hope you're hungry because," The guests turned their attention to the doors which swung open and the entire wait staff entered with trays of hors d'oeuvres. They were also stripped to the waist. Joel noticed Morgan marching along with the others, a big smile pasted across her face. The Bishop followed Joel's eyes and admired the young beauty.

"God and his many wonders. And this is where I make my exit." The priest shook Lisa's hand once again and left the ballroom.

* * *

An eerie silence hung over the Biopharm lab. The room was trashed, equipment and liquids tossed helter-skelter. The intruders were gone. Emile's shirt was torn and his hair was tussled but he looked relatively unscathed. Not so, Roger. Emile was sitting over the researcher, trying to suppress the flow of blood from his head with some gauze. After a moment, Emile dropped the bloody gauze next to the lifeless body and made the sign of the cross.

CHAPTER 11

It was just after eleven that night when Lisa and Joel climbed into the back seat of an Uber to discuss the events of the evening.

"Some cocktail party," said Lisa. "Is that typical of Biopharm? Everybody running around half naked day and night?"

"Just on the coffee breaks." He noted the perplexed look on her face. "I swear I've never seen anything like that. Somebody's crazy idea of marketing a new product initiative, I guess."

"Hope at least it raised some money." She shifted in her seat and shifted the conversation at the same time. "I never did get to meet your boss."

"Not missing much."

Lisa snuggled closer to him. "And to invite a bishop there as well."

"If you wanna call him that."

"Why do you have such contempt for him?"

Joel stared out the window. "He's been around my family ever since I can remember. Whenever my parents argued, he'd show up to mediate, always running interference. I don't know if he had anything to do with their break-up, but I've always had a bad feeling about him."

Lisa reached over and placed her hand affectionately on his leg. "You never really told me about your mother. She has the same condition as that pianist?"

Joel nodded but avoided her gaze. "And there are things you haven't told me about your family either."

"Hey, hon,' I'm not trying to fight with you. I'm trying to get to know you. That's what people do when they're a couple." Lisa didn't want to put any more pressure on him. "We've been together six months now. After the 'honeymoon stage' all your shit comes out and you either deal with things or you break up. I don't want to break up."

She reached out to take his hand again. Joel hadn't been in a relationship of this depth before, but instinctively he knew Lisa was right. He cupped her hand in his and relaxed.

"Short answer. My mother had this condition since birth. I guess she leaned on her faith to help her cope, but I think it also drove the family apart."

"What do you mean?"

"My mother always believed she and her family had a special calling. Yes, she had a hereditary condition but the other aspect of her heritage was this claim on an ancient relic."

"The Judas Robe?"

"It was always very vague. But my folks would argue about it, what does it do, where was it, how can we cash in on it. It hovered over us like a curse. My brother, Gordon, wound up doing alcohol and drugs. My sister, Colleen used to cut herself. When I was seventeen my dad split and took them both with him. I haven't seen them since."

Lisa turned to face Joel directly and offer her support. "And you were left at home with your mother?"

"The courts said I was too young to leave."

"Was it crazy/terrible there?"

Joel softened a little upon reflection. "Well, she always took care of me, even when I got sick. So —"

"So, you dedicated yourself to finding a cure for your mother's illness while hating her at the same time? That's a real mind fuck. I can understand why it's so hard for you to leave Biopharm, knowing that they're supporting your project." Lisa paused to gauge Joel's response. He appeared less agitated and more open, so she continued. "But you said you haven't spoken to your mom in years. Maybe now is a good time."

"It's complicated." He stiffened again.

"Always is when it's family. But obviously you love her or else you wouldn't—"

Joel's phone buzzed — a message. He looked at its face and decided not to answer.

"Your brother again?"

"No, my lab partner, Roger."

"Can we forget about work for a minute?"

Joel acquiesced and shoved the phone back into his pocket without answering. He loved Lisa but there was no way she'd understand his family. Maybe he wasn't destined to have a typical life, or for that matter, happiness. Maybe he wasn't worthy. But the night of surprises was not over.

"I met your friend, Sofia today," said Lisa, trying to draw him out again. Joel's face darkened in response. "She stopped me on my way to classes."

"Lisa, whatever she said, don't believe her. I don't even know her."

"I'm not jealous, if that's what you mean. We talked awhile, actually. I think you should seriously consider what she has to say."

Joel shifted his body toward the door. Knowing that his girlfriend was being dragged into this quagmire added another level of anxiety. The tone of his voice changed, became more distant.

"Listen, Lisa, maybe you're right. With my studies and my job and all, maybe we should take a break, for now at least."

"Joel, I'm not stupid. I know you're trying to protect me, but..."

Joel sat up straight. "Maybe you don't have a say in it."

Another buzz from his phone announced a second text message. Joel pulled the phone out of his pocket, glanced at it, and froze. Lisa saw the ashen look on his face and asked.

"What?"

"The lab was broken into, everything destroyed. I'm going to drop you off home and—"

"No, you're not. I'm coming with."

"God-dammit, Lisa!" he shouted.

Staring into her eyes Joel knew she wouldn't budge. And he was just too exhausted to argue. He gave directions to the driver who made a quick right turn and headed toward the Biopharm offices.

Fifteen minutes later they arrived at the building to find three police cruisers and an ambulance parked outside with lights flashing. Joel told the driver to continue another fifty yards before stopping. Then he and Lisa got out to assess the situation from a distance. That's when they heard a surreptitious whistle. Joel and Lisa turned to find a female standing in the shadows about twenty feet away.

"Sofia?" Both said at the same time.

She gestured for the couple to join her.

"There was an incident, an attack on the laboratory," she whispered.

"I know," Joel replied. "I got a text from my partner, Roger. Where is he? Is he all right?"

"It was me who messaged you from his phone." Sofia showed Joel the phone she used. "Roger is dead. So is the security guard."

Joel looked dumbfounded. "Roger? Phil? I don't believe it. Why would anybody—?"

"We should go somewhere else to talk," she said. "It's not safe here."

"This is crazy!"

He took several angry steps in the opposite direction until Lisa caught his arm. "Joel!"

"This woman, whoever she is, I think you should hear her out!"

Joel shot a glance at Sofia who waited anxiously for them to make a decision, "No! She's caught up in the same crazy shit as my family. It's like a disease. I don't want anything to do with it and I don't want you to have anything to do with it either."

"Well, you're in pre med. How do you treat a disease, Joel? You diagnose it, find its source and cure it, the scientific method. If it's a hoax, then you debunk it. One way or the other, you need to deal with it."

Joel took a minute and looked up and down the street to make sure they weren't being watched. He felt as if he was caught between an oceanic riptide pulling him out to sea and a tidal wave bearing down on him. Lisa was right. This wasn't going away and he could no longer ignore it. The insanity had spread beyond his family and was causing innocent people their lives. If he really wanted to solve the problem, the best thing would be to get it all out in the open, debunk it as she said. Even if that meant exposing family secrets. With a nod he agreed to Lisa's suggestion.

"Okay. Where?"

Sofia led them down the street, skirting the shadows until they arrived at the nearest watering hole, The Lazy-Eyed Lawyer. They huddled in a booth far enough away that no one could eavesdrop on their conversation. A waitress came by to take their drink orders.

"Beers all around," he said.

"What kind? We got..."

"Whatever's on tap, thanks."

The waitress understood they were there to talk and left them alone.

"All right," said Joel to Sofia. "What the fuck is going on?"

Sofia leaned in. "You already know. Someone is after the Judas Robe."

"Which doesn't exist."

"Neither does all this carnage around you."

"All right. And by someone you mean—?"

"He's a priest, a bishop by the name of Promane."

Lisa took a double-take. "Now wait a minute.

Sofia stared at Lisa. "What did you find out?"

Lisa looked sheepishly at Joel, feeling guilty for going behind his back.

"He was a cleric who lived during the Spanish Inquisition."

"Spanish Inquisition?" said Joel.

"I told you, Sofia and I met earlier, I did some research in the stacks. He was an actual person."

"Yeah, 500 years ago. Are we telling ghost stories now?"

"Let's deal with the facts. A few nights ago Andy was killed at a party you were supposed to attend. Tonight, your company was broken into and your partner was killed. Obviously, somebody using his name is behind all this, coming after you."

Sofia said, "Not to kill you, to scare you."

"Scare me into what?"

"Into exposing the robe, revealing where it's hidden."

"The robe is a myth my mother made up. Like the chalice or the golden fleece. Jesus Christ!"

99

The server came over and laid all three drinks on the table. "I can see you're busy so," she laid the bill on the table. "That'll be $16.49."

Joel stuck his hand in his pocket but Sofia beat him to it and presented a twenty-dollar bill.

"Keep the change," she said.

"Thanks." The server smiled and sashayed away.

"Can we backtrack a bit?" asked Lisa. "Sofia, what's so special about this robe that people are willing to kill for it?"

Sofia drew a breath. "According to the bible, the body of Jesus was claimed from Pilote by Joseph of Arimathea who, with the assistance of another man named Nicodemus, buried the body."

Joel said, "But it's called the Judas Robe."

"After Judas hung himself," said Lisa. "the body fell from a tree and his guts spilled out. Later he was buried in a Potter's Field, if I remember my catechism correctly."

"You're saying somebody stole Judas's robe after he died?" asked Joel. "Why?"

"Because," replied Sofia, "some believed he was not a traitor, he was the catalyst for Christ's ascension to sainthood, a hero in his own right. And those people believe his robe has some transcendent power."

"Sure, and Poseidon had a trident, Zeus had a thunderbolt, Thor had a hammer. Why isn't anybody looking for them?" Joel paused to wait for an answer that he didn't expect would be forthcoming, and then continued. "Plus, you haven't explained who you are."

Sofia ignored Joel's question and turned to Lisa. "Did you do the research on Bishop Promane as I asked? "

"Uh-huh. One bad-ass character, second only to Thomas Torquemada."

Joel said, "You didn't tell me anything about that."

"You didn't give me a chance."

"And the other priest, Father Sanchez," continued Sofia.

"Not much I could find about him."

A man's voice rang out, "Maybe I can be of help."

"Emile?" said Joel.

The three were so involved in their conversation that they did not notice the elderly gentleman walking up to them. Lisa caught Sofia giving Emile a smile as she grabbed a chair and gestured for the caretaker to join them.

"You two know each other?" Joel asked her.

"We go back."

The caretaker took a seat, caught the server's eye, and gestured for her to bring another beer.

CHAPTER 12

Who are you?" asked Joel suspiciously. Before Emile could answer, the waitress brought over a beer.

"I assume?" she said.

"You assume correctly," answered the caretaker with a smile. He fished a few dollars out of his pocket and passed it to her.

"I love the way your hair cascades over your ears," he said. The waitress giggled at the compliment and touched the curl in her hair."

"Thanks," she said.

"But those lovely looks will not last forever. Enjoy your youth while you can."

"Damn, you were so close," she replied as she walked away.

The caretaker smiled again, took a large gulp of his beer, belched, and turned to Lisa.

"Excuse me."

"Emile, what the hell is this all about?" asked Joel.

"You both have questions. Let me answer them to the best of my ability," said the caretaker. "This man Sofia asked you to research, this Emilio Sanchez, he was born in the city of Valencia in 1446. He began his apprenticeship in the priesthood at the age of 14 and became a cleric at 22. The church provided him with an education to prepare him for his calling. His chief duties were to educate children, minister to the sick, and pray for the masses."

"What has this got to do with —"

"Joel," said Lisa, shushing her boyfriend in an effort to allow the caretaker to continue.

"It's pertinent, I assure you." Joel nodded and the elderly gent continued. "In those days the Catholic church held great power. But there was always the threat of other faiths encroaching upon their territory. In 1478 Pope Sixtus IV instituted an order to bring the strays of the flock back into the fold."

"You mean the Inquisition."

Emile nodded. "It began in Europe and migrated to Spain. However, it was all a ploy. The strays they referred to were mostly Jews. The official argument was that the church was trying to save the Jews from eternal hellfire because of their rejection of the savior, Jesus Christ. The truth was, Spain was struggling financially. The Jews of that country were financial leaders. Under the guise of saving them from damnation, the real plan was to expel them and confiscate their wealth."

Emile took another drink and paused to let the information sink in before he continued.

"There were a number of Jewish families in Father Sanchez's village living under this threat. Some of the lucky ones escaped early. Other, more proud Spaniards, refused to leave. One such family was the Garcias. The law, at the time, allowed Jews to remain if they renounced their religion and became what was known as *'conversos'* citizens who converted to Christianity. If not they'd be put to death. Sebastian and Adelina Garcia were a proud, stubborn couple who wanted to remain in the town of their ancestors."

"I still don't understand what this has to do with Sanchez and Bishop Promane and us," Joel said.

The caretaker raised a cautioning hand, begging for patience. "One night, a patrol rode into the village and rounded up all the Jewish families. The next day, Sebastian and Adelina were brought before the council for questioning. However, any accusation made by the inquisitor was damning in of itself because in those days you were considered guilty until proven innocent. Those under suspicion were given the opportunity to confess. If they refused they would be accused of heresy and automatically sentenced to an *auto de fe.*"

"A what?" asked Lisa.

"Translated, it means, 'Act of Faith.' Presiding clergymen would deliver castigations, confinement to dungeons and all manner of torture. After that, those who reconciled were punished even further—their property was confiscated and they were banished from public life. These were the were the lucky ones, the ones who lived. Those who did not confess were burned at the stake or strangled."

"So you were screwed no matter what," said Lisa.

Sofia nodded as a grim confirmation.

"Upon the Garcia's' arrest, Father Sanchez went to the judiciary and told them that, as a family friend, he was assisting in their conversion. After several days of petitioning, the parents were allowed to return home. Sebastian returned, minus three fingers. As for Adelina," the caretaker paused to gather his words, "she would not speak from that day forward. There were special 'treatments' for women."

"I'll bet."

"Fearing for his family, Sebastian presented the priest with a scroll he had in his keeping for many years. It was written in an unreadable language but he felt it was an important religious document and that if the priest offered it to the church, his family would be spared. Father Sanchez agreed do his best." Emile paused again. His face darkened with the knowledge he was about to disclose. "Father Sanchez, however, did not present the scroll to the church as he'd promised."

"Why not?" asked Joel.

"He had to be sure it had value, something he could trade for the family's freedom. The scroll was written in Aramaic, ancient Hebrew. Since he could not interpret it himself, he put out the word for someone who could. A short time later he was approached by a man who said he could read the parchment."

"What did it say?" Joel asked again.

"It spoke of a robe that was taken from the body of Judas after he was buried."

Joel bristled at the mention of the robe. This relic had become the bane of his family and he was eager to dispel its authenticity.

"It was a fraud, wasn't it?"

"Joel," said Sofia. She had been silently monitoring the conversation, making sure that Joel and Lisa were following Emile. She calmly and quietly beseeched them both to be patient until he finished his story.

Joel sat up straight, leaned in, and waited to hear more.

"Lemme guess," Lisa said, "The interpreter snitched to the church."

Emile nodded. "Promane had Sanchez's apartment searched and found the scroll before the priest could even offer it. Promane interrogated the priest, assuming that if he had the relic, he also knew the whereabouts of the robe."

"Did he? I mean, was the robe's hiding place written in the scroll?" Emile lowered his head as an admission of guilt. "No, but..." The caretaker shifted uneasily in his chair. "Having been born in the village and brought up in the priesthood, Father Sanchez was privy to many of the secrets of the local monastery, one of which was talk about an ancient relic." Emile took another gulp of beer. "He had a suspicion."

"And he wouldn't give up the robe for the Garcias' lives?"

Emile glowered and his voice turned defensive. "The artifact was not meant to be used as a political tool, especially by someone as despicable as Bishop Promane." The caretaker slumped back in his chair.

Joel shook his head in disbelief. "Wait a minute, wait a minute. You're talking about it as if—"

Emile gave Joel a look that warned him to stop interrupting. "In any case," he continued, "Father Sanchez was 'persuaded' to reveal its hiding place. The story goes that Promane plundered the monastery and stole the relic. And the priests in the monastery, they all died."

The caretaker stared off into the distance as if he was reliving the actual moment. His face slackened and the weight of its impact showed in the weariness of his eyes.

Joel gave Lisa a dubious look as if to say his caretaker friend might be a little crazy. Instinctively, Lisa reached out and took Emile's hand to comfort him. Emile 'woke' from his reverie and smiled at her. "Fortunately, as soon as Promane laid hands on the artifact, he lost it. Soldiers of the Order of Christ had followed him and confiscated the relic."

Again, Emile fell quiet but the frown on his face remained.

"That's not the end of the story, is it?" said Lisa.

"After the Order escorted Father Sanchez back to the village, he arranged for Sebastian and Adelina to escape through what would be referred to today as an underground railroad."

"And their children, too, right? The whole family?"

The caretaker took a deep breath as if he was about to admit a confession. "A family of four on the road would be too suspicious to the authorities. The priest placed the children with a Christian family hoping to smuggle them out at a later time."

"Tell me there's a happy ending."

Sofia picked up the thread. "As soon as they left town, the parents were apprehended and killed."

"My God. And the children?"

"They lived, they even flourished. Just before the Order of Christ was dissolved in 1789, they placed the robe into the hands of the Garcia children who had been adopted by the Christian family. After what they suffered, the Order felt it was the right thing to do. And they've kept it all these years."

Joel blinked as if seeing something for the first time. "Wait! Are you telling me the Garcia children are my ancestors?"

Emile and Sofia nodded in unison.

Joel got up and walked around the table nervously, trying to comprehend the impact of this story. Lisa reached out to him but Joel kept pacing, processing the information.

After a moment Lisa asked, "So what happened to the two priests?"

CHAPTER 13

The church on Sumach Street had been abandoned for six years, another casualty of secularism in modern North American society. Parents who had been brought up in the faith a generation ago had a hard time convincing their children of the merits of regular attendance. The miracles described in the old and new testaments had lost their meaning for those living in the age where communication traveled at the speed of light and a pair of jeans could be purchased online and delivered the next day. Hellfire and damnation had long since lost their threat. If someone had a hankering for a religious fix, it was as close as their television, internet, or cell phone.

Although the church paid no taxes, there were costs in the upkeep of the property, building maintenance, staff etc. The public could no longer be counted on to support the aging institution. When the building was put up for sale, Bishop Newman purchased it and started his own order. He never advertised for members. He never had to. His method was through word of mouth. At first, most people he approached were looking for handouts or a place to sleep for the night. But once they arrived, Newman offered more than just food, shelter, and the need for comfort. It didn't take long for word to spread.

Tonight was the 'night of the gathering.' More than 200 members attended in the main sanctuary. They came from all walks of life, rich, poor, educated and otherwise. The church renovation was not yet finished but the first thing Newman did, was make the sanctuary functional, for his purposes. It was restructured in such a way that the pews were built in a circular fashion around the room. The pulpit and altar stood in the center, giving the followers a 'theatre-in-the-round' experience. This night the attendees stood about, murmuring in excited tones. They were all here because what was promised was nothing short of a revelation. At Eight O'clock the sounds of a Gregorian chant was piped into the sanctuary. It featured multi-voiced a-cappella voices sung in unison by a male choir, beginning with a simple melody that flowed into a complex structure. The repetition of liturgical phrases was mesmerizing, hypnotic.

A door opened and in strode Bishop Newman dressed in a raiment of royal purple and black, a cowl drawn over his head. The look combined aspects of the dramatic, the spiritual, and the mysterious. The bishop stared neither left nor right, but straight ahead as if peering into another realm. The look on his face was solemn and fervent. The procession behind Newman included Belle and two males who, in turn, were followed by a dozen acolytes dressed in dull, grey robes. Their pace was slow and measured, like actors taking the stage and the flock watched their every movement with rapt attention. When they reached the podium in the middle of the sanctuary, they paused. Newman lowered his cowl and addressed his congregation with a beneficent smile.

"Welcome all to 'the gathering.' You are here of your own will. Those who choose not to participate may leave now."

Newman scanned the eyes of every person in attendance. The few who could not meet his gaze honestly, turned and left. The chanting ceased and soft choral music began to play as the priest continued.

"For some, this is your first night, your initiation. For the rest, I welcome you back." Newman smiled lovingly at several pregnant women in attendance. "You are here tonight, we are all here tonight, to meet our God. Not all of you will succeed, but know that the process will have begun. Myself, Sister Belle, and a few of the righteous will be your guides. Trust us, do as we say, and his truth will be revealed."

With that, Belle slipped off her robe and climbed up onto the altar, naked. Her two counterparts did likewise. All three were clean shaven from head to toe and blessed with the glorious physiques of Greek Gods. The attendees began humming along with the melody of the music and the room was soon filled with an intoxicating sound. The three acolytes turned to the bishop. He loved this part, knowing that no one made a move until he gave his permission. He nodded and they slowly began to intertwine their arms, legs, and torsos like serpents, undulating in a slow, hypnotic rhythm. The congregants watched in rapt attention, their pheromones literally raising the temperature of the room. Newman played the ritual like a conductor of a symphony, gesticulating when to pick up the rhythm and when to segue into the next segment. One by one each follower reached for the person next to them and began their 'devotions.' Shirts, pants, skirts and underwear dropped to the floor. People melted into one another and erotic moans filled the hall.

Newman reached across the altar to the tithe or collection box. From inside he brought out a small ampoule. He opened it and placed it under Belle's nostril. She sniffed the contents and her eyes flew back into her head. Newman passed the same ampoule to her lovers. The amyl nitrate only took a few seconds to kick in. The rhythm between the three began to build intensely as the drug transported them to a new high. Their lovemaking became ferocious, animalistic. Others in the room were eager to join in but would have to wait their turn. One of the two males sharing Belle cried out in ecstasy. Newman crouched over his face.

"Yes, Jesse. Tell me what you see."

Jesse could not respond, overcome by the euphoric experience. As Belle began to climax Newman opened a second ampoule and placed it under her nose. She breathed in the vapors and shuddered. She kicked away her lovers and began to writhe on the altar until she peaked and fell silent, almost catatonic. Newman whispered in her ear, "Are you with him, Belle?" An ephemeral smile played across her face. "Greet your lord," he whispered. Her eyelids fluttered as if she had been overcome by rapture. Newman turned to the others in the room and shouted, "Glory!"

"Glory!!" they shouted back as members mounted one another, eager to experience the passion they had just witnessed. Newman obliged and offered each couple the drug. Upon their climax he exclaimed, "Reach out. Praise him, touch him!"

The room became a mass of gyrating bodies, moaning and writhing in complete abandon. The combination of the chanting, the sights and sounds of the group lifted them all to a level of euphoria few had ever experienced. Belle lay still on the altar, awash in her own intoxication. Newman drew close and whispered.

"Do you see the lord, Belle? Is he there? Tell me!"

Newman's voice was filled with urgency. But Belle's altered state prevented her from expressing herself. Wherever she was, it was beyond words or language. The bishop stepped back, frustrated. He'd tried this exercise many times with her only to reach a similar pinnacle and fall short of his goal. God, it seemed, was always just beyond his reach. As eager and compliant as Belle was, she was not the right cipher. He looked around at all the others caught up in sexual abandon. Perhaps one of them.

CHAPTER 14

"A few moments more," said the caretaker. "and all will be revealed, I promise."

Joel looked at Lisa with frustration. She reached for his hand and made him sit. Then she turned to Emile and nodded.

"The night Promane stole the robe from the monastery, he brought Father Sanchez along to guarantee the veracity of his claim. Neither knew the knights of the Order of Christ were nearby."

"They were tipped off?" asked Joel. "By whom?"

"Father Sanchez was the town priest and beloved by many. When he was arrested, some of the guards in the fortress where he was held sent word to the knights who followed Promane to the monastery. After the bishop stole the robe from the monastery, he returned to his men in the field. Under darkness he wrapped himself in the robe and chanted a prayer. Something happened. The robe...turned color, a bright orange-red. And it glowed, illuminating the man like, like he was on fire." Emile looked enthralled by the vision he described as if he was actually witnessing it. "That's when the knights attacked."

"And they killed him?" asked Joel.

The caretaker shook his head. "While his guards were defending themselves, the bishop fled from the killing ground, but not before he was wounded. He dropped the box containing the robe and Captain Domingos, leader of the order, recovered it."

"And the bishop?" asked Lisa.

Emile and Sofia gave each other guarded looks before the elderly gentleman proceeded.

"There was a more urgent matter back in town."

"What?"

The caretaker and Sofia shifted uneasily. Sofia nodded for Emile to continue.

"Father Sanchez would have gladly died and taken the secret of the robe to his grave. But as an assurance of his word, Promane kidnapped a ward of the priest, a young girl, and threatened to kill her if the priest lied."

"Fortunately," Sofia said, "she was rescued. Afterward, the two fetched her younger sister and the three of them returned to the priest's home to plan their escape."

Sanchez continued. "Fourteen days it would take to cross the country from Granada into Portugal. With the aid of friends, they began gathering supplies for the long trek. On the second night of preparations there was a knock on the door."

"Somehow," said Sofia, "Promane survived his wounds and made his way back to the village. He was lying half dead on Father Sanchez's stoop."

"And they let him in?" asked Joel.

Sanchez replied, "The younger of the sisters reminded the priest of his Christian duty and regrettably, he relented. Though wary, they provided the bishop with nourishment and rest. He even seemed humbled, appreciative."

Sofia sighed with regret. "But the next day, little sister was...changed."

"Changed, how?" asked Lisa.

"Her innocence was gone," said Sofia.

"Are you saying the bishop raped her?" asked Joel.

"Worse. In her place stood a creature - someone more knowing, calculating, devious. And of a base, carnal nature."

"Well, their first mistake was letting the snake inside," Joel said.

"Don't you think I know that!" yelled Sofia.

Her response was so abrupt that Joel and Lisa jumped.

Joel said, "Uh, you just went from third person to first person."

Sanchez and Sofia locked eyes on Joel, daring him to believe his own conclusion.

"Look, guys," Joel said with a derisive laugh, "If you're saying what I think you're saying, you two are certifiable and the Judas Robe is the least of our..." Emile raised his hand to stop Joel from finishing his thought, then continued. "Somehow the bishop's prayer in the field that night invoked some kind of supernatural... what I'm trying to say is, he found a way to cheat death and pass his 'gift' on to others."

"You're Father Sanchez?" said Joel. He slammed his hand on the table loud enough to attract the attention of everyone in the pub. Sofia cautioned him to keep his voice down. "C'mon," he said. "This fairy tale just keeps getting crazier and crazier. I'm a scientist for fuck's sakes. Prove one thing you've said is true, just one."

The caretaker reached into his pocket and pulled out a small, dirty container the size of a sardine can. He placed it on the table amongst the glasses of beer and opened it. A foul stench escaped, so rancid that Joel and Lisa had to hold their sleeves over their noses. After the initial shock, the two leaned in to view the contents of the box; a man's blackened, fossilized, pinky finger.

"What the hell?"

"When Promane came to my home that night," continued, Emile. "he was wounded from the battle, this digit dangling from his hand. I found it necessary to amputate."

Lisa's eyes widened with a new awareness. "You're Emilio Sanchez. You're the man you asked me to research!"

Sanchez nodded with a smile, closed the tin, and slid it across the table. "Take this, prove its validity, and you'll believe."

"You both would have to be over 500 years old."

"All I can tell you is there was a metamorphosis of some kind, a combination of bodily fluids, unholy deeds and prayers that a chaste priest should never have experienced. Whatever this power was, it came from Promane and was transferred to Sofia and her sister, Belle. And myself."

Joel turned to Sofia, "Funny, you don't look a day over twenty-three."

Sanchez continued, "Perhaps Promane's power comes from the robe, perhaps from the devil himself, I don't know. But I'm telling you this because *we* no longer matter. Promane needs to be stopped before—"

"You say that as if... Wait a minute; Newman?' Newman'?"

Father Sanchez and Sofia nodded.

Joel looked at Lisa and his eyes rolled. His girlfriend gave him a look as if to say, 'stay with it.' "All right, let's say for the minute that this fairy tale is true. What's this guy's end game?"

"We're not sure," answered Sofia. "It may be that, with the robe, he wants to unite all the factions of the church under one banner."

Sanchez said, "Or his intention is to proclaim Judas as his patron saint which would turn the whole concept of 'Jesus as savior' upside down. One thing we know for sure is that your mother is in serious danger. As is your entire family."

"Crazy, crazy, crazy," said Joel.

I can't say I disagree with my boyfriend, I mean, we're both scientists. May I?"

Sanchez nodded. Lisa took the container and slipped it into her pocket.

CHAPTER 15

Mother Natalie sat in her quarters, staring into the mirror. She gently traced the outline of her face with her finger beginning at her left ear, down along the jaw bone to her chin, and back up to her right ear. Bishop Newman had been a Godsend, lending her emotional support through all the ups and downs of her life. He even helped raise the funds for her facial reconstruction which included several skin and bone grafts, as well as dental implants. Natalie's features now were more palatable and gave her a measure of confidence when it came to dealing with the general public. But there was a price to pay. Along with the surgeries came a physical discomfort that came roaring back at all hours of the day and night. No amount or prayer or meditation could alleviate the pain. Only opioids could do that. Soon, she became dependant on the drugs which at times caused her to feel upset and unfocused. She was careful to conceal her addiction from everyone around her because she needed the safety of the convent, not just to give her purpose in life, but to help protect the relic.

Natalie's health was on a downward spiral and she knew the day would soon come when she would have to pass on the guardianship of the robe. The problem was that she had alienated her family who became fed up with what they believed to be a religious obsession. She had intimated knowledge of its existence but none had actually seen it. Thus, they all assumed it was a figment of her imagination. If anyone took her seriously it was her husband, Eugene, who only wanted to get his hands on it so he could sell it. As far as her son, Joel was concerned, the stories served to confirm the family's suspicions that his mother was a head case and had been for years. Now at this late date, Natalie was left with only one option.

The nun reached for the pharmaceutical bottle hidden in her drawer and shook out two pills. Then she went to the computer to Google the prescription and read its efficacy rate. She studied the information, then shook out three more pills, and grabbed a glass of water.

* * *

Lisa and Joel left the pub and decided to walk home. There was so much information to digest that neither said anything for a full five minutes. The streets at this time of night were almost deserted. The traffic and the wind diminished to the point that every sound, from the patter of raccoons running across the street to the siren from a distant ambulance felt amplified and ominous. With heightened awareness, the couple looked suspiciously into the faces of each person they passed, concerned they might be an approaching threat.

"You know what would have made their story better?" asked Joel. "Popcorn. I mean, I haven't heard bullshit that like that since—"

"I know," Lisa replied. "For someone to claim to be 500 years old."

"Lunatics, crazy as the people that killed Andy."

"Worse," agreed Lisa.

"You have that finger?"

Lisa patted her front left pocket and nodded.

* * *

It was Rasmus who found Natalie at about 3:30 a.m. Some kind of canine sixth sense awakened him and compelled him to make a beeline to the nun's room. Sister Beatrice heard the pitter-patter of Rasmus's scratching and whimpering out in the hall and roused herself.

"Rasmus, quiet! Go back to bed!" she shouted.

But the dog continued. Beatrice stumbled out of bed and into the hallway to find the animal pawing at Natalie's door. The nun immediately took it as a sign of trouble and knocked on it herself. After getting no reply, she started to pound.

Mother Natalie, are you okay? Mother Natalie, open up!"

That brought other members. They all huddled outside in their bed clothes asking each other what to do next. Finally, the Mother Superior appeared. There were no locks in the dormitory but Natalie had pushed her dresser up against her door. It took a minute or two of struggle until Mother Superior and the others succeeded in entering the room. There they found Natalie laying unconscious on her bed, arms crossed. Mother Superior felt for a pulse and found a faint beat. She shook the woman and called out in a sharp tone.

"Natalie, wake up! Can you open your eyes, dear?"

There was no response.

"Oh my, my! What happened?" asked one of the sisters.

Whispers of 'heart attack' and 'stroke' echoed throughout the room. One of the nuns noticed the prescription bottle lying on the floor and picked it up. The Mother Superior surmised what the unconscious nun had done, at which point she slapped Natalie across the face.

"Natalie, Natalie, open your eyes, damn it!" She shouted to the others behind her, "Somebody call 911!" She turned to the closest nun. "Help me get her up and walk her."

The two women picked Natalie up under her arms and shuffled her around the room while another used a cell phone to call the emergency line.

"Water!" said the Mother Superior.

Sister Beatrice ran down the hall to a washroom and hurried back with a glass of water. The Mother Superior opened Natalie's mouth and tried to force the liquid down her throat in an effort to upchuck the pills. The half-conscious nun let the water dribble down her chin. Fifteen minutes later, three emergency responders arrived with a gurney. They laid the nun back on her bed and the attendants took over the room.

"Everybody back up, please," he said. Then he called out his assessment to his partners. "Shallow breathing, finger nails turning blue."

"Who found her?" he asked.

"Rasmus did," said Sister Beatrice, pointing to the cocker spaniel that was pacing nearby. "Then I came running. I'm Sister Beatrice. My room is next door. The door was barricaded so I called for help and when we entered, we found her there."

"I was called," said Mother Superior in a take-charge voice, "we stood her up to try to get her walking, keep her alert."

Good," said the second attendant. Then he leaned in to his partner and whispered. "You know what 'dog' spelled backwards is?"

His partner smiled and said, "Sure do and it's not 'overdose'". At the mention of the word 'overdose' a chorus of whispers rose up again.

The first attendant began rubbing Natalie's arm. "What's your name, dear?" Can you tell me your name?" Then he rubbed his knuckles against her upper lip. Her lips puckered in response, a good sign.

"Naloxone?" asked the second attendant.

"Nope, she's breathing," he answered. "Bring the stretcher over. Who's her next of kin?" asked the second attendant while he and his partner wheeled the stretcher to the bed.

"We have her son on record," answered the Mother Superior, "He was just here a day or two ago."

"Call him."

"It's four in the morning," she replied, "And as I recall, they had a difficult relationship to say the least."

"She may not last the night. If she was your mother, wouldn't you want to know?"

The attendants lifted Natalie onto the gurney.

"Make some room, please," said the third attendant as they wheeled the nun out.

CHAPTER 16

The next morning Natalie awoke in pain. She touched the sore area in her arm to find an intravenous drip attached. Then she coughed to clear the dryness in her throat. She opened her eyes and realized she was lying in a hospital bed. She fought the impulse to panic and remained still while she forced her brain to catch up with her circumstances. She assumed the soreness in her throat was the result of the hospital staff having to pump her stomach. She gently probed her arm again but made no attempt to pull the needle out or call for help. She willed herself to wait patiently until a nurse finally entered the room ten minutes later.

"Good morning. I'm Nurse Ratched." The nurse waited for a response but there was none. "Sorry, I like to begin my day with a little joke. My real name is Louise. And you're?"

"You can call me McMurphy," came the hoarse reply. The nurse smiled at her patient's quick wit.

"You have a sense of humour, good. Do you know where you are, McMurphy?"

"Well, if you're a nurse then I guess I'm in a hospital."

"Good. Do you know why you're here?"

"Yes, and one more 'good' and you're going to lose a gold star from your morning rounds."

"I like my patients a little feisty. So, good." The nurse glanced at her patient's chart and continued. "So McMurphy, we're going to start with a few simple exercises and go from there, okay?"

"Good."

Nurse Louise took out a flashlight and asked Natalie to follow the beam of light with her eyes. She followed it left and right as requested.

"Perfect," said the nurse.

Then she took the nun's pulse and following that, her blood pressure.

"Have I had any visitors?" asked Natalie.

"There have been enquiries from the nuns of your order."

"No one else?"

"Are you expecting anyone in particular?"

"No."

"Well, your first visitor should be your doctor anyway. I'm going to report back to him and he'll be in to see you shortly."

"That would be *good*, Louise."

"Stay feisty, Natalie."

Nurse Louise smiled with genuine warmth and then she exited.

* * *

Professor Brown stood at the front of the hall, giving a lecture. A reprieve from the violence of the past week seemed to have calmed the campus to the point that many of the students had returned to their classes. Joel and Lisa sat next to each other, listening to their prof.' But their minds were anywhere but on their studies.

"You know Bishop Newman's baby finger is missing," she whispered.

"That's not unequivocal proof," Joel said. "There are no photographs of Bishop Promane, are there?"

Lisa shook her head. "The first Kodak camera was invented just before 1890, so no. Which means we'll have to get a sample of his DNA."

"Or I could go over to this church and cut off his other pinky," he answered.

Even through his humor Lisa could see the turmoil Joel was going through so she put her hand on his and turned her thoughts to the lecture. Joel's cell phone rang just before they got home the previous night. A hospital administrator informed him that his mother had taken an overdose of drugs but would recover. He resisted the urge to run down there immediately. The question wasn't whether or not he should visit her, but how long he could hold off before he felt he had to. Because, after his discussion with Sofia and Father Sanchez, he would seriously have to entertain the notion that everything his mother had inferred over the years might be true, which meant he and his entire family was wrong about her. Not that he believed any of the people he'd recently met were actually immortal, but some seriously sketchy people believed Natalie had an ancient relic in her possession worth a lot and would kill for it. And if that wasn't enough, he had to face the fact that his mother was addicted to drugs. He tried to reason with himself that perhaps it was the drugs that were responsible for her delusions and paranoia. But that wouldn't explain the murders and the mayhem around campus. No, for that to happen everyone in this bizarre passion play would have to be on the same trip.

"So according to quantum physics," said Professor Brown, "our infinite universe is expanding infinitely."

A student put up his hand to add, "And according to that same theory an object may be in two places at once."

Brown responded, "If so, the question follows, are there multiple universes?"

Morgan said, "So there might be another version of me?"

Brown grinned, "Even quantum physics isn't prepared for that, Morgan."

There was a smattering of laughter throughout the study hall. Everyone knew the two were sleeping together. Joel was lost in thought and missed the joke. The professor had glanced at him more than once in the past hour, aware that his mind was elsewhere. But before the professor called him out on it, Lisa raised her hand to distract him.

"So, in those universes, would there be copies of us doing what we do except for minor variations, I mean based on time and space?"

"Perhaps," said Brown.

"And in those universes, science and medicine may be at different stages of their evolutions. There may have even been the same famous people who lived somewhat different lives; George Washington, Hitler, Jesus, Judas. And what if in that universe Judas was the good guy and Jesus was the bad guy?"

"Sounds like an episode from The Twilight Zone," said a student.

"Are you just tossing out ideas or is there a point you're going to make, Lisa?" asked Brown.

"Well, if in alternate universes the good guys are the bad guys, how would we measure good or bad?"

The room began to percolate with questions.

"Yeah, what would be the reference point, the base line?"

"And would there be one God for all the universes or would each have its own?"

Before anyone could answer, the bell sounded.

"No answers," replied Brown, "but I love the questions. Keep 'em coming, we'll pick up on them next time."

The students packed up their laptops and books and the hall began to empty. Joel remained sitting silently until Lisa gently nudged him.

"So?" she asked.

"Okay, okay," he said, gathering his books and standing up. "I'm going."

"I'm going with you."

"Definitely, not."

This time Lisa did not argue. She just smiled, pleased that at least he'd made a decision.

* * *

It was about 2:00 p.m. when Joel arrived at the hospital and strode up to the information desk.

"Natalie Gardiner, please? She was admitted last night?"

"And you are?" she asked.

"Her son."

The receptionist nodded and consulted her computer, "Room 420," she replied with a warm but officious voice. "But she can only have one visitor at a time and there's already someone in there. If you'd like to wait..."

Joel did not wait for the receptionist to finish her sentence. He marched down the hall ignoring the receptionist's objections until her voice faded in the distance. If it was one from the flock of sisters, she'd have to be the one to leave. However, as he approached his mother's room, he heard another voice that drew his attention, coming from his mother's room, a male voice.

"A temporary setback. You've overcome more than this."

That voice made every hair on the back of Joel's neck stand on end. He entered the room to find his mother propped up in the hospital bed with an IV attached to her arm. She looked tired but alert and calm.

"Hello, Joel," replied Bishop Newman.

The bishop was standing off to the side, near Natalie's bed, the hand with the missing digit stuffed in his pocket. Joel frowned, dismayed at his presence. Then he realized an opportunity and brightened.

"Hello, bishop, nice of you to come," he said as he wedged himself between the priest and his mother's bed.

"Mom, how are you?" asked Joel, taking her hand.

Natalie pointed to her irritated throat.

"Sore throat?" he asked as he poured her a glass of water. "Here."

She shook her head to indicate she didn't want the drink but pointed to a pack of lozenges on her bedside. Joel passed the lozenges to his mother and handed the glass to the bishop.

"Do you mind?" Joel asked as he moved closer to his mother. Reluctantly, the bishop took the glass. "If you don't mind, Bishop, I'd like to speak to my mom privately."

Insulted, the bishop put the glass on the tray. "Excuse me? Your mother was admitted at three this morning. Half the day has gone by. I've been here for nearly two hours and the moment you step through that door you dismiss me?"

"I don't answer to you."

"That kind of defensive response is generally used to mask guilt, son."

"I am not your son." Turning to his mother, he asked, "Mom, what happened? They said it was about your medication."

What Joel really wanted to know was whether she tried to overdose or not. The Bishop read between the lines and offered an explanation. "God never gives us more than we can handle."

"Really?" Joel asked. "Then why do over 40,000 people commit suicide every year?"

The bishop bristled at the response. He was not used to being challenged. "You want to get real, Joel? We are all mirrors for each other. It's not me you're angry with. You're angry with yourself for having neglected your mother." The bishop suddenly changed his demeanor and smiled at the patient. "Natalie, I'll leave you in the capable hands of your son and we'll pick up later when you're feeling better."

Bishop Newman turned and exited the room briskly.

"Could you have been any more insulting?" Natalie said after the priest left.

"I see your voice has recovered. What did he want?"

"To see how I was, naturally."

"Never liked that guy," Joel said with a sneer. "Look, we need to talk."

Joel discreetly took the glass from the tray and slipped it into his jacket pocket, careful not to smudge the bishop's prints.

"Why do you think I sent for you?"

"Sent for me?" It took Joel a minute to understand her inference.

"I took five pills. A lethal dose requires eight or more. I Googled it."

"So, you didn't try to take your life. You just wanted my attention? Jesus, why couldn't you pick up a phone like a normal person?"

"Because the last thing you said to me, Joel, was that you never wanted to see me again."

Joel's first response was to lay into her for scaring him to death by staging a suicide. Then he remembered Sanchez's words last evening; that his first consideration should be toward his mother. His anger turned to self recrimination.

"I'm sorry. I didn't mean it..."

Joel actually did feel horrible knowing he'd put his mother through all this just to get a 'face to face' with him. If she was going to be honest, it was only fair he do the same.

"That man," he said, referring to Bishop Newman, "What if he's not who you think he is?" Natalie opened her mouth to speak but raised his hand to stop her. "Let me finish. He's not here for your benefit. Never has been. Newman might not even be his real name."

"Is that the reason for stealing the glass?"

Joel shrugged. "And he might be guilty of a lot more. " Joel lowered his voice so only she could hear. "This relic you spoke about, the robe your family's kept all these years, you must've known that to me and everyone it always sounded crazy."

"But now?" Natalie used her arms to push her body to a more alert position. "What's changed?"

"Let's say for the minute it did exist."

Natalie started to tear up.

"Why are you crying?" he asked.

"Because after all these years, you believe me."

"Don't cry, Mom."

He handed her a Kleenex and she wiped her eyes. When she calmed down, he continued.

"I didn't say that, exactly. It's just that life has thrown me some pretty strange curves lately and certain things have been brought to my attention."

"Such as?"

Joel looked around. People were walking back and forth past her door. There was no privacy. "Not here."

Natalie nodded and then said, "After they release me, come over, we'll talk." Joel nodded. The conversation had led to a moment of peace and reconciliation for them both. "Speaking of strange," she said warmly, "Can I get a hug?"

Natalie reached out, and for the first time in years, her son drew close and they hugged. "Mmmm, I could get used to this 'strange.'"

CHAPTER 17

Bishop Newman exited the hospital, saying goodbye to all the staff and thanking them for their good work. He thought back to Joel's indignant reply which wasn't unexpected. Neither would it alter the priest's plans in any way. His machinations had been put in motion long before the boy was even born. Careers had been derailed, families torn apart, and peoples' lives sacrificed, all for a higher purpose. One disgruntled whelp would not stand in his way. As soon as Newman reached the sidewalk, a black town car pulled up and he climbed inside. The car headed south along the busy avenue.

Bishop Newman was not the only one on a mission. Sofia was following him from a discreet distance. Both had taken great pains over the years to avoid each other because each time they met there was a battle, two serpents trying to swallow each other. Today, Sofia had no intention of confronting the priest. All she wanted was for him to lead her to the one he had enthrall.

On his way out of the hospital Joel stole a plastic bag from a service tray and wrapped the drinking glass inside it to preserve Newman's DNA. Then he called his girlfriend and asked her to meet him on campus. They met at the food court and kissed. When they sat down, Joel handed over the evidence.

"Think you can get DNA off a glass?" he asked.

"I'm not sure, but I'll find out."

"We can't afford to screw this up, Lis.' Not saying that this is going to give us definitive proof that Newman is a 500-year-old priest but we might find out if he has another alias or guilty of something somewhere. Who do we know who could run these kinds of tests?"

Lisa shrugged and contemplated, "Cops use DNA matches all the time when they're looking for a suspect, don't they? I have a cousin studying police forensics. Give it to me."

Joel hesitated for just a moment. "I know he's a cousin, but do you trust him?"

"Sounds more like, do you trust me? Maybe we should go back to using condoms."

"What? How do you equate.... point taken." Joel smiled apologetically and handed her the plastic bag. She shook her head, pissed over his lack of trust.

Newman's town car stopped in front of a small factory. The sign on the building read, 'Glass Masters.' He exited and was met by three burly men who led him into the factory. Sofia had no idea what she'd find in there but even with her considerable abilities, she worried about her chances if there was a confrontation. She decided to sit back and wait, until after twenty minutes, her curiosity got the better of her. She climbed out of her Corolla and scooted around back to a discreet entrance. As she approached the back door, she heard the rumbling of a truck pulling out of the cargo dock. She dashed behind a large industrial bin just in time to see a 'Glass Masters' truck leave the premises with the bishop sitting in the cab with the driver. Sofia was about to run back to her car when the other three factory workers emerged and climbed into their vehicle. By the time they'd left the yard, Sofia realized she'd never be able to catch up to them in her car. Instead, she went inside to glean what information she could.

The sprawling warehouse was filled with all matter of machinery and lift trucks. The buzzing saws and drills echoed through the building like a flock of angry metallic birds. A dozen workers criss-crossed the grey industrial floors in masks and overalls to protect them against the air that was thick with dust and odors akin to sulfur. Sofia held her breath and proceeded until she came upon a large open area that smelled even more acrid. She watched workers carry fifteen-foot sheets of colored glass from shelves to large tables.

"Hey, you can't be in here without protective wear," said the middle-aged foreman.

He took her by the arm to escort her back the way she came.

"Uh, yeah, sorry," replied Sofia. "I was looking for...my name is Layla Bradbury. I'm from the university doing my thesis on glass manufacturing, part of the Ecological Environment Strategy Initiative.

Your company is actually up for an award for your efforts in minimizing your global footprint."

"Don't know nothin' about that. You wanna speak to anybody in the head office you're gonna have to make an appointment 'cause you can't be here without protective gear."

"Not a problem. Don't wanna get you into any trouble." Sofia let the manager escort her a few steps before turning back to him. "Look, I've come such a long way, maybe I can ask you a couple of quick questions? What's your name?"

The attractive young woman smiled in such a coquettish way that the manager could not refuse.

"Doug Murgle. Shop steward," he said, puffing out his chest a little.

"Right. The shop steward is like the boss of the place, isn't he, Doug?"

"Well, not the top dog, but..."

"What I was wondering was, is if you could break down the process into maybe four or five basic steps..."

"We don't make glass here. We just colorize it."

"See? That's exactly what I'm talking about," she replied with a purr in her voice.

"I could get into a lotta shit if...." Doug looked around to make sure they weren't in harm's way and no one was watching them. "Okay, quick, the large sheets we rack up in that corner over there and then bring 'em to that table over there where they're cut into pre-ordered shapes. Those shapes are taken to another table and laid on top of a pattern where they're soldered together."

Sofia held her sleeve against her nose. "Is that what that smell is?"

"Yep, solder bein' applied to the copper tape around each shape."

"So a company places an order and then you cut it into a pattern for them?" she asked.

"Yep."

"You must get a lotta churches."

"A shitload."

Sofia noticed the St. Christopher's medallion on his chest and reached out to admire it. It was a crude attempt to gain favor but it worked most of the time.

"As a matter of fact," he said, "we just finished a big job for a church."

She nodded enthusiastically for him to continue. She leaned in close enough that Doug could catch the scent of her perfume. Her fragrance was such a welcome change from the stink in the warehouse that he couldn't stop himself from talking.

"You know St. James?"

Sofia shook her head. "Nope, don't think so."

She fondled the medallion, encouraging the conversation.

"They mothballed it a few years ago and then this new priest buys it and starts to remodel. He was just here."

"Really. He buys the glass and you cut it into the shapes he orders? Like all the traditional figures — Christ, Mother Mary, Elvis?"

"Yeah, sometimes," he said with a chuckle. "But that's the interesting thing. This guy took the flat sheets to do his own design work." The sound of honking blared from one of the lift trucks, reminding Doug of his job. "Look, I gotta get back—"

"Sure. I don't want to keep you."

"No problem," he said. "But if you ever wanna get together, you know, to talk about art and craftsmanship and shit like that over coffee or somethin'."

"Yeah, I'd love it. How's Thursday about 5:30?" Sofia asked.

"Yep, I can do that. There's a bar at the corner—"

"I saw it driving up." Sofia reached out to shake Doug's hand. "Always nice to meet someone who knows their stuff and is so willing to share."

"See ya, Thursday, Layla."

Sofia offered a smile that held a promise she'd never keep. Then she made her way back through the rear exit, climbed into her car, and booted it out of the parking lot.

* * *

Lisa had a class to attend but the DNA testing was too urgent a matter to ignore. After she left Joel, she messaged her cousin and asked him to meet her at the entrance to the campus library. Barry Laver, a short slim nerd of about twenty-two, was waiting when she arrived.

"Hey, cuz, how you doin'?" said Barry. "I never see you on campus."

He hugged her and kissed her on the cheek.

"I know, I know. Classes are nuts, the work is crazy."

"I reserved us a study room," he said.

"Great."

The two sauntered down the corridor together.

"How're your folks?" Barry asked.

"Fine, family is good, thanks," she said with a casual shrug. "Yours?"

They arrived at a study room surrounded by windows where they could be seen but not heard. They entered, shut the door, and set their knapsacks down on the boardroom table.

"You know," he replied with a sigh. "I miss those days when the whole family got together, Christmas, Easter. They were the best."

"I know. It got hard after your folks split."

"Well, that's the thing. They're split but still living in the same house. I mean, they're trying to make it work, but..." he said shifting his weight from one leg to the other. "I guess Mom's okay."

Lisa could see that family life was a difficult subject for Barry. But if she expected a favour of him she knew she'd be obliged to lend a sympathetic ear. Unfortunately, Barry was never one to tell a story in a linear fashion.

"And your dad?" she asked.

"That's the thing. He's still seeing 'her' on the side."

"Her?"

"She quit stripping. Works in retail now."

"Oh." Lisa had no idea who 'she' was and wasn't going to ask. "Anyways, you were always such a wiz at things and you're studying forensics, I knew you were the guy to ask. I was wondering, is it possible to get DNA from a fingerprint?"

"Depends on how long the finger remained on the surface. Gotta be at least 60 seconds to leave some residual matter. I'm living in an apartment off campus now, ya know. Dad threw my ass out."

"Your father threw you out of your own house? Why?" she asked.

"You know he travels a lot."

"Computer software, right?"

Barry nodded. "He came back early one night and caught me with Charlene. Went ballistic."

"I don't get it. Charlene is your girlfriend. You two were together and he got pissed? Why?"

"Turns out he was banging her too."

"He was banging your girlfriend? Jeez," Lisa said, blinking.

"That's what the whole thing was about," said Barry, staring at the floor. "It was my own fault."

"Why was it your fault?"

"Dad says it was because I brought her around. Her just being there, seduced him, ya know? Couldn't help himself. That's what he told Mom anyway. They had a big fight and he said it was best if I left for their sake. So..."

"Sorry," Lisa replied awkwardly.

"Not so bad. At least the bastard's payin' for my room and board and tuition."

Lisa let the silence hang for a moment. Then she brought out the glass wrapped in the plastic bag for Barry to examine. "Anyway...."

Barry picked up the bag gingerly to avoid compromising the evidence.

"Mmm," he said. "The good thing is, smooth surfaces have the best retention. But it didn't end there."

"Huh?" said Lisa, wondering what he was referring to.

"Dad's still seeing Charlene. And he threatens to cut me off if I say anything to Mom so there's not a lot I can do."

"A real piece of work, my uncle," replied Lisa. "So, how long would it take to get the analysis on the glass?"

Barry looked at her sideways. "Someone try to rufy you?"

"No, Barry, I'm in a relationship with a guy..."

"*He* try to rufy you?"

"No. He's a real nice guy."

Barry held the glass up. "So what's this all about?"

"Someone else, and he didn't try to rufy me either. I'm just looking for a match."

"A match to what?"

Lisa brought out the small sardine can from the knapsack. She opened it up and Barry stepped back from the stench.

"Whoa! Are you telling me you think the fingerprint on the glass came off that gnarly old digit?"

"Or whoever owned it. That's what I need to find out."

"Are you kidding? This thing looks like it's a hundred years old. There's no way—"

"I know but, how soon?" she pressed. "It's really important."

"I wish I could say but that's kinda the problem."

"What is the problem?"

"Charlene calls me whenever she has a fight with Dad and she comes over and before you know it, we're back together and then my dad comes over and then my life goes sideways and I can't cope."

"Boy, do you need a break. Look, if you do this for me, maybe there's something I can do for you."

"What?"

"I know a guy. Trust me."

Lisa packed the sardine can and the glass into Barry's knapsack and zipped it up.

"I'll give it a go, but—"

"Call you in a couple of days," she said.

Lisa gave Barry a peck on the cheek. They hugged and Lisa left the study room to mull over how she might help her cousin.

***

St. James church was a solid structure built over a hundred years ago and currently in the midst of renovation. Stacks of two by fours lay piled high in the parking lot. The lawn and hedges had been recently cut, but the paint on the bricks had faded and there were bald spots on the roof where shingles had fallen off. The original stained-glass windows were faded and barely intact.

Sofia sat in her car across the street in a strip mall parking lot, watching the premises. The Glass Masters' truck was parked in the church lot. She climbed out of her car and strolled to the back of the building to find it abuzz with activity. Some people tended a garden, others carried lumber into the church, while others enjoyed a smoke and a chat. Sofia sauntered casually toward the back door, nodding to the people as if she belonged. No one questioned her even when she entered the church. She heard sounds of construction and voices emanating from a multi-purpose room down the hall so she tip-toed along the corridor and peeked inside. There, she saw half a dozen people dressed in casual work clothes, helping with the renovations. The three men from the truck were moving a large colored pane of glass over to a large table. In the midst of it all stood a person directing the work, the person she was looking for, her sister. She was easy to spot, dressed in black leather pants and a white halter top. Another woman walked past Sofia and strode up to Belle.

"He wants you," she said discreetly.

Belle nodded and directed the workers to place the glass pane on the cutting table. Sofia retreated to an alcove to avoid being seen. Her sister sauntered out of the multi-purpose room and down the hallway to a set of stairs which led to the basement. Sofia followed at a discreet distance. The basement featured a long hallway with closed doors leading to several rooms on either side. At the end of the hall was the rectory. Sofia noticed the door ajar. She crept close enough to peek though the opening.

Bishop Newman was standing behind his desk playing Jenga, a game which consisted of a tower of wooden bricks that stood a foot or so high. The prelate studied the tower and carefully removed one of the bricks in such a way that left the structure intact without it collapsing.

"The glass is being cut?" he asked.

"As we speak," Belle said.

"The pattern just as I'd laid out?"

It will be magnificent."

"What other progress?"

Belle looked away, afraid to look at the bishop directly. "Since our last contact..."

The bishop stopped playing the game and furrowed his eyebrows. "You promised me all it would take would be a few insignificant deaths."

"The mother is in the hospital, reachable any time we choose. I could—"

"You'll do nothing! I cannot risk her demise until we recover it. And the son?"

"His lab has been trashed, his partner, neutralized, and his research scuttled."

"Completely?"

Belle hesitated. "The notebook with the formula...is missing," she waited a beat and then added, "We don't know if there were any other electronic files." She grew pensive for a moment and then brazenly suggested, "We should just grab him off the street and—"

"That's not how you play the game, Belle. You build your opponent up, give him everything, family, wealth, a life worth living. And then slowly, you take it away piece by piece." The bishop reached for one of the Jenga bricks and withdrew it causing the entire tower to collapse. "Every shred of hope gone, until they have nothing left to cling to. That's when they make mistakes. And that's when I reclaim what is rightfully ours."

"Command me. I'll do whatever..."

With a single swipe of his arm the bishop sent all the pieces flying across the room. "You've done enough! I'll take care of this."

Footsteps signalled the approach of several people as they trundled down the basement stairs. Out in the hallway, Sofia looked to find a place to hide. She tried one door after another until she found one unlocked. She opened it and found herself in a near-vacant room. The only furniture in here was a mattress that lay on the concrete floor and next to it, a plain side table. She listened as a trio strolled toward the rectory. From inside the room Sofia heard the voice of a secretary.

"Bishop, Maggie and Samuel are here for their meeting."

"Folks, come in."

The couple in their early twenties approached with beaming smiles.

"Belle, that will be all, thank you," said the bishop. Belle nodded and left. "So you two are to be married," she heard the bishop declare with delight.

Inside the bare room, Sofia heard the secretary and Belle walk down the corridor toward the stairs.

"Everything all right, Belle?" asked the secretary.

Belle did not answer. Sofia cracked open the door in time to see her sister storm up the stairs followed by the secretary. When they were gone, Sofia peeked back down the hall to find the bishop's door closed. Then she headed upstairs toward the sound of her sister's abrasive voice.

"Why aren't these pews locked in place?" she said. "The paint on those walls looks like it was done by a bunch of retards! What's wrong with all of you?"

Sofia crept down the corridor toward the sanctuary. At the entrance she peeked inside to see the innovative structure of the space and how the pews sat in a circular fashion around the altar. As people scurried every which way to satisfy Belle's demands, Sofia waited until her sister wandered within whispering distance.

"Belle?"

Belle's eyes opened wide with surprise and then she turned to her. "Sofia. What a pleasant surprise. How long has it been?"

"Since the Bay of Pigs incident."

"You were on the wrong side of that one too as I recall."

Sofia nodded to the renovations, "Impressive."

Belle smiled. "You came to persuade me of the error of my ways. You came to point out that everything he stands for is selfish and everything he does is for his own good. That he treats me and his followers like cattle, am I right?"

"Actually, I wanted to know where you picked up that cute little blouse."

"Barcelona. You like?"

"Belle, you're my sister. Whatever fork in the road we took all those years ago, whatever differences we have, our bond can never be broken. For us, there will always be a way to at least talk."

Belle glanced at the busy workers and left the sanctuary so that she and her sister wouldn't be overheard.

"A man is running," Belle said. "Is he running to catch a bus or is he running from the murder he just committed? That is as much as we know about him and as much as we know about God. We don't know where either came from or where they are going. But at least we know the man exists. We can see him. The only thing you know about God is what is written in some dusty old books or what you believe him to be through your own limited perceptions. But the bishop is a visionary leading us all to experience the one true lord. He, alone, is the way. Join us."

Belle reached out to her sister. Sofia sighed and did not take it. She knew there was no argument that would sway her so she responded the only way she could, "I love you, Belle." With that Sofia turned and left. As a parting shot Belle called out to her. "When you're ready to hear the truth..."

* * *

Marie Champlain stood at the front of her boardroom like Captain Queeg preparing to quash a mutiny. In front of her sat a dozen disgruntled suits itching to take her down at the slightest sign of weakness.

"We know about the break-in, Marie," said one of the execs. "As promising as this discovery sounds the integrity of the project has already been compromised."

"Equipment was destroyed but replaceable. Nothing of value was taken," she assured everyone.

"We all know, historically, about two-thirds of new drugs fail to meet prelaunch expectations for their first year and under-deliver for the next two," said another exec. "We can't afford to lag behind in the market. Where are the notes for this revolutionary formula?"

"Safely under lock and key. No one but myself has access to them." A few of the members put up their hands to object. "And don't even ask because if you think I'm going to risk any more attempts at corporate espionage..."

"What if something happens to you?"

"Then I guess it's in your best interests to make sure nothing does." She looked at them to let that little kernel sink in before continuing. "Gentlemen, ladies, the universal blood formula is the holy grail of the medical industry. Its profits will exceed anything we've put on the market to date."

"All well and good, Marie, but we need proof, we need to see some conclusive results."

"And you will. When I'm ready."

***

Barry Laver lived in the basement apartment which consisted of little more than a bedroom, kitchenette and bathroom. Charlene, his girlfriend, was sitting at the kitchen table with a glass of coke when she heard a knock on the upstairs door. She stood up and climbed the stairs to open the side door of the house. Barry's father, Conrad, stood there offering a bouquet of flowers and a warm smile.

"Is the lady of the house in?" he asked in his most endearing voice.

With a deadpan face, she turned and walked back downstairs as Conrad followed. When they reached the bottom floor, he put down the flowers and grabbed Charlene from behind."

"Did I miss you!" He said passionately, putting his hands all over her.

Charlene turned around and pushed him off gently but firmly. He looked quizzically at her until she nodded to the man sitting at the kitchen table in the corner.

"Who the hell are you?" Conrad asked. "This is my son's place."

"Which makes it crystal clear that it's not yours," replied Father Sanchez.

Conrad took a couple of threatening steps toward the old gent. "What do you want?" he said, pissed off.

"I'm a priest come to ask you if you believe in God."

"No. Now get out."

Sanchez stood up and moved toward Conrad as if leaving. But instead of passing the man, Father Sanchez grabbed Conrad by the scrotum and squeezed. The priest's grip was so firm that Conrad froze in pain.

"Fair enough. Do you believe in this?" asked the priest.

Barry stepped out from the bedroom to face his father.

"I've just had a lovely chat with Charlene and your son, Barry," continued the priest. "I am about to have another chat with your wife, unless you leave, never to return or bother these two again."

Barry crossed over to Charlene and put his hands protectively around her shoulders.

"Because then I'll have to pay you another visit," continued Sanchez. "With me will be your boss, a phalanx of lawyers and the tax department. I don't think anything more needs to be said, do you?"

"No," said Conrad, gasping for breath.

"Oh, sorry, there is one more thing. Since you're the one who kicked your son out of his own home, you'll be paying for his room and board and tuition not just for this year but until graduation."

Conrad nodded.

"Thank you for your understanding," said the priest. "Go with God."

The priest relaxed his grip at which point Conrad took a huge breath. He adjusted his pants, gave a disparaging look to the young couple, and hobbled back up the steps. The three waited until they heard the side door close. Then Sanchez turned to Barry.

"Looks like you have some spare time to help out your cousin, Lisa, now."

"Thanks," said Barry and Charlene.

CHAPTER 18

Joel paced the floor of his apartment with the phone in his hand while trying to fend off Lisa's questions.

"Where can we meet?" he asked his mother. He put his hand over the cell and whispered to his girlfriend.

"It's a family thing. Two hours tops," he said.

"You can't keep shutting me out, Joel," she said.

"I'm not shutting you out. It's just... it's a delicate situation." Joel returned to his telephone conversation. "When?"

Lisa was not about to let it go. "Sofia told me about Father Sanchez before you even knew about him. I was there when he told you the whole story. This affects me as much as you."

"I'm sorry you were dragged into this, babe, but—"

"Do you really expect me to sit back while you make decisions that affect my life as well as yours?"

Joel replied into the phone, "Sure. See you then." He clicked off and turned to Lisa. "This is not about us. It's something that began long before you and I ever met."

"I see." Her curt answer told Joel he'd just stepped over a line.

"Babe, it's just a meeting with my mother. You wouldn't want me around when you're hanging out with your mom, would you? I'll be back in a couple of hours tops and fill you in then, promise."

"Sure. I'll just sit here and keep dinner warm 'til you get back."

Joel smiled weakly. He took a step over to kiss Lisa but when she backed away, he left the apartment.

***

The upcoming Halloween events were generally a welcomed balance to the chilly nights and the overwhelming demands of school. Orange and black banners flapped in the wind all along the downtown core. Store owners dressed their windows in macabre displays, each one trying to outdo the other. Pubs advertised parties for students to get drunk, spend their money, and blow off steam. But on this moonless night, as Joel tramped through the downtown streets, he felt lonelier and more detached from life than he had in months. Up until a week ago there was promise in his future. Now there was only angst, and the feeling that every day was bringing him closer to some kind of vague, impending catastrophe. He hated lying to his girlfriend but he felt like his life swerving was out of control, like he was a hostage trapped on a runaway train. It was up to him to try to prevent the train from crashing.

Joel arrived at St. James's convent twenty minutes later and knocked on the front door. Sister Gabrielle opened it and offered him a polite smile. She invited him in and led him to the ante room without saying a word. There, he waited another five minutes before Mother Natalie appeared.

"You ready?" Joel asked his mother.

He had arranged to take his mother to meet with Father Sanchez and Sofia to get a first-hand account of what he'd learned to date, another fact he'd kept from Lisa. His plan was to study all three in the same place to determine if their stories meshed. After that, he'd have a clearer idea as to how to proceed. He told himself he didn't want Lisa there in case there was any danger. Truthfully, he didn't want her there clouding his judgement.

"Before we go," his mother said, "come with me."

"We don't have time. We have an appointment..."

Mother Natalie waved her son's objection off and Joel had no choice but to follow. Minutes later, someone else knocked on the door of the convent. It was odd to have one visitor this time of night let alone two. Sister Gabrielle, who was nearest the door, reluctantly answered.

"Hi, 'scuse me," Lisa said in a plaintiff voice. "I was hoping I could speak with someone."

"It's after 7:00 p.m., young lady. You can call back tomorrow and make an appointment if you like."

"Sorry, it's really important, a personal matter. My father has been on a respirator and my sister has just given instructions to the hospital to pull the plug. But that's like killing him and it's not right, is it? I really need to speak to someone."

"What do your family members say?" asked the nun.

"Mom died two years ago. There's just me and my sister, Lucy, and she hasn't seen dad since she left home. Isn't there anyone who can give me five minutes?"

Lisa fidgeted nervously, wringing her hands and pleading with her eyes. Sister Gabrielle considered the young woman's plight and wondered, what would Jesus do? In spite of her better judgment, the nun allowed her in. It was a half-baked plan but Lisa refused to be left out of the loop by her boyfriend. As soon as Joel left their apartment, she called a cab and followed him. But what she was going to do from there, she had no idea.

Mother Natalie led Joel down a long hall to a staircase which led to the basement.

"Where are we going?" he asked. "I told you..."

"If this man, Sanchez, waited until now, he can wait a little longer."

Before Joel could object, she turned on the light and descended the staircase. As obstinate as he knew his mother to be, Joel also knew she would not be wasting his time.

"Look, Mom, I'm, uh, sorry."

"For what?"

"For the things I said."

"You've barely said a word since you—"

"Over the years, I mean."

"What, that you thought I was a religious freak? A bat-shit-crazy nun?"

"Truth is, you didn't give me much choice."

"Because I didn't have a choice."

Lisa followed Sister Gabrielle to the ante room and waited while the nun fetched one of the other sisters. She counted to ten and peeked into the hallway. With no one in sight, she scurried down the corridor in search of her boyfriend and his mother.

When Joel reached the bottom of the stairs, he found himself in a fully finished basement with hardwood floors and pot light fixtures, a pool table and a dining area with seating for a dozen or so people.

"The building was a hospital originally," said Natalie, "And this used to be a lounge area for the doctors."

"And that?" asked Joel, nodding to a formidable looking wooden door.

Natalie grinned like a mother about to give her son a birthday present. She took out a key, unlocked the door, and gestured for Joel to follow her inside. They crossed the threshold into a large wine cellar. Hundreds of bottles sat on shelves five feet high by twenty feet long against two brick walls. Between them were several large barrels, mostly for ornament's sake. At the end of the long center aisle Joel could see that it split left and right, presumably to store additional product.

"Those doctors knew how to live," said Joel.

"Actually, this wine room was built by us. Climate controlled and everything. The church has a long history with wine as an investment tool for resale. Do you know much about wines, Joel?"

"That most of them are overpriced. That the most expensive are owned by rich snobs, bought and sold like rare art. I'm more of a beer guy myself."

"Ever heard of Dom Perignon?" Natalie selected a bottle and brought it out for Joel to view.

"Who hasn't? Top shelf champagne."

"Yes, but did you know it was named after a Benedictine monk who lived in the sixteen hundreds?"

"The guy's name was actually Dom Perignon?"

Natalie nodded and showed him the label. "Yes. He didn't discover champagne but he did help perfect it. It happened by accident, you know. One of the by-products of fermentation is the release of carbon dioxide gas—"

"Which when trapped inside the bottle, causes intense pressure," replied Joel. "Basic science. Anyways, if that's all—"

"Right. The pressure inside those weak French bottles often exploded causing a royal mess. If the bottle survived, the wine was found to contain bubbles, something that the early Champenois or wine makers considered a fault. A fault! Can you imagine?"

Joel looked toward the cellar entrance, indicating his boredom and eagerness to leave.

*　*　*

Sister Gabrielle knocked on a few of the apartment doors until one sister finally answered. After explaining the young stranger's dilemma, Sister Boniface put on her habit and followed her colleague back to the ante room only to find it empty.

Sister Boniface scowled. "Sister Gabrielle, you should know better."

Sister Gabrielle's brow furrowed. "I'm sorry. Jesus made me do it. Maybe she wandered off somewhere."

Both women scowled and turned on their heels to begin a search. Meanwhile, Lisa scampered from room to room, trying to find her boyfriend. When she heard angry footsteps approaching, she looked for a hiding place. She noticed the basement door ajar and the faint sound of her boyfriend's voice below.

"Accidents are how a lot of medical advances are discovered," Joel said. "But we don't have time for a wine or a science lecture right now."

"I didn't bring you here for that."

Natalie placed the champagne bottle back on the shelf and strode down the center aisle, disappearing around the corner. Lisa slipped off her shoes and crept down the flight of stairs. When she reached the bottom, she saw Joel's back as he perused the rows of bottles. Lisa knew the two were not here to sample wines. But what then? A confidence? A betrayal? Silently, she slipped behind the pool table and waited. A moment later, Natalie came back into view carrying a small wooden box. By the sobering look on her face Joel knew the contents did not contain another bottle of wine. And because of that he was thankful Lisa was not here. Natalie strode up her son, her face a mask of solemn intensity. Slowly, ceremoniously, she opened the lid, watching the look on his face to gauge if she'd made the right decision. Inside lay a weathered, yellow cloth with dark burgundy streaks. Lisa craned her head around the table to see what they were looking at but was blocked by Joel's body. Natalie studied her son while Joel studied the garment. Whether this cloth was a gift from heaven or hell, Joel had no idea. But he was compelled to learn more.

"Judas' Robe?" he asked. It's actually real?"

Natalie nodded. With a mixture of hope and fear, she offered the cloth to him and held her breath in anticipation of her son's reaction. Joel tentatively reached out for the fabric. When he held the cloth in his hands, his heart beat faster and he rocked backed back on his heels. A feeling of dizziness came over him and he had to steady himself against a wall. Watching his reaction, Lisa's hand shot to her mouth to stifle a cry. Joel wondered if this wretched piece of fabric could actually be infused with something beyond the physical realm, something holy. After a moment he placed the cloth back in its container and calmed his heart. Natalie closed the lid without saying a word.

"All the stories, everything you told me, it's true?"

Natalie nodded and a sublime look spread across her face. Without another word she turned and tread back down the aisle with her package, leaving Joel to contemplate the experience. He rubbed the sweat off the back of his neck and shook his head in disbelief. From her vantage point Lisa could sense that he was genuinely shaken, that what he'd just seen had fundamentally touched him. A sudden ruckus above broke the contemplative moment. The upstairs door opened and several nuns came trudging down the steps accompanied by their beagle, Rasmus. Lisa crept into the wine cellar and hid behind one of the large barrels just a few feet from Joel.

When the nuns reached the bottom, they were surprised to find Joel standing there.

"Excuse me, young man..." said Sister Boniface sharply. "No one is allowed down here. I'm going to have to ask you to..."

As Rasmus ran over to sniff Joel, Mother Natalie appeared from around the corner.

"Sorry, sisters," she called out, "This is my son, Joel."

A couple of the women were aware of Natalie's past and her family. The others lifted their hands to their mouths in surprise. 'Son'?

"Immaterial, Mother Natalie," said Sister Boniface. "This area is off limits."

Rasmus sensed another figure hiding behind one of the barrels. But as soon as the dog began to wander over it was called back.

"Rasmus, back here!" said Sister Gabrielle.

The dog obeyed and the nun scooped the animal up in her arms.

"Forgive me, sister," replied Natalie. "My son is somewhat of a wine connoisseur."

Joel gave his mother a sideways glance and then played along with her. "Did you know Dom Perignon was a Franciscan monk?" he asked the sisters.

"Yes." replied Sister Boniface. "We all did."

Natalie said, "I haven't seen my boy in close to two years. Selfishly, I used the opportunity to bond with him. My apologies."

"We'll deal with that later, Mother," interjected Sister Boniface. "Right now there is a more serious problem. We have an intruder."

"An intruder?" Natalie said.

"A young woman. She gained access to the convent a few minutes ago, claiming to need some spiritual advice. Then she disappeared."

"What did she look like?" asked Joel.

"Nervous creature in her twenties," said Sister Gabrielle. "Too slim for her own good in my opinion, about five-foot five."

Joel shook his head as if the description didn't register. But he wondered whether it could be either Sofia or Belle. Mother Natalie shifted nervously, worried that whoever this person was, might be after the robe. She glanced at Joel and then to the sister.

"No one here but us," she replied with a vague smile. "Have you checked all the rooms upstairs thoroughly? The lavatory?"

"Well—"

"Why don't we all go up?" suggested Mother Natalie. "Perhaps whoever it is, has returned and is waiting where you left her."

Mother Natalie ushered everyone out of the wine cellar, shut the lights, and locked the door behind her.

"Could you have been followed?" she whispered to her son as they walked back up the stairs.

"Don't think so. Do you think—"

"What I think is that now would be a good time to meet your Father Sanchez."

The group tromped back up the wooden steps and closed the basement door behind them. Lisa stood in the pitch black. Whatever Joel had seen was challenge enough. Now she had to deal with breaking out of a locked wine cellar. She listened to the clatter of heavy shoes walking back and forth along the halls above her, and the opening and closing of doors for the next fifteen minutes. When the noises ceased, she relaxed. Fortunately, Lisa had her cell phone with her. She turned on its torch, searched the walls, and found the light switch which offered a soft, mellow glow. At least she wouldn't be stuck alone in the dark. Next, she tried the door and realized it was locked from the outside. She resigned herself to staying there overnight, turned the light off, and decided to wait until someone had a yen for a glass of Chardonnay.

CHAPTER 19

The Barking Pig was one of a dozen pubs that dotted the university campus. There was nothing special about this particular watering hole which is why Joel chose it. Like most pubs the Pig catered to a mix of students and teachers. Neon signs flashed the names of popular beers and spirits in the dim light. Bob Seeger and the Silver Bullet Band played "Night Moves" over a group of obnoxious jocks who drank over their team's latest basketball win. Another table hosted a foursome discussing their current scholastic projects. Scattered around the room were a few guys trying to build up enough courage to score with a few girls.

Joel and Natalie entered and spotted Sofia and Father Sanchez sitting at a table against the wall.

Natalie turned to her son and asked, "So who do you think the woman was who crashed the convent?"

"Who knows. Could be totally unrelated." They traded unconvincing looks. "Okay, Mom, now remember we're all on the same team."

The two wound their way through the boisterous crowd until they reached Sanchez's table. The priest, who wore civilian clothing, stood and offered his hand.

"Mother Natalie?" he said.

"Father Sanchez," she replied, refusing to take his hand. Joel rolled his eyes at his mother. Sanchez smiled and gestured with his outstretched hand for her to sit next to him.

"This is my friend, Sofia," Sanchez said. "Joel, I believe you two have already met."

Joel nodded and all four sat down with nervous anticipation.

"Spirits?" asked Sanchez.

"I'm not a drinker," replied Natalie.

Joel smirked at the thought of the extravagant wine cellar he'd just had a tour of. Sanchez called out to the barmaid.

"Miss? A pitcher of beer," He turned to his companions, "When one comes to a bar it's wise to drink or you arouse suspicion."

"Where is Lisa?" asked Sofia.

"Couldn't make it," Joel said.

Natalie turned to her son, "Lisa? Is that your girlfriend?"

"You'll meet her some other time."

"I like her," Sanchez said.

The waitress sidled over to the table carrying a pitcher and four glasses. Father Sanchez paid for the drinks and waited until the girl left before he spoke. "Mother Natalie, I want you to feel free to express yourself knowing that Sofia is as cognoscente of the matter as I am.

"Good. Then as far as I'm concerned, you're *both* fools."

"Mom!"

"I don't know what my son has told you, but—"

Sanchez laughed. "Bishop Newman did a splendid job on you, didn't he? Paying for your surgeries, lending you his shoulder to cry on when your marriage fell apart. Even finding you refuge in the convent where you currently reside. As much as he's done for you, he is also the cause of your troubles."

Natalie frowned and her back stiffened. "I've been here for thirty seconds and inside that brief time you've disparaged a dear friend and a lifelong confidante." She stood up to leave. "My son is a good boy, Father. Sometimes a little too trusting for his own good."

"Sit," Sanchez said. "Sit!" he repeated in a commanding voice. "If after I've said my peace, you choose to leave, I'll have no quarrel with you."

Reluctantly, Natalie took her seat and hoisted her glass to take a long gulp of beer.

Sanchez continued. "I could impress you with some historical facts such as how Pope Pious 12 was complicit in the attempted assassination of Adolph Hitler. Or who was behind the death of Princess Di. Even then you would have your suspicions about me. But maybe something closer to home. Your father, Albert, was a functioning alcoholic who died from a fall. Your mother was agoraphobic. Never admitted her fear of the outdoors for fear of relinquishing the Robe to those who sought it."

"The robe is a myth," Natalie said.

"A myth your family and their ancestors took great pains to hide for over a thousand years," Sofia said. "Ever since the day it was entrusted to them by the Order of Christ."

Natalie shook her head. "I know of no such order. Nor did my family—"

"Your family came from Spain in the 1100s," continued Sofia. "I know that because so did we. They escaped to Portugal, and then to England, and finally to America." Sofia turned to the priest. "Why are we playing this game, Father?"

Father Sanchez gently touched Sofia's arm.

"Patience, Sofia. Mother Natalie must be certain that we are on her side. This robe 'that does not exist,' is not the golden fleece, it does not give you the ability to bend steel in your bare hands or leap tall buildings at a single bound. Am I right? It is a coarse piece of cloth, yellowed with time, and streaked in blood, the color of rust."

Natalie stared into the eyes of the priest, watching for any tell-tale glimmer of deceit. The fact that Sanchez had been correct up until now worried her. Natalie needed an ally she could trust but her vow to keep the secret of the robe prevented her from acknowledging anything this priest said.

Father Sanchez knew he would have to provide some kind of overwhelming evidence if he was going to convince her to trust him. He pulled back his shirt sleeve to reveal a series of scars embedded in his arm.

"Oh, my!" said Natalie.

"A gift from Bishop Promane, the man you know as Bishop Newman."

"Don't be absurd. I've seen scars before," said Natalie, recovering from the awful sight.

Joel stared at the priest's arms knowing that the scars were so deeply embedded that no tattoo could have made it.

"You recognise these, Natalie?" said Sanchez.

Natalie looked closer at the scars on Sanchez's arm and took in a sudden breath. "The alpha and the omega," she replied with shock.

"The what?" Joel asked.

"The first and last letters of the Greek alphabet."

"The beginning and the end," added Sanchez, completing the thought.

Natalie leaned in, "But how do those marks..."

Sofia took up the story, "Bishop Promane, the grand inquisitor at the time, arrested a priest and charged him with aiding and abetting a family of Jews trying to flee the Inquisition." Sofia gave a nod to her comrade. "What he was really after was the robe. The man sitting before you withstood horrible torture to keep its whereabouts a secret. When Promane couldn't break him, they tortured me."

Sofia lifted her skirt to reveal the same wretched marks on her inner thigh.

Joel, who had been staring at Sanchez's arm, almost stuttered, "I, I, know that mark."

"Of course you do. It's a ubiquitous sigil in Catholicism."

"No but, I've known it all my life," Joel slowly raised the sleeve of his arm to show his birthmark, the same mark that Sanchez and Sofia bore.

Father Sanchez and Sofia nodded knowingly. Mother Natalie was still in a state of denial. To believe Sanchez and Sophia meant she'd have to question her unwavering loyalty to Bishop Newman. Could he have been so deceitful all this time and she so naive? Certainly, Joel never liked him.

"I hate to disappoint you," she said, "but I don't have any mark remotely similar. Listen, I know what you're getting at. But let's say for argument's outrageous sake that my Bishop Newman is your Bishop Promane. If he is already immortal, what would he want with the robe? What more could he hope to gain?"

Sanchez replied, "Throughout history the major religions of the world have vied for superiority - Hindus, Muslims, and all the Christian sects. Each believed the world would be a better place if people worshipped God under their auspices."

"It would make people easier to govern, to manipulate," added Sofia.

Sanchez continued, "Let's remember the ultimate mission of The Inquisition. It was conceived to wipe out all threats to Catholicism and ensure that their brand of Christianity ruled globally."

"The robe?" asked Joel.

"The singular physical piece of proof of God on earth," said Sanchez. "Whoever possesses it would have the power to solidify all the factions under one faith."

"And whoever owned it could anoint himself as leader of the church," continued Sofia.

Over the next twenty minutes Father Sanchez explained in further detail, the history and relationship between himself, Promane, Sofia, and her sister, Belle. When he was done, the group sat silently absorbing the information.

"Pity Lisa isn't here," said Sanchez. "She was instrumental in confirming much of this. Where did you say she was?"

"I'm not sure right now," Joel replied.

"I understand you don't want your girlfriend involved, Joel, that you're protecting her," said Sanchez, "but just because she is not here doesn't mean she's not in danger. Mother Natalie, only you know where the robe is and whether it's safe. It's up to you to leave it in its resting place or move it before Promane finds a way to acquire it. Do not underestimate his cunning or his resources."

One of the young couples at a nearby table was groping each other so passionately that a few others shouted, "Hey, get a room!" The couple giggled, stood up and left, taking their advice.

"One other thing, Joel," said Sanchez, "The discovery you made at Biopharm, the universal blood typing, it is imperative you see it realized."

"It wasn't me. I mean I had the general idea but I had no clue as to which enzyme…"

Sanchez grinned just enough to tip the boy off.

"You're the one!" Joel said. "You discovered the enzyme and wrote it in my notes!"

Sanchez nodded. "Your foes are powerful. The church has money, Promane has money. You'll need money too, a lot of it. The royalties from that discovery will provide a financial legacy your heirs will need to ensure the safekeeping of the robe for generations. Do we have a pact?"

Joel promised himself before this meeting that he'd listen to see if all the stories from all the points of view meshed. He had to admit that what he'd heard felt like the coming together of the sides of an isosceles triangle, one supporting the other in perfect symmetry. That, and the additional knowledge that Sanchez had completed Joel's research, convinced him that these stories, however incredible in nature, made a certain logical sense. And then there were the scars they had in common.

Joel turned to Natalie, "So, Mom?"

* * *

It was after Eleven O' Clock when the amorous couple from the pub arrived at the church. After informing Belle of what they'd overheard, Belle hurried down the hall to find Bishop Newman who was supervising the assembly of the cut glass over the pattern that lay beneath it. The primary form was that of the bishop on bended knee reaching his hand to the heavens.

"Nice likeness. Where am I?" she asked.

Promane pointed to an area off to the side where a pile of colored pieces was being assembled.

Belle smiled and disclosed the information she'd just learned. "Joel and his mother met Sanchez and my sister."

"Damn!" Newman's brow furrowed and he exhaled a long breath. "Time to exercise our demons."

CHAPTER 20

Joel and his mother said their goodbyes to Father Sanchez and Sofia outside the pub and pledged themselves to a common cause, that of keeping the robe safe and secure. Joel and his mother strolled down the vacant streets, watchful of any strangers.

"You're lying, I know you are, about the sigil," Joel said to his mother.

"Don't get me wrong. I've waited a long time for this day, but I'm not one hundred percent convinced about these people or their story."

"Kind of ironic, isn't it?" He said. "That I'm the one trying to persuade you that something supernatural might be going on."

Natalie smiled at her son and took his arm as they continued along the street. Whether the robe was other-worldly or not, neither could deny that people had died and more would follow unless the Judas Robe was secured against their foes.

"You have somewhere else you can hide it if you need to?" he asked.

"No," replied Natalie.

"No? What?"

"No, I don't have another place."

"What the hell, Mom? I mean, you must have known one day—"

"The plan is, and always was, that whoever took possession of the robe would be the one to protect it. That way only one person in the world would know its whereabouts. That's how it's been done for centuries."

"You didn't write it down, where exactly you hid it in the wine cellar?"

Natalie shook her head.

"So lemme ask you something; what if something happened to you, what then?"

"I suppose it would be lost until someone found it again. And if it was never found then that would be God's will."

Joel pondered the sobering thought. "What you're saying is, you're loading all this shit onto me by myself? Where the hell am I going to stash it?"

"You'll think of something," she said, hugging her son's arm.

They continued along the downtown streets knowing that a new course of action would have to take place, and soon. His mother glanced at her son from time to time, seeing the worry in his eyes. She knew how difficult this was because she had carried the same burden as had her ancestors, for centuries. She felt a mixture of sadness and pride knowing Joel was finally accepting his legacy. When they arrived at the convent, they had much to think about but little to say.

"We'll talk tomorrow?" Joel asked.

"Tomorrow," she answered, and kissed him lightly on the cheek.

"Sleep tight, Mom."

Mother Natalie entered the building and hurried to her room fighting the thousand little worries that fluttered about in her head. She removed her clothing and prepared for bed. But no matter how she tried to distract herself, the worry for her son would not abate. She reached under her nightgown and looked at her inner thigh. There was the birthmark, the sigil, as it had always been. Everything Father Sanchez said was true. In addition to her failing health, in addition to the extra strain she'd placed on Joel, she now had to deal with the fact that Bishop Newman had been her enemy from the day she laid eyes on him.

The next twenty-four hours would be pivotal for Joel. In addition to deciding what to do about the robe, there was Bishop Newman's role in all of this and the impact it would make on his mother. When he thought about what everybody wanted and all the machinations that had been put in place, it was overwhelming. And then there was Lisa. He knew she was smart, but he had no idea how resourceful she could be until she'd unearthed all that information about the robe and everyone connected to it. And the way she'd orchestrated the proofing of the

DNA samples from Bishop Newman, he was in awe. But in doing so she'd also put herself in harm's way and he couldn't allow that. Joel began spinning thoughts and turning over a dozen different scenarios in his mind until, by the time he arrived home, he'd devised a plan to keep her out of jeopardy. He'd tell Lisa that Sanchez was a liar and a fake, that the old man had concocted an elaborate scheme to con the clergy at his mother's convent. His purpose was to gain the trust of the nuns in order to steal some of the religious artifacts they'd amassed over the years, and sell them on the black market. Joel refined and rehearsed his story until it sounded plausible. Still, he knew, that might not be enough. To ensure that Newman would never threaten Lisa, he'd have to sever his relationship with her completely. It was the only way. Except, when Joel returned to their dorm just after 2:00 a.m., Lisa wasn't there.

* * *

It was deep in the night, the doors to the wine cellar were locked, and there was no guarantee when anyone would open them. Lisa extracted her phone from her pocket again and flicked on the torch. She hunted for the switch on the wall but worried that a glimmer of light might escape and inform someone upstairs she was there. She left the light off and used the torch to guide her down the corridor. She wasn't sure how long it would last so she hurried, making a mental note of everything she saw. She passed row upon row of bottled wine stacked on either side of her. It was obvious by the sheer volume that this particular religious sect wasn't as penniless and impoverished as they made themselves out to be, though that wasn't what she was curious about. It was the artifact Mother Natalie revealed to Joel. Was it actually Judas' robe? Lisa's cell phone buzzed. It was Joel. This could solve one problem but it would only lead to another. If she told him to come get her, she'd be admitting that she followed him against his wishes. She let the phone ring.

* * *

Panic set in as Joel searched the campus for Lisa. She was not at home, she was not picking up her cell phone, and none of their dorm neighbors had seen her. He called Morgan but got no response. Frustration and worry nagged at him like a thousand tiny gnats. Why would Lisa be out at this time of night, and where would she be? Unless she was in trouble. With nowhere else to go Joel raced across the quad to the adjoining dorm building and knocked on Morgan's door. After a few minutes the sleepy-eyed co-ed opened up.

"What the fuck, Joel?" she said. "It's like, three in the morning."

"Yeah, I know. Lisa's missing. Is she here?"

"No."

"Have you seen or heard from her?"

"No."

"I've checked our building, all the bars've closed. I don't know where else to look. Can you check your phone? Maybe she called and you didn't pick up."

"Wait here," she muttered as she closed the door. A moment later he heard a man's groggy voice asking questions. Joel recognized it. Morgan returned to the door.

"Sorry, Joel, nothing. But I'm sure she's okay."

"Thanks. Oh, and tell Brown not to expect me back in class until I've found her."

Morgan offered up a guilty smile as Joel hurried down the hallway. He emerged from the building and jogged around the campus hoping to spot her returning from wherever. After another hour he returned to his apartment hoping she'd be home.

With nothing else to do, Lisa decided to search for the item that had held so much fascination for her boyfriend. She remembered that the container Natalie showed Joel was about the size of a shoebox. She'd seen the nun go to the back of the room, turn the corner, and return with it. Lisa retraced the nun's footsteps to the back wall where the aisle split into a 'T.' Additional shelving extended three feet in both directions. She turned right and searched the obvious places first, behind the wine bottles, under shelves, and inside drawers. The battery on her phone was running down and the strength of the light began to dim. She got down on her hands and knees to look for any trace that might reveal a hiding place. Feeling her way around with her free hand, she came upon some cement granules on the floor at the base of a wall. She pushed and pulled a few bricks, finding two of them loose. When she removed them, she found a small cavity in the wall. Unfortunately, the torch went out and she was left in total darkness. Undaunted, Lisa reached into the hole and felt around until she located something. She grabbed it and pulled out a small box.

Lisa weighed the heft of the container in her hands while weighing the consequences of opening it. Her fingers trembled as if knowing that when the contents were revealed, the object inside would have a serious impact on her life. But there was no choice. She took a breath and opened the box. Could this be the single piece of physical evidence of God on earth that Father Sanchez spoke of?

CHAPTER 21

Life in the convent began every morning promptly at 5:00 a.m. The sisters rose for the first of two prayers which took an hour and half in total. At 7:00 a.m. they took breakfast in the main hall, the sounds of which had awoken Lisa. It was pitch black in the cellar. The cold, hard concrete on her hands and face informed her that she'd fallen asleep on the floor at one point, with the box tucked under her arm. She sat up and stretched to get the kinks out of her shoulders and neck. Then she reached into her pocket for her phone and pushed herself into a standing position. Lisa pressed power hoping there would be at least a glimmer of incandescent light from the phone. Nothing. She picked a direction and used her hands on the nearby shelves to guide her toward a wall, any wall. Stumbling along, she noticed a small ribbon of light peeking under the main door about fifteen feet away. Using the shelves, she stumbled toward the luminous strip. A minute later she congratulated herself on finding the entrance to the wine cellar. Next. Thinking back to the previous night she remembered the light switch and felt around until she located it. She switched it on and shielded her eyes until they adjusted to the light. Her next thought was of the robe. She turned back and rushed back to the box lying on the floor where she'd awakened. Gently, she opened it. Now she could see the relic, a dull, yellowed robe with dark stains running through it. It looked old enough, and when she brought it to her nose, it did have a musty smell. But beyond that there were no other distinguishing marks or proof that this was the actual relic. And then a more urgent need pushed the former away; she was hungry.

In the upstairs dining hall, the talk was all about the woman who schemed her way into the building the night before. No one knew what she wanted, where she went, or if in fact she was still on the premises. This was the second time in a week the convent had been broken into and everyone was on edge. Residents were told to keep a sharp lookout for intruders or anything that might be missing. Mother Natalie listened intently to the gossip and kept her mouth shut.

After breakfast, the daily chores began. Some of the nuns began their cleaning duties while others opened the school for the children. The rest began rounds in the palliative care unit. Sister Baptiste was in charge of distributing fruits and vegetables which were stored in the basement. After breakfast, the young novice tread lightly down the stairs to gather food for the school children and the elderly. That's when she heard a whimpering behind the wine cellar door.

"Somebody in there?" she asked. She was answered with more whimpering. "Who's there?" asked the novice.

"Someone unworthy of your pity."

Sister Baptiste joined the convent only four months ago. She could have gone directly to her superiors upstairs but she felt this might be an opportunity to test her faith. "What is your name?"

"Is suicide truly a sin?" asked the plaintiff voice. This was not the kind of reply the noviciate was expecting, and it threw her.

"Suicide?" Sister Baptiste's heart skipped a beat. "What's your name, dear? Please."

"I mean, if there was no other way? Wouldn't God still receive me?"

A trickle of red liquid began to pool at the bottom of the door and it made the novitiate tremble.

"There is always a way," she said with a tremor in her voice. "Are...are you hurt?"

"A little," came the reply. "But it will be better soon."

The voice sounded so frail that Sister Baptiste began to panic. "Stay where you are, Move away from the door. I mean, don't do anything."

More dark red liquid poured through the bottom of the door. The young nun searched on the wall for the key and found it hanging on a hook a few inches to the left of the door.

"I'm going to unlock the door. Step back." The novitiate inserted the key into the lock. "Almost there."

Sister Baptiste turned the key, praying she wouldn't be too late, and pushed open the large oak door. Lisa yanked it at the same time and the young noviciate stumbled through the doorway. Lisa grabbed her by the lapel and shut the door.

""Take off your clothes," said Lisa. "I'll probably burn in hell for this."

The young nun froze with fear.

"I mean it!"

The novitiate began to tear up while she reluctantly removed her cowl and habit. Lisa removed her own pants and top at the same time. The novice's entire body shook nervously.

"Relax," said Lisa. "I'm not going to hurt you."

A moment later, Lisa emerged from the wine cellar dressed as the novice. She shut the door and locked the young lady inside. "I'll tell the others upstairs. You'll be out in no time, promise. And I'm sorry."

With the box in hand Lisa leaped up the stairs and made a beeline for the front door. She kept her head down as she hurried along the corridor past several nuns. She was only a few yards from the exit when an alarm sounded.

Lisa froze, and then in the guise of the novice, shouted, "Lock all the doors, lock all the doors!" She ran to the front door to lock them, but fled outside instead. As she burst onto the street and kept running, she chanted to herself, "Hail Mary full of grace, hail Mary full of grace, hail Mary full of grace."

Lisa hopped onto the first bus that came along and rode it until she'd reached another neighborhood. She jumped off and strode into a coffee shop. She used the washroom before buying a coffee and croissant and sat at a table that had an outlet to charge her phone. Customers glanced her way and she smiled back. She must have looked a curious sight and giggled to herself as to what might be going through their minds. Lisa checked her phone messages to find Joel had left over a dozen. She ignored them, still pissed for having been cut out of the loop. Then she remembered the DNA evidence she gave her cousin. She rang Barry up, but he didn't answer. She gave herself a minute to enjoy the croissant and coffee and satisfy her hunger which allowed her to concentrate on what to do next. Lisa reached for the small wooden box sitting next to her on the bench, desperate to know the origin of its contents. If the robe was the real thing, she needed to understand its history and who she was dealing with. The obvious place to start would be with Bishop Newman. She doubted it would be difficult to track him down. She took another swig of coffee and Googled the Biopharm phone number. It was a curse, this enquiring mind of hers.

"Hello? Human resources, please?" she said into the cell phone. "Hi, I was at the Biopharm cocktail party the other night and this marvelous Bishop Newman was there and I heard what he was doing for the less fortunate. I'm calling because I'd like to make a donation to his parish. But I didn't get his contact info so I was hoping..."

Lisa rode another bus back to campus and entered her apartment a little past 10:00 a.m. to find the place empty. She sighed with relief at not having to deal with Joel just yet. She took off the stolen habit and showered and after, put on some makeup, a pair of jeans, and a shirt. She slipped her IPad into her purse and hurried out again. Lisa waited another 15 minutes for a bus and climbed on. Searching for privacy, she walked past mothers and their crying babies, several students, and business people. She ignored them all, sat down, and put ear phones on to discourage any random conversation. Then she took out her IPad and studied the notes on Judas Iscariot she'd placed in The Cloud. It seemed odd that for such an infamous historical figure there was precious little information. Nothing was mentioned about the man's past before he took up with Jesus. All the world knew about him was based on his betrayal of Christ and the aftermath, the giving back of the 30 pieces of silver, his decision to hang himself, and his burial in Potter's Field. That was essentially it. It was as if the man was parachuted into the story and forgotten after he'd served his purpose. So why would his robe be the one piece of physical evidence of God? That question led to the next, whether Bishop Newman truly was Bishop Promane? And if so, that presented a thousand more questions.

Lisa's heart began to thump harder than a Salvation Army drum on Christmas Eve.

The alarm went off and Joel shot up in bed. He wiped his eyes and looked at the clock, 7:30 a.m. He felt the other side of the bed and realized Lisa was still missing. He climbed out and shuffled to the bathroom to shower and shave. Everything felt mechanical, a serried of muscle memories, but he needed to rely on them because his every other thought was of Lisa. In the gaps and spaces of those thoughts, scraps of conversation from the night before floated through his brain like untethered balloons. Each nugget of information led his mind to conjure up one tortuous scenario after another. Somehow he finished getting dressed and searched the apartment looking for Lisa's timetable but couldn't find it. He cleared his mind to make a mental list of where she might be and set out to find her.

* * *

Professor Brown was in the lecture hall arranging his notes when he lifted his eyes to see Lisa enter. He wondered whether or not to say anything about Joel looking for her last night but decided against it. Maybe she was with some other guy the night before. It was common enough for couples to hook up and break up over the course of a week let alone a term. In any case it was none of his business. He did, however, catch Morgan's eye and made a gesture to her. Morgan took his suggestion and shifted over to sit next to her girlfriend.

"Lisa, you okay? Where were you? Joel was all over the campus last night looking for you."

"Oh, uh, I had this thing to do and after, I decided to crash at a friend's."

Morgan nodded. She'd used the same vague excuses herself on more than one occasion.

"That's what I figured. So are you gonna, call him, text him?"

Lisa gave off a cool vibe and shrugged, "Yeah, a little later."

Morgan nodded, "I get it. If you ever want to talk, you know, you can always call me."

Lisa shot her a sideways glance. "And the next time you decide to hook up with one of our Profs you can tell me."

Morgan's back stiffened. Lisa's retort was uncharacteristically cruel. Whatever happened to her the night before had a profound effect on her.

"Well, sorry for caring," Morgan said and moved away.

Brown noticed the frosty rebuff and shook his head over the spat. To distract them both he called the class to order. "All right," he said smartly.

As the lecture continued, Lisa grew more and more oblivious to the topic. The stunning events of the previous night were gnawing at her so viciously that she felt that if she had to sit there one more minute, she'd scream. Instead, she grabbed her stomach as if having a sudden attack of cramps, picked up her things, and hurried out.

A single sheet of paper was tacked on the front door. Written upon it in magic marker were the words, 'Welcome to St. James Church – under renovation.' A cacophony of sounds from saws, hammers, and drills echoed throughout the building. Lisa entered to find a busy crew of parishioners putting finishing touches on the interior, painting walls and cobbling together the wooden frames and pews.

"Hi there," Lisa said to the nearest woman. "I'm looking for Bishop Newman?"

"Are you here for confession?" she asked.

"What? No," she replied, somewhat taken aback.

The woman smiled and explained. "Don't be offended. Most strangers are here to receive some kind of penitence. In the eyes of the lord we are all guilty of one sin or another, aren't we?"

Lisa hesitated, unsure of how to respond. Another woman noticed her reticence and strode over.

"Hello. Can I help you?"

"Like I told this girl, I'm here to speak with Bishop Newman."

"Do you have an appointment? It's just that we're very busy, getting ready for the blessed opening."

"I met him the other night, at a company party. Biopharm Pharmaceuticals? Through my boyfriend, Joel Gardiner."

Belle smiled back, without showing any sense of recognition.

"And your name?" the second woman asked.

"Lisa."

"Hi, Lisa. I'm Belle." Belle offered her hand and Lisa accepted.

"Come with me, we'll see if the bishop has a moment." Belle led Lisa out of the sanctuary and down a hallway. When they were alone Belle whispered, "Don't be upset with Angela. Sometimes the 'newbees' are the most zealous."

Lisa decided that arguing the point would get her nowhere, so she simply smiled and nodded. Belle led Lisa through a doorway, down a set of stairs, and along the basement hallway to the rectory.

"Bishop Newman?" Belle called out as she knocked. "We have a visitor. Do you have a second?"

"Come," he replied.

The two women entered the small, officious room. Lisa looked around to see a filing cabinet, desk and two chairs. A host of liturgical books sat on shelves and various surfaces around the room. Pictures of the Pope and Jesus hung on opposite walls. Newman looked up from his papers and recognized the girl immediately.

"Lisa, isn't it?" he acknowledged with a warm smile.

"I'm impressed," she replied.

"I have a talent for remembering faces."

When the bishop offered his hand, Lisa hesitated, unsure of whether to shake it or kiss it.

"A handshake will do," said Newman with a grin.

Lisa laughed uncomfortably and shook the priest's hand. The first thing she noticed was his missing baby finger and a small tingle ran up her spine.

"And to what do I owe this pleasure?" asked the bishop.

Lisa gestured with her eyes, indicating that she would rather speak to the priest alone.

"Belle," said Newman. "Now might be a good time to take care of that matter we spoke of earlier."

"Certainly, Bishop," said Belle, getting his drift. And with that she left.

"Forgive me," he continued. "We're all so very busy preparing for our opening. You and Joel, of course, are invited."

"Thanks. So, you're restoring the church? I saw everyone working so hard upstairs."

"Not restoring, remodelling. Modernity has many advantages, better medicine, technology. And with the internet it seems that man can almost get along without God."

"Oh, I wouldn't say—"

"But it has its drawbacks, one of them being, crisis of faith. This particular church ran into hard times a few years ago and was vacated. I was fortunate enough to purchase it and here we are."

"It's going to be a Catholic church? I remember mine being more ornate."

"Our version is anchored in the classic, but with a few modern touches. I feel it's important to have something to offer the people to help them deal with the issues of the day while keeping a sense of tradition."

"Which kind of brings me to why I'm here, Bishop."

"Your concern for your boyfriend?"

Lisa nodded. This was not the reason for her visit but she figured the more she could keep the bishop talking, the more she'd learn. Maybe even give himself away.

"He was a little rude the other night, and I wanted to apologize for him."

"No need. How long have you two been together?"

"About six months." The bishop kept his gaze on her, almost demanding that she continue. "He's a great guy but not always easy to read. And he doesn't talk much about his early years, his family." The bishop nodded in such a way that she knew he was aware of his circumstances. "I, uh, he mentioned you were the family priest."

"Correct."

"I was hoping for any insight you might be able to offer."

Newman took a seat and indicated that Lisa sit across from him. He reclined slightly, causing Lisa to lean in and hear him.

"I'm in the unique position of having known Joel Gardiner and his family for more years than you've been alive. I was there when his mother married, gave birth to her three children, and I was there to counsel her when her marriage collapsed and her family dissolved."

"I've never met Joel's mother. He said she had a condition."

"Ectodermal dysplasia, yes. With a number of surgeries, we were able to help her lead a more normal life. But that didn't heal the other wounds."

"Other? Psychological, you mean?"

Newman nodded. "When one has an ailment or disfigurement you naturally ask, 'why me, God?' Natalie's rationalization was in the belief that she had a special purpose. Specifically, that God had given her a mission."

"What kind of mission?"

"In her case, to protect a relic."

At the mention of the relic, Lisa's heart beat a little faster and fought to stay calm.

"What kind of relic?"

Bishop Newman smiled. He paused for a moment and turned his attention to some mail that was sitting on his desk.

Lisa tried another tack. "You're telling me the woman has mental issues, that she's crazy?"

Newman dropped the mail and fixed his eyes on hers. "You must appreciate that as a close family member, I would never betray a trust. All I can say is, through her fervor and steadfast belief, she ended up alienating her entire family. Her husband and children left her a little more than two years ago. Joel, who was the youngest, remained but under very strained conditions. A year later he severed ties with her altogether. I managed to get Natalie shelter in the religious cloister where she currently lives. I'm sure he didn't mention it but I was also instrumental in getting Joel into the faculty of medicine.

"Really?"

"I don't say this to brag. If I brag at all, it's about Joel who had the drive and the smarts to get where he is today."

"And yet, when he talks about you— "

"Yes, I know. I've always tried to look out for the lad, but when he was younger, he got it into his head that I was partially responsible for the breakup of his parents' marriage." Lisa's intent stare begged a little more information out of Newman. "In simple terms he equated his mother's delusion with the church's influence on her. And since I was the church's representative..."

Lisa considered that if Newman was Promane, he was hiding it well. Still, after 500 years, he should be a master at anything he put his mind to. He had successfully derailed the discussion of the relic and made everything about Natalie and her family, almost as if the Judas's Robe was the fiction of a demented mind.

"That explains a lot, thanks." She was about to stand up when a thought struck her. "Oh, Bishop, while I'm here, Joel and I were having an argument maybe you could settle."

"If I can," replied the priest with a smile.

"The character in the bible, Judas?"

"Fascinating subject. Before we start, when was the last time you made confession?"

Lisa laughed nervously and drew back. "Why is everyone here so obsessed with confession?"

Sensing her discomfort, Bishop Newman stood up. "It's stuffy in this little office of mine. Why don't we get out of here?"

Newman crossed to the door and gestured that Lisa follow him out of the rectory. As he led her down the hall he picked up where he left off.

"Ever been to a wine tasting?"

Lisa held her breath, wondering if he was alluding to the wine cellar she'd just escaped from and the article she'd stolen from it. "On occasion. Once or twice."

"Do you cleanse your palate before the tasting or do you swallow whatever is offered straight away? Confession is a cleansing of sorts, that when done properly, allows for a clearer head and a more balanced perspective."

Lisa expelled her breath slowly and relaxed. The bishop wasn't referring to the relic she found. Or was he teasing her, baiting some kind of trap for her? They reached the stairs that led to the main floor and Lisa grew guarded again. Confession entailed being alone in a small room with a priest and there was something about all this that made her uncomfortable.

"Don't worry, Lisa. We don't force anyone to do anything they don't want to do," he said with a benign smile.

Newman led her up the stairs. When they reached the main floor, instead of going to the sanctuary where the confessional was, Newman led her out the back door. When they emerged, she was relieved and fascinated at the same time. In front of her stood a tract of land that included a large garden populated with all kinds of trees, flowers and vegetation. The foliage was fading in the autumn weather but a number of people were still tending the grounds.

"It's a sanctuary I find as serene out here as the one inside," said the bishop.

As he led her on a casual stroll down the patio stones, Lisa felt like the interview she initiated had been hijacked. She still didn't know what to make of this man who made her feel warm and relaxed one moment, then jittery as a coke addict the next. Further into the yard the couple came upon two parishioners, kneeling. When they finished their prayers, they stood up and walked back, "Blessings, Bishop," they said as they passed the priest.

"My children," he replied.

Lisa noticed this patch of ground had rows upon rows of small glass shards that stuck six inches out of the ground.

"What are those?" she asked.

"A garden like this provides an abundance of fruits and vegetables. But none of it can grow without sustenance."

The bishop fished around in his pant pocket and showed Lisa a few seeds. Then he bent down on one knee and dug a small hole with his fingers.

"We dig a little hole and place the seed in the dirt. At the same time, we say a prayer admitting our sins, and then we bury them along with the seed. Growth through redemption.

"The exercise serves two purposes. One, to help produce nature's bounty next season and two, to set us free of our burdens."

Lisa's brow furrowed over the bishop's obtuse observations and folded her arms. "And Jonah was swallowed by a whale, and the seas parted, and Jesus was killed and then came back to life. Do you and the church expect people to believe these fairy tales, literally?" Newman gave a slight nod, acknowledging her question. "Because it's a fact," she continued, "that a whale does not have an esophagus large enough to swallow a human being." Newman did not answer. Lisa's blood was up and felt compelled to continue her questioning. "Let me ask you straight out; do you believe Judas was a real person or was he a character the church made up to help promote the myth of Jesus? I mean, just how do you all separate fact from fiction?"

Newman folded his hands as if pondering an age-old question. "Good points, all of them, and issues that folks have asked themselves for centuries."

Lisa could feel her fingernails digging into the palms of her hands with frustration. Finally, she unclenched her fists and shook off the tension. "Thanks for the talk. Very enlightening," she said in a voice tinged with sarcasm.

She was about to turn and leave the grounds when Newman reached into his pocket and pulled out a shard of glass similar to the ones in the ground. Then he took a grease pencil from the same pocket and wrote her name on it.

"Lisa, I want you to take a moment to contemplate all your questions and anxieties."

"Really, as you can see, I'm not a believer."

"Then it can't hurt, can it? What have you got to lose?" he asked.

The bishop handed Lisa the shard. She took another calming breath, closed her eyes, and went along begrudgingly with his request. When she attempted to hand the glass back to the priest, she accidentally stumbled and sliced Newman's wrist with it.

"Ohmygod!" she cried. "I'm so sorry. I must've lost my footing."

Lisa stared at his wrist. She was sure she had cut deep enough into his skin, but although the skin had separated, there was no blood, not a single drop. Newman ran his other hand over the wound, soothingly.

"That's alright, dear. No harm done."

Lisa couldn't believe her eyes. She focused on his eyes to study his reaction when she asked him her next question. "How old are you?"

The bishop shook his head. To him it was like a child trying to outsmart a sophisticated adult. He reached up into an apple tree, twisted off the fruit, and handed it to her. She noticed the cut on his wrist had faded to a scratch and she blinked as if her eyes were lying to her.

"This apple, is it just a fruit we consume?" he asked.

Lisa's voice grew tight with anger and frustration as she ignored his question and pursued her line of thinking. "There was a bishop who lived in Spain a long time ago, a Bishop Promane."

"Or is it a symbol of the source of all knowledge as the bible teaches?"

Lisa stared back at him, her eyes burning into his. "Your cut just healed in front of my eyes!"

The bishop gazed back at Lisa with an air of pure calm.

"You've been disappointed by the empty words of your church, your schooling, and your family, haven't you, Lisa? They've all demanded you accept the dogma with blind obedience. You have a sense of faith but you're not religious. You want to believe but you need proof." The priest took a step closer to her as if he was about to impart a deep secret. "What if I could give you what no other prophet has ever been able to, a glimpse of the one true God?"

Newman's Svengali-like gaze was so intense that Lisa began to tremble; afraid she might evaporate into thin air if she didn't leave immediately. "Thanks for the talk. Gotta go."

With that, she hurried out of the garden and across the street to the parking lot. When she reached her car, she climbed in and watched her hands tremble on the wheel. She hoped a minute to herself would calm her nerves but her whole body felt the prick of a thousand tiny shocks. She started the engine and booted it out of the parking lot, hoping that distance would calm her. Cutting the bishop on the wrist was a spur of the moment decision. It wasn't a very elegant experiment but the opportunity presented itself and she had to know. The thought of it frightened her. It frightened her because, as a scientist, she was being forced to consider that many of the laws and rules she lived by might be false. Was it possible this man could be 500 years old? The corollary to that inferred the robe might also be real. And she had it.

Where the hell was her cousin?

CHAPTER 22

Marie Champlain had been marshalling her forces all day, overseeing all the disparate aspects of her corporate plan to bring the universal blood formula to market. After several heated discussions she finally convinced her board of directors that this discovery had to be the priority for their company. She drew up a list of her most astute scientists and assigned them to the task of helping to hunt down the key enzyme from Joel Gardiner's notes. Then she informed the legal department to prepare for patents and consider all the other auxiliary facets for the upcoming project. She learned her lesson a long time ago with regard to leaving the fate of such an important find in the hands of too many people. It resulted in corporate thievery and prolonged, expensive law suits. She assigned the workload in piecemeal so that each scientist and each department had an individual task. No one had any idea of the connection between their work and the one next to them. That way, no single person or cell could jeopardise the integrity of the entire program by stealing the information. It was after 8:00 p.m. when Marie exited the elevator into the dimly-lit garage. At this late hour the staff had gone home and the garage was deserted. Her mind was so preoccupied that she was unaware of the girl until she reached her car.

"Miss Champlain?"

Marie turned around to find a slim, attractive red head in her twenties wearing a black body suit.

"I don't know you and my day is done," she replied curtly. "If you want to speak to me book an appointment with my secretary during business hours."

With that, Marie clicked her key fob to open her car door, but it wouldn't work.

"You need to keep Joel Gardiner on the project," continued Belle.

How did this stranger know about Joel and her project, she wondered? "Who are you?"

The young woman just offered a condescending smile.

"Okay, then," said Marie, placating the stranger. She tried her fob again without success. Sensing danger, Marie clenched her car keys between her knuckles, ready to use them as a weapon if necessary. Then she turned back to the female, aggressively.

"There are cameras in every corner of this garage. Also, the security guard knows I've clocked out. If I'm not out of here in—"

"It's important that Joel stay with the project."

"Repetition does not make your message more urgent. It only makes it boring, dear. I don't know who you are but if you don't want me to call security and put your ass in jail you better open this car door immediately!"

Belle didn't budge. Four of her comrades who had been hidden in the dark until now came out from behind various pillars. Marie's agitation turned to fear when one of them pulled a knife. Marie dug into her purse for her phone and tried to dial 911. Before she could, one of the men strode up and wrestled it out of her hand.

"Ouch!" she yelled.

The thug pulled back to slug her, making her flinch. But in the last second, he placed his finger over his lips to 'encourage' her to be quiet. Then he grabbed her purse spilled the contents onto the concrete.

"What the fuck?!"

The thug gave Marie an icy stare and she recoiled. Belle sifted through Marie's belongings and found her driver's license.

"Marie Champlain. 2648 Walker Point Drive."

"So, you know where I live. Big deal. I've been threatened before by much smarter than you. My lawyers—"

"Men with paper? Do I look like someone afraid of paper?"

Belle nodded to her cohort holding the knife who advanced on Marie. The executive knew she was no match for a thug with a serious weapon like that. All she could do was crouch on the ground in a defensive posture and scream. But instead of attacking, he walked past her. Marie swivelled around on her knees and watched the thug puncture all four of her tires. She relaxed for a moment, hoping that the worst was over. That's when the thug advanced on Marie and slashed her across her forearm.

"Owe! Are you all crazy?" Marie shouted at Belle.

"No argument there," replied Belle with a smirk. "Joel Gardiner stays on the project. Sorry if I bored you."

Belle waved at the cameras in the ceiling and led her crew out of the garage. As soon as they were out of sight Marie began shivering and allowed tears to stream down her face. After her nerves settled, she picked up some Kleenex that had spilled out onto the ground and pressed it against her wound. Then she stuffed her belongings back into her purse, got to her feet, and scurried to the elevator. By the time she returned to her office the fear had morphed into rage and she called building security to report the assault. Two guards rushed up with a first aid kit. One tended to her wound while the other reported the attack to the police.

The next morning Marie sat in a detective's office wearing a short sleeve blouse and a white bandage on her arm. She'd told the officer everything she could remember about the attack the previous night. He'd taken her statement and reviewed the security video.

"Unfortunately, there was nothing," said the detective.

"What do you mean, nothing? I was there. They were there, something had to be recorded." Marie said with a mix of surprise and fury.

"The cameras...the lenses were smudged with paint. Nothing in the garage area was recorded."

"Well there must've been some DNA at the scene, detective. Fingerprints and such. I've seen enough CSI programs to know—"

The detective shook his head. "There are no fingerprints, there's no knife. Some partial footprints which we are working on, but... and we'll check any CCTV cameras in and around the property. We've got the descriptions you gave us. It would help if you could tell us what they wanted."

Marie's eyes shifted away from the officer as she considered what to say. "I... I'm sorry."

"Well, is it corporate or personal?" he asked. Marie remained mute. "Ms. Champlain, you came to us. There's not much we can do without your cooperation."

Marie stood and straightened her posture. "Thanks for your help, detective."

It was almost noon when she arrived at the parking lot where her loaner sat. Her insurance agent had arranged a Cadillac while the tires on her Mercedes were being replaced. As she closed the door, she was accosted by another young woman at her window.

"Got any spare change?"

"Get away from me!"

"Joel Gardiner stays on the project, got it?"

"Yeah, I got that memo last night when your pals slashed my fucking tires. Don't you people talk to each other?"

Sofia tried not to look surprised by Marie's exasperated response. Instead, she said nothing and walked away thinking, someone else wanted to keep Joel on the project as well, the bishop, no doubt. For once both sides wanted the same thing, but for totally different reasons.

* * *

Two days had passed since Joel last saw or heard from Lisa. He'd crisscrossed the campus several times, visited pubs and restaurants they frequented, and asked around. When he cornered Morgan, she just shrugged, unwilling to get mixed up in any drama. He'd gone on to alert campus security and spoken with the police who took his statement, promising to look into it. Each night he came home hoping to find her there, but no such luck. He was going out of his mind with worry. And although she was his chief concern, it wasn't his only one. His studies and pledge to find a cure for his mother's affliction weighed heavily on him as did the robe. And although he couldn't prove it, he knew the two were linked. He racked his brain, trying to think of some way to be more proactive. One idea that crossed his mind would be to just take the robe and run. If someone was holding Lisa, at least he'd a have a bargaining chip. After he got her back he could deal with the rest. If in fact she was lost to him forever, he might choose to run away and live in obscurity for the rest of his life. Or he could take Father Sanchez's advice and remain with Biopharm to cash in on the universal blood formula. Its dividends would make his family rich enough to fight his enemies for generations. He smiled to himself thinking of becoming a modern-day Bruce Wayne, but without the bat cave and the sweet gadgets. It also meant dealing with Bishop Newman on a regular basis, the Joker to his Batman. Which brought his mind circuitously back to his mother and Lisa. This fucking robe was a curse! He needed an objective opinion and the only opinion he respected was Professor Brown's. Joel strode through the campus to Brown's office. Half way there, his cell phone rang. He looked at the screen to find a phone number instead of a name.

"Hello?"

"Joel? It's Marie Champlain. I'd like to discuss your future. Can you come by the office now?"

"I don't think..."

"Try to keep your thinking to a minimum until we've had our chat."

"Ms. Champlain, I've got a lot of things on my mind—"

"There's nothing more important than this, I assure you."

"My girlfriend's been missing for two days."

"Trust me, Joel, love only clouds the mind. See you within the hour."

Marie hung up. As if Joel didn't have enough stress to deal with. But in that moment he found clarity. He realized his biggest, overall concern was for Lisa. Everything else could wait. He postponed his discussion with Professor Brown and returned to his apartment to look for any other clues as to his girlfriend's whereabouts. When he arrived, he was stunned by the sight in front of him; there she was, sitting in a chair, sipping a glass of wine.

"Miss me, hon?" she asked.

CHAPTER 23

"Lisa! Where the hell've you been?" asked Joel.

"Glass of wine, Joel?" she asked.

Lisa offered him the glass but he refused. Instead, he strode over to her and hugged her fiercely. When he didn't feel the same emotional response, he pulled back and stared at her.

"I've been worried sick. Are you alright? What happened to you?"

"I'm not big on wine myself, but in the last couple of days I've acquired an appreciation for it. Ever since your visit to your mother's convent."

Joel's eyebrows arched with surprise. "You followed me?"

"They have quite the collection down in their wine cellar. I know because I spent the night locked up inside it."

Joel paused, feeling guilt being heaped upon him.

"I called you a million times. Why didn't you pick up or message me? I could've gotten you out." The wry look on Lisa's face told him the questions he was asking were superfluous and the time for subterfuge was over. He knew that if he expected her to be honest, then he would have to be as well. He took a couple of paces to gather his thoughts and turned to her using a softer, more conciliatory tone.

"There was a reason I didn't want you involved."

It was Lisa's turn to be aggressive. "You kept me in the dark about a lot of things."

"Listen—"

"Bishop Newman for one."

Joel's face went white. "What about Newman?"

Lisa walked into the bedroom. Joel turned to watch her leave, worrying that this conversation was going to get a whole lot more uncomfortable.

"Since I couldn't get any information from you," she said from the other room, "I decided to pay him a visit."

"You went to see Newman? You shouldn't have done that. I know you're pissed at me, but..."

"He's building a church, you know. He has big plans."

"Whatever he told you, it's a lie."

Lisa emerged from the bedroom with her glass of wine in one hand and the robe in the other. Joel's jaw dropped. She crossed over to the kitchen counter where the two bottles stood. "Red or white?" she asked again. "Red, I think. It'll help bring back the color to your face."

Joel stood frozen to the spot, unsure of what she had in mind or what to do. Lisa poured him a glass and wrapped the robe around her shoulders. "Chilly in here," she said as she brought him the wine.

He accepted the glass and said, "You need to give me that right now."

"Do you know what this can do, Joel? Do you have any comprehension what this means?"

She whipped the robe behind her and ran around the room, acting like a superhero, the cape dancing behind her in the breeze. Joel began to sweat, worrying if the robe really had any power. And whether that power might make Lisa as crazy as Joel's mother.

"Lisa! Take it off! It doesn't belong to you."

"You're right. It belongs to everyone. It belongs to the whole world."

"Babe, listen to me, you have no idea..."

Joel reached out to stop her from running, but she pulled away and hissed at him like a snake.

"Yes, I do! I spoke to my cousin this morning. He did the DNA analysis on the petrified finger and the glass you gave me. Guess what? Match! Bishop Newman and Bishop Promane are one in the same. And the corollary to that means this robe is genuine too."

Joel stepped a little closer but Lisa dropped into a defensive stance and he backed off. "I'll make you a deal. Hang onto it for now," he said, "But we need to know more about it. I don't want anything to happen to you."

"Why?"

"Because."

"Because why?"

"Because I love you."

"You never said those words to me before."

Lisa relaxed her stance and petted the cloth affectionately. "This is one nifty little miracle worker." She took a sip of wine and smiled at Joel, like a God indulging a mere mortal.

CHAPTER 24

After leaving several messages for his mother, Joel finally connected and convinced her to come over to his apartment. When Natalie arrived, she entered to find Lisa sitting on the couch. Joel showed his mother to a chair and he took his place next to Lisa, to show her support. Strolling to her chair, Natalie noticed the bottles of wine standing on the counter and recognized the labels. She glanced at Lisa, knowing she was the interloper in the convent the other night, but said nothing. There were just the three of them and they all knew what happened. The trio sat uncomfortably for a moment.

"So, this is Lisa," Natalie finally said. "Lovely to meet you, dear."

"And you," Lisa replied in a reserved manner. The younger watched the elder in the same way a mongoose watched a cobra.

"Would you like some tea or something, Mom?" Joel asked.

"Or a glass of wine?" suggested Lisa.

Joel squeezed his girlfriend's hand, suggesting this was no time for snide remarks.

"You didn't invite me over for drinks, or for that matter, to meet your girlfriend, did you?" replied Natalie.

"Well..." Joel shifted his weight and leaned in. "The other night when I visited you, I thought I was alone. Believe me, I had no idea—"

Natalie gasped in mock surprise. "You were followed? By whom?" Then she turned to Lisa and asked, "Which do you prefer, the red or white?"

Lisa ignored the question and reached around to pull the robe out from behind the couch, placing it snugly in her lap. Natalie's amused gaze turned suddenly frosty.

"Where did you get that?"

"You know exactly where I got it," Lisa replied with a smug look. "Just to be clear, I never wanted anything to do with your little intrigue. But I got pulled into it because I was concerned about your son. Then I was shut out, so I make no apologies."

"You trespassed on private property and stole a priceless relic. And that's just for starters."

"If this robe is what you claim it is, then it's my guess you've broken a higher law."

"Young lady, you have no idea what you've done or what you've set in motion!" Natalie stood up. "Now give it back!"

Lisa remained in her seat and posed defiantly. "Something like this doesn't belong to you, alone. You have no right—"

"Both of you!" Joel yelled. "We're past trading blame now. We need to focus on what to do next."

"The main thing is, to keep the robe from Bishop Promane," said Lisa.

"Bishop who?" asked Natalie.

"Your Bishop Newman. I met with him at his church. He's got some big-ass plans and they all involve this piece of cloth."

Mother Natalie shook her head. "You don't know what you're talking about. I've known Bishop Newman all my life. After one meeting you think—"

"I slashed his forearm," Lisa replied, proudly.

"You what?!" said Natalie.

"There was no blood. And in a matter of minutes the wound disappeared. Father Sanchez was right. Bishop Newman and Bishop Promane are one in the same."

"Who the hell is Father Sanchez?"

"Lady, the time for playing ignorant with me is..."

A rock smashed the window and sent splinters of glass everywhere. The three of them dropped to the floor. Thirty seconds later another missile crashed into the apartment. This one hissed and emitted a cloud of gas.

"Smoke bomb!" shouted Joel. "Stay on the floor."

All three wrapped clothing around their faces to protect themselves from the smoke. Joel crept to the front door but Natalie pointed at the shadows that appeared under the transom. "Joel," Natalie whispered, "Is there a fire escape, another way out?"

Joel shook his head. Lisa choked out a command, "Call Spencer and have him set off the fire alarm."

Joel fumbled for his cell phone and made the call. "Spencer, emergency, man! Those freaks who killed Andy a few days ago? They're back. I need you to pull the fire alarm ASAP. No joke!"

"This is what I've been dreading for years," said Natalie, trembling with fear. She turned to Lisa. "You have no idea what you've set in motion."

Before anyone could say another word, the fire alarm went off. Joel and Lisa crawled to the front door but Natalie held out her arms and stayed them with a warning. "Wait!"

Choking and sputtering, she held Joel and Lisa back for 30 seconds before allowing them to leave the apartment. When they burst out of the flat, smoke escaped with them into the hallway while a dozen or so students gathered around, more curious than afraid.

"What happened, man?" asked one student.

"Overcook the mac and cheese?" asked another.

Joel scanned the hallway to see if the bishop or any of his people were about, but he didn't spot any strangers. Lisa coughed and hacked as if her lungs were burning! "Fire! Everybody out!" At the sound of, 'fire' everyone bolted like a frightened herd of cattle toward the nearest exits. Joel, Lisa and Natalie melted into the crowd.

Natalie tried to keep up, but after a few fumbling steps, she began to pant. When they reached the stairwell, she was jostled in the scrum. Joel and Lisa supported her on either side and assisted her down the steps, protecting her from being jostled. When they emerged into the fall night, Natalie noticed three strangers standing down the block, watching everyone who came staggering out.

"This way!" the nun said, directing Lisa and Joel to flee in the opposite direction.

"The robe!" cautioned Lisa who, in all the chaos, had forgotten all about it.

"We can't go back now," answered Natalie.

"Mom, we have to!" replied Joel.

"Trust me, let's go," answered the nun.

Natalie spoke with such authority that no one questioned it.

"Where do we go?"

Before his mother could answer, a cab pulled up. All three stepped back, afraid it was their pursuers. Until the door swung open and Sofia poked her head out. "Get in!"

Without skipping a beat, the three hopped into the back of the cab to find her and Father Sanchez waiting for them.

"How did you know?" asked Joel.

"While Promane's people have been watching you, we've been watching them," she replied.

"Nice to see you again, Mother," Father Sanchez said to Natalie.

"Where to?"

"Saint James Convent," she said, trying to stifle her cough. The cab sped off.

* * *

Along the way Joel, Lisa, Natalie, Father Sanchez and Sofia confirmed their suspicions about the robe and who they believed Bishop Newton really was. Natalie listened intently and said nothing, partially because whenever she tried to speak, she would gasp for air. Father Sanchez called ahead to make arrangements. By the time they arrived at the convent Sister Beatrice was waiting for them at the front door. From there they were ushered to a small anteroom.

"Sister Beatrice, my medicine?" asked Natalie.

The nun nodded and hurried out of the room. The mood amongst the group was filled with tension and anxiety.

"What if the people who attacked us at my apartment found the robe?" said Joel.

"Whatever happens is God's will," replied Natalie with a rasp.

"Joel, our first priority should be your mother's health," said Father Sanchez.

Sister Beatrice appeared with several small bottles and a glass of water which she handed Mother Natalie.

"Thank you, sister," said the nun as she searched the bottles to find the correct pill. Then she swallowed it with the water. Everyone watched the Natalie's breathing begin to calm and regulate.

"Perhaps some tea?" asked Sister Beatrice.

"Yes, thanks," replied Father Sanchez as he led her out of the room and closed the door behind her.

"It's all over, isn't it, if they have the robe?" said Joel.

Lisa and Joel stared at each other anxiously. All their efforts had resulted in failure. Then Mother Natalie reached under her coat and pulled out the cloth. "As I said, it's God's will."

"Well done!" said Sanchez with a twinkle in his eye. "Now, we need to find a place to secure this, a better place."

"You mean," said Sofia, "In the next hour? Promane and his followers will waste no time—"

"We can't stash it here again," said Joel. "Those bastards have killed so many innocent people. Can you imagine what they'd do if they got inside this place?"

Sister Beatrice knocked on the door and carried a tray that included a kettle, and several tea cups, and biscuits. The trio looked at the innocent nun, knowing Promane and his zealots would spare no one once they got inside these walls.

"Sister," said Natalie, "The wine sale we had a few months back..."

"Yes?"

"Do we still have the bags?"

"The bags? Hundreds, I'm afraid."

She set the tray down and Sister Beatrice helped pour the tea for each person. "I always thought my idea of selling those heart shaped biscuits with inspirational sayings would have been a better option. I did have a degree in marketing before—"

"And it was a marvelous idea. Call all the sisters to the great hall," said Natalie. "We're going to need everyone's help."

"I'll dig up my recipe!" sang Sister Beatrice as she left in a run. Natalie did not have the strength to tell Sister Beatrice her cookies were not going to market.

* * *

Bishop Newman and Belle stood in their new sanctuary along with the congregation, admiring the renovations. The wood fixtures gleamed with polish, the pews were aligned in perfect symmetry around the altar, and the lighting offered a proper, solemn mood. Belle stepped up to a rope that hung from the ceiling. The bishop genuflected and she pulled the cord which caused a large cloth to drop from the ceiling. The room lit up like a Hollywood sound stage from the brilliant array of colors that shone through the newly- installed stained glass windows. The glorious design depicted a priest on his knees, offering a robe to God. Next to the prelate stood a smaller character, his female consort.

"This should get his attention," the priest whispered to himself. Then he turned to his congregation. "Children, I have built you this magnificent house to be closer to your God. Our dreams are almost realized. One more step and our mission will be realized."

Several followers entered with small baskets and began to hand out pills and ampoules to the congregants. These were the same drugs used by the followers who now salivated with the promise of ecstasy coursing through their veins.

"For us to begin our ascension to God, the Robe must sit on this altar," the Bishop said. "Tonight, each of you will play a vital part in its return. Sister Belle will assign your tasks and before this night is over, you will all have earned a place at His side."

Belle took one of the pills in her hand and swallowed it, followed by breaking the ampoule and inhaling its contents. Everyone else did likewise.

* * *

The long table in the convent's great hall was filled with piles of empty brown paper bags. The frail nun spoke determinedly as she addressed the dozens of sisters who stood before her.

"We have known each other for years," said Mother Natalie. "What I'm asking of you may sound like a simple exercise but, trust me, it will be instrumental in combating a great, perverse evil. May His spirit be with you."

The sisters formed a line and each one took an identical bag. Father Sanchez noticed Lisa standing off to the side and approached her.

"Lisa, when you had possession of the robe, at any time, did you place it on your body?"

Lisa smiled beatifically. "Let's say I'm a believer."

Father Sanchez frowned with deep concern.

***

The university campus was generally alive this time of evening with students criss-crossing the grounds on their way to night classes or pubs or hook-ups. But a curfew had been put in place to protect them from the marauders who were still at large. Normally the students would be up in arms about such restrictions but nobody objected because they all feared for their safety. Security guards and police made regular rounds but the grounds were so large that they could not be fully monitored. And that made it easy for Newman's followers.

Belle led a squad of dark cloaked figures down the street toward the campus, flitting in and out of shadows like a pack of strung-out ninjas. Once her followers were in position, Belle dispatched them in twos and threes. They entered the dorm buildings and stormed the hallways terrorizing everyone they came in contact with. One group spotted a couple dallying by their door, lips locked in a sensual kiss. The male sensed predatory eyes on them and, like any half-drunk sophomore, shouted a challenge, "What the fuck? Can I help you?"

Taking it as an invitation, the intruders grinned maliciously and charged. The female screamed and ran into her room, locking her door. The male was not sure whether to stand his ground or run. His hesitation cost him and they pummelled him mercilessly. The scent of his blood filled their nostrils and drove the wild-eyed intruders to an even greater state of savagery. They kicked him unconscious and howled like blood thirsty wolves before tromping down the corridor in search of more victims. Sounds of violence alerted other students who hurried back to their rooms and barricaded their doors. But some of the hellions carried crowbars and after four or five attempts, broke the doors down. The panicked students retreated into their bathrooms only to be cornered and beaten. Others ran out to their balconies and tried to leap to the ground or to adjacent apartments.

The exercise was designed to create chaos and havoc and it worked exceedingly well.

Their relationship had lasted almost three months but the initial spark between Morgan and Professor Brown was beginning to wane. The difference in age and sexual stamina had given Brown a case of performance anxiety. In his youth he could perform two, three times a night. Now, he had one good shot in him and he worried whether that was enough to keep his lusty young lover satisfied. The truth was, he liked Morgan a little too much and was afraid of losing her, which of course led to more anxiety.

"What's wrong?" she asked Brown as he slid off her sweat-soaked body.

"Nothing, nothing," he replied.

"If you're having trouble..."

"No, no. It just takes me a while to, you know, regroup. I'll be good in a minute or two."

Brown turned the music on the radio to another channel and threw a sheet over himself. Morgan suspected it was the 'age thing' but she didn't want to pressure him. The truth was, she liked him too.

"S' okay," she said softly. "Maybe we could add a little something to playtime."

"Like what?"

"Like a toy, like another player?"

"If you're into it. Uh, boy or girl?"

"What's your pleasure?" she replied.

They were interrupted by a shuffling sound outside her front door.

"Do you have a surprise for me?" Brown asked in a sing-song voice.

Before she could reply Brown threw on a robe and swaggered to the front door. Maybe adding a third person was a blessing in more ways than one. It would renew his sexual vigor as well as give him some much-needed recuperation time. Regardless, he'd head out tomorrow and invest in a package of Viagra. When he reached the door, he convinced himself he was up for any challenge.

"Who is it?" shouted Morgan from the adjacent room.

Brown opened the door to find two greasy looking thugs with menace in their eyes. Then he heard the maniacal screams and shouts for mercy from victims down the hall. Brown tried to slam the door shut on the assailants. "Morgan, call 911!" he shouted. But the intruders muscled their way in and began to beat the professor. After receiving two savage punches to the head he blacked out.

Morgan surprised the goons by running at them with a baseball bat and screaming like a hellion. She managed to break the arm of the first one, but the second one grabbed her from behind and slammed her headfirst into a wall. A minute later she was lying unconscious next to her lover. The intruders stood over their prey fueled with adrenalin and a thirst for more.

"Let's just do 'em!" said one.

The other snarled back, "Can't, we got orders."

The orgy of terror engulfed the entire dorm block. Blood lust and carnage swept through every floor. Limbs were broken and heads were smashed. It wasn't long before sirens filled the air and every available police cruiser and emergency vehicle was dispatched to the university, which was exactly what the bishop wanted.

On the other side of town, Newman stood high on a hillside overlooking St. James convent. His own brigade of drug-fueled miscreants stood awaiting his orders. The bishop's ears keyed in to the sounds of sirens speeding toward the campus and he smiled as if he was listening to a symphony. That distraction meant there would be little if any resistance where he was currently planning to attack. The priest signalled two of his men who crept down the hill and stationed themselves on either side of the convent's main doors, crowbars in hand. But just before the Bishop could signal his men, the doors flew open and out marched nearly fifty nuns, carrying the same identical bag.

"Which one?" asked one of Newman's followers.

The bishop blinked, unsure of how to answer. For once he was flummoxed. Any one of them could be carrying the relic in her bag.

He rephrased the question in his mind, pursed his lips, and bellowed, "A place in paradise for the one who finds the robe!"

His followers shrieked and barreled down the hill after their prey. In their frenzy they pushed the nuns to the ground, tore at their clothes, and ripped the bags from their hands. Newman watched from his vantage point, eagerly awaiting to see which zealot found his prize.

Natalie, Joel, Lisa, Father Sanchez, and Sofia were not among those on the streets. They were scrambling through a tunnel system under the convent. Their shoes clacked against the cobblestone floors as Sister Beatrice led the way in the darkness with only a small candle in hand.

"It was a hospital first, you know," Sister Beatrice whispered as if she was giving a tour. "The architects who built it just after the First World War also built this tunnel as a means of escape in case we lost the war."

"Clever people," said Father Sanchez.

"Of course, the war never reached these shores," she continued. "In time, more modern hospitals were built and this building was repurposed as a convent and then as a school. Now all three reside under one roof."

"Enough with the tour. How much further?" asked Natalie, gasping for air.

"Almost there," replied the sister.

Sanchez peered ahead to see a different gradient of black in the darkness. He glanced behind to see Lisa and Joel helping his struggling mother navigate the dark passageway.

"Joel, you all right?" he called.

"Right behind you, father."

The group reached the end of the tunnel to find a cement wall. In the center of the wall stood a sturdy metal door. Mother Beatrice produced a set of keys and unlocked the door. It opened up to a small garden on the other side with a patio table and chairs that the nuns used for quiet reflection. The garden itself sat at the end of a cul de sac which was encircled by a grove of mature trees. The only way out was a road that led into a residential development past the woodland. Father Sanchez stepped out onto the patio and listened intently. He and the others could hear the fracas on the far side of the building, but all was quiet and peaceful here.

"Pray my sisters are all right," whispered Beatrice as she looked over her shoulder.

"God will protect," replied Natalie, with less assurance in her voice than she'd hoped to convey.

Joel used his phone to call in the attack to the police.

Father Sanchez surveyed the area ahead of him and when he was satisfied, signaled the others to emerge from the tunnel.

"Which way?" Sanchez asked Joel.

"About six blocks east," he replied.

"Good. Hurry," said Sanchez.

Joel escorted his mother by the arm but she only got another ten feet before she had to squat and catch her breath. The ordeal was more than her frail body could take.

"Joel!" shouted Sanchez when he turned to see them pause.

"Gimme a minute," he said to the priest as he knelt down beside his mother.

"We have none," the priest replied urgently. "Every minute we waste—"

"Then go without us."

"For fuck sakes," Lisa said. She took her phone out and pressed an app. A moment later she announced, "Uber in three."

Reluctantly, the group had no choice but to wait. Sanchez kept scanning the woods and the street while Lisa tracked the limo on the digital map in her phone. Every once in a while a cry would rise above the din a few blocks away and the group would wince, knowing someone was being assaulted. When the town car finally pulled up, the group bid Mother Beatrice goodbye and hurried over to the vehicle. A moment later it was Beatrice who cried out. Two of Newman's thugs had sneaked through the foliage and grabbed her around her throat.

"Go!" she yelled to her comrades.

"Into the vehicle!" Sanchez said.

Lisa and Joel helped Natalie inside the car while Sanchez and Sofia ran back to help Sister Beatrice. Sanchez grappled with one of the thugs while Sofia crippled the other with a few savage kicks to the kneecaps and midsection. Three more of Newman's men bolted out of the woods and joined the fray. Father Sanchez pushed Beatrice back into the tunnel. "Lock the door!" he said. When he heard the lock bolted into place, he and Sofia turned to face the trio who glared at them like crazed animals. A split second later there was a sudden screech of tires and a town car slammed into all three of them, knocking them over like bowling pins. Joel had commandeered the car from the Uber driver who was now curled up in the passenger seat.

"Let's go," he shouted to his friends.

Sanchez and Sofia stepped over the maimed assassins and broken patio furniture and climbed into the vehicle which sped off down the street, into the night. Bishop Newman and several of his men burst through the wood thicket a minute later to find his men writhing on the ground. A small setback, he thought. The robe had finally been flushed out and the wheels were in motion.

CHAPTER 25

"I am Uber," cried the driver. "We don't carry money. But whatever I have, you can take."

The driver dug his hands into his pockets and threw all the coins he had into Joel's lap. Then he leaned on the passenger door to get as far away from him as possible. Joel ignored the plea and continued driving down the residential street.

"We're not the bad guys," he said.

"No, no, of course you're not."

Mohammed Malek was nearing the end his shift when he got the call. Even though it was after dark, he knew the area well and felt there was no safer district in the city to pick up a fare. When he saw Joel waiting at the entrance of the cul de sac, Mohammed dutifully came to a stop. It wasn't until Joel approached him on the driver's side that he became suspicious. And it wasn't so much the threat of a knife or a gun as it was being caught on the wrong end of a cell phone video. Any adverse publicity that reflected badly on the company might ruin the driver's livelihood. In any case, Joel opened the door, shoved the driver over while apologizing for hijacking the vehicle. Thirty seconds later, Joel jumped the curb and plowed the auto into three of Newman's bullies, knocking them all to the pavement. Mohammed screamed so loud that he could have been the one mowed down. When Joel's people climbed into the car, they found the poor driver hunched over in the corner, reciting prayers.

"It's all right, son," said Father Sanchez from the back seat. "What's your name?"

"Mohammed," replied the terrified driver.

"We're not going to hurt you, Mohammed. And we don't want your money."

The driver turned pleadingly to the priest. "What *do* you want?"

Sanchez tapped the back of Joel's seat. "Joel, slow down."

Joel ignored the priest and continued tearing along the roadway, searching for whatever street had the least traffic.

Joel asked, "Mohammed, are you Muslim? You believe in Allah, right?"

"Of course."

"If you asked him to save you, would he?"

"I, I don't know," replied Mohammed as sweat poured down his face.

"Slow down, Joel," Lisa said.

Joel persisted, "Do you think Allah is powerful enough to stop me from ramming this car into a wall?"

"Joel, what're you talking about?" asked Lisa. "Stop terrorizing the man."

"If it is his will that I should die," replied the driver, "then, I will die."

"Here's what I don't get," continued Joel. "We do crazy things in the name of God. Nations attack other nations, enslave their people. I just hit three people with your car. Where the hell is God?"

Natalie sat up as best she could and warned her son, "Joel, if you don't stop this lunacy right now..."

Joel turned to his mother. "You got divorced even though God sanctioned your marriage."

"Your father left us."

"Because he couldn't stand all the religious bullshit you shoved down his throat. He took my sister and my brother and left me with you."

"Because you were sick. I nursed you back to health."

"You're a very good mother who loves her son very, very much," said the driver, trying to curry favour.

Everyone in the car began shouting at Joel to pull over. he ignored their pleas and kept careening around every corner.

"And for all your suffering, Mom, what has God ever done for you? Nothing! How about you, father?" Father Sanchez stared blankly at

193

Joel's reflection from the rear-view mirror. "And don't tell me God works in mysterious ways. Or he has a plan for us all but we're too dumb to understand it...or, or, 'free will'? Every time a catastrophe happens it's God's will and he gets a 'get out of jail' pass. Not fair!" Joel knew he was rambling but he couldn't stop himself. "Religious leaders are so quick to blame us whenever we do something wrong and give God the credit when things go right. But what has He done but kept silent? A Muslim kills a Christian, a Christian kills a Jew. They all kill in the name of God and say, 'look here in the bible, in the Koran' – God is telling us to kill in his glorious name. That's what's all so fucking crazy."

"Joel, please slow down!" said Lisa as she held on to the others for support.

"What do you want, Joel?" said Father Sanchez in his most calming voice.

"I want to know, what kind of God do we have here? Is he an angry old man with a beard seeking vengeance on his enemies or a soft puffy cloud giving comfort to the world or does he not give a shit about anything down here?"

No one said a word. Joel had driven himself literally and figuratively to the edge. Everyone was worried that he might crash the car and kill them along with him.

"No takers, eh? What about you, Mohammed?"

"I believe—"

"Forget what you believe. We all believe something. What do you *know*?"

Sweat soaked through the Mohammed's shirt. "I, I don't know...anything."

Mohammed began to weep. He assumed he'd been hijacked by some religious freak and this mad man behind the wheel was going to end his life as easily and quickly as the ones he just mowed down. Before Mohammed could say another word, Joel pulled the car to a stop. Sweat dripped from his forehead and his fingers clutched the wheel.

"Get out," he said through clenched teeth.

"You're not going to kill me?" asked the terrified driver.

"You're the only person who told me the truth. So, no."

Mohammed pulled the door handle and slipped out of the car. The group watched him fall onto the ground, pick himself up, and scramble down the street. This last exchange released a lot of tension and gave everybody a much-needed break.

"You happy now? You get your answer?" asked Sanchez.

Joel nodded, "As much as I ever will, I guess," he said, completely drained of purpose and energy.

"Now what?" said Lisa.

Natalie began to cough and hack profusely. Joel glanced back at his mother who was sitting askew on the back seat. "My mom needs a doctor."

"Nowhere we can be found," said Natalie. "Promise me."

With the Bishop Newman's fanatics and the police looking for them, the foursome knew they couldn't go home or anywhere they'd been before. Joel put the car into gear and drove aimlessly through the streets for another thirty minutes until they passed a non-descript motel. They ditched the vehicle, pooled their cash, and took a couple of rooms. Inside, they pulled the drapes, purchased some pastries from the coin machines, and planned their next move. The ordeal had taken its toll on Natalie who lay propped up uncomfortably on one of the double beds.

"You knew what Newman was planning years ago," Joel said to Father Sanchez. "You could've warned us way back then and avoided all this."

Natalie spoke up in the priest's defense. "You never listened to me, Joel. Thought I was crazy. Even if Father Sanchez had a note signed by Jesus himself you wouldn't have believed him."

Sanchez added, "If it means anything, I do regret the inconvenience this has caused you all."

"Inconvenience? Look at my mother!"

"Joel, stop arguing or we're never going to get out of this," Lisa said. "Father, why do you think the bishop made his move now? He could have come after Joel's family anytime."

"The universal blood formula is intended to extend life immeasurably," replied Sofia. "A discovery like that would be a huge threat to a man who believes he has the exclusive rights to immortality."

Joel turned to Father Sanchez, "You were the one who provided the key to that formula. This is all your fault."

"My intention," replied Father Sanchez calmly, "was only to neutralize the bishop's power until such time as—"

Natalie said, "You're missing the point, all of you. We're here because my ancestors foresaw a day when the robe might prove the existence of God and unite the world."

"Not 'unite,' I'm afraid," the priest replied. "Dominate. The church's mandate was to spread the word and convert."

"I've dedicated my life to my faith, and I'm not going to turn my back on it now."

Sofia glanced at Natalie and said, "Your perspective is a little skewed."

"What does that mean?"

Sofia turned to Sanchez and said, "Tell her, father."

"Now is not the best time."

"Oh God, what else?" Natalie began to cough uncontrollably.

"Get her some water," said Sanchez.

Joel hurried to the bathroom and brought back a glass.

Natalie slouched on the bed but her voice still had the strength to demand, "Tell me. I deserve to know."

Sofia took a seat in a chair. "There are certain aspects to your ancestry, aspects that have been kept secret for good reason. You were raised Catholic but your actual lineage—"

Sanchez took a step closer. "Sofia?" he said, interrupting her. Sofia stopped. Sanchez sat on the bed opposite the nun and picked up the story. "I told you the story, about all those years ago when Bishop Promane tortured me to get me to disclose the location of the Robe."

"Yeah, and the monks died but the knights from the Order of Christ saved you."

"And three nights later Promane 'turned' Sofia, Belle, and me."

"Please? Before I expire?" Natalie said.

"During the Inquisition," continued Sanchez, "I told you about some in our village who had very few choices; either convert to Christianity or perish.

"The Garcia's, yes," said Natalie.

Sanchez nodded. "After I arranged passage for them from Portugal to America, I asked them for a favour, to smuggle out an artifact."

The gist of what Father Sanchez was implying began to ferment in Natalie's mind. "Garcia, Gardiner..." And then she connected the dots.

"But isn't Gardiner you father's name?" asked Lisa.

"My mom was a stubborn woman and never changed her maiden name," Joel said. "Family pride, eh, Mom?"

Natalie could not contain herself any longer. "You're telling me that my ancestors are not of The Order of Christ, they're not even Catholic. They're...Jewish?"

"As Jewish as Jesus," offered Sanchez with a weak smile.

"Well, God never ceases to amaze, does he?"

"Look, folks," Joel said, "I don't think it's a matter of whether we celebrate Easter or Passover. If the bishop gets his hands on the robe—"

"Agreed," said Sanchez. "We need a plan."

"We need to take care of my mom first," said Joel to his mother who was clearly suffering. "Anything I can get you, Mom?"

Natalie fingered the gold cross that hung around her neck. "Maybe some chicken soup?"

* * *

By 8:30 the next morning The Biopharm offices were humming with activity. Joel and his entourage, Father Sanchez, Sofia, Lisa, and Mother Natalie, who had regained some of her strength, paraded through the foyer. As they passed, one of the clerks joked, "A priest, a nun, and a hooker walk into a lobby..."

The group approached Susan, the effervescent young receptionist, who smiled at seeing Joel's handsome face. She'd had a crush on him ever since he started working there as an intern. She also recognized Father Sanchez who had been employed as a janitor and thought about the odd pairing.

"Hey, Susan. How's it going?" said Joel.

"Hey, Joel. They told me you left."

"Rumors, you know. We're actually here to see Marie Champlain."

She looked over the group. "Uh, you have a meeting, all of you?"

"Yep."

Susan buzzed Marie on the company phone. "Hello, Ms. Champlain. Joel Gardiner is here to see you... and he has several guests." Susan waited for a response and then answered, "Yes, ma'am." She hung up the phone and said, "If you'll go to Boardroom B, she'll be with you in a few minutes."

"Thanks, Susan."

Susan watched Joel lead his odd group down the hall and wondered whether the lean young man wore boxers or briefs. She was sure he'd look hot in either.

Marie sat back in her office chair and smiled to herself. This was exactly what she had been angling for. Of course, he was a little late but nothing happened without a little push and pull. Now she could take the development of the formula to the next level. She called her legal staff on the phone.

"Paul, those nondisclosures I had you draw up for Joel Gardiner, make half a dozen copies and bring them to my office, stat."

Joel and his people entered the boardroom and helped Natalie into the most comfortable chair. She was running under her own power, but just barely.

"There's a kitchen, sleeping quarters, and best of all it's secure," Joel said to the others.

"You sure she'll agree to it?" said Father Sanchez.

"She'll have to. Trust me, it will give us all the resources we need and time to plot our next course of action. It's also the best place for my mom."

"I don't like it," Sofia said. "The bishop is on the board of directors. We'd be right under his nose."

"Which is the one place he won't be looking."

The door opened and Marie Champlain entered, followed by her lawyer. The first thing she noticed was the frail woman seated in the chair usually reserved for her.

"Ms. Champlain," Joel said, "I'd like to introduce you to some people. You know Lisa, of course, my girlfriend."

"We've met," replied Marie dryly.

"And this is my mother, Natalie."

Marie nodded courteously to the frail woman. Although Marie knew the pianist at her cocktail party had the same condition, the ravages of the disease manifested in Natalie disturbed her.

"I want you to know we are doing everything possible..." Marie assured her.

Natalie waved her off as if to say, 'cut the crap.' Marie then cast a disparaging eye in the direction of the other two in attendance. "Joel, you know our work here is strictly confidential."

"The blood formula wouldn't have been discovered without this man," Joel said.

"This janitor?" asked Marie incredulously.

"Here, he's a janitor. In his country, Father Sanchez was both a theologian and a biologist."

"And this woman?" asked Marie.

"His research assistant, Sofia Vargas."

"I'm sure," she replied, making an instant judgement about the beautiful, young female. "In any case, Joel, you were to be in this office twenty-four hours ago."

"Sorry," replied Joel without an ounce of remorse. "My mother's health comes first."

Marie nodded and glanced once again at the ailing nun. "The question is, why are you here now?"

Father Sanchez replied, "Ms. Champlain, as you are no-doubt aware, a medical discovery of this nature would be an enormous boon to the world."

"No doubt. But everybody wants something, Father, priests included. What do you want?"

"Nothing more than what was promised," said Joel. "After we develop the formula to create a universal blood type, we go to work on the cure for ectodermal dysplasia."

Turning to Natalie, Marie said. "You know, even if we work day and night—"

"It's not for me," Natalie said. "But for others like me."

"Very magnanimous of you, Mother..." the executive replied.

"Natalie will do."

"What else?" asked Marie, turning to Joel.

Joel continued, "I don't know if you know, there were some deaths on my campus."

"Yes, tragic," Marie replied with little emotion.

"We can't stay there anymore. Too dangerous. In order to continue our work uninterrupted, we'll need to stay here on the premises, for the sake of the project and to care for my mother."

"And by 'uninterrupted,'" said Sofia, "we mean, no one is to know we are here."

"Benefits me as much as you, dear," replied Marie. "But I've been in business long enough to know negotiations begin with the small victories."

"Ten percent royalties on sales of the formula we manufacture," said Joel. "In perpetuity."

Sanchez raised an eyebrow at this. Joel was shrewder than he looked.

"Biopharm pays all its employees a generous salary," Marie replied. "Any discoveries belong exclusively to the company. It's standard in the medical industry, the electronic industry, even the advertising industry. We have not nor will we ever provide participation shares."

A tiny grin grew across Joel's lips. "As an intern I do not receive a salary." He let that hang in the air a moment while Marie bit her lip ever so slightly. "Let's say, a hundred thousand a year each for each of us until the product is on the market. Then the royalties kick in. It's a nothing investment for you."

Marie didn't flinch at his demand. She was expecting much higher figures. But it wasn't in her nature to capitulate so easily.

"Sliding scale on the royalties," she replied. "Ten percent to start, reduced to five percent after ten years, reduced to two percent after that. Of course, I'll have to ratify all this with our board."

"I'll even allow you to use my likeness on the bottle," quipped Father Sanchez.

"I'll take that up with the board as well."

"Which brings me to the most important part. On your board there is a man by the name of Bishop Newman. He is to have no knowledge of our agreement or that we're even on these premises."

"Professional discourtesy?" she joked.

"Let's say he does not act in the best interests of either you or us."

Marie nodded. She knew the bishop better than most. Joel held out his hand to shake. Instead, the lawyer handed him a ream of papers.

"It's a non-disclosure. Sign them, please, all of you."

Joel did as he was told and passed the papers along. The lawyer collected the originals and handed the others their copies. Joel shook Marie's hand and led his group out of the room to the elevator in silence. When they entered, Joel pressed the button for Sub Level 6, inserted his security card, and the elevator kicked into action.

"Limbo, purgatory, eternal damnation," Joel joked as the car descended to the lower levels.

"What was all that negotiating about?" asked Natalie.

"I couldn't make it too easy for her," replied Joel. "I mean, Marie wasn't expecting to get this for nothing."

"Whether you know it or not you did yourself a great service," Sanchez said. "The Order of Christ had the financial support of the church in its time. You have nothing and your family is going to need a great deal of money in the future."

"I didn't do it for the money."

"Nevertheless," countered Sanchez.

"You think your boss can be trusted?" Sofia asked.

"She's all about the money. As long as we give her what she wants. But I'll remind her, if we get the faintest hint of Newman skulking anywhere around here..."

Lisa's cell phone rang. She looked to see the name, Morgan, illuminated on the screen.

"Don't answer," said Joel. "From this point on we're cut off from everybody."

Lisa considered Joel's request and ignored the call.

CHAPTER 26

In the days that followed the crew began their work in earnest. They severed all ties with the outside world, family and school included. Lisa told her parents she applied for and received a grant to study in Eastern Europe and would keep in contact. Joel had an easier time. There were no other family members beside his mother to deal with. Letters of a hiatus were written to the university on behalf of Joel and Lisa. Neither could risk giving authorities any excuse for their prolonged absence for fear it might lead Newman to them. All other research projects at Biopharm were moved to a separate floor and access to Joel's lab was restricted through a set of key cards and thumbprint I.D. After a while, concern over Bishop Newman diminished, leaving them to focus on the development of the blood formula. Natalie was given comfortable quarters and attended to by a team of doctors and nurses.

Father Sanchez led the research assisted by the others in whatever capacity they could offer. Joel and Lisa remained cordial but their romance waned. Whenever he asked her about her experience with the robe, Lisa refused to answer. Eventually, he stopped bringing up the subject altogether. They took to sleeping in separate rooms and kept conversation limited to their work. Sofia watched the two grow apart and felt sympathetic to the couple. She also worried that if Joel became isolated and depressed, he might lose his commitment to the project. One day, during a lunch break, she took him aside.

"Your mom seems comfortable," she said in a casual manner. Joel nodded. "You and Lisa, not so close these days."

"Yeah, well, she needs her space, as the cliché goes."

"She'll come around, Joel. The past few days have been very traumatic. For everyone." Joel nodded without further comment. "How about the rest of your family? Father, siblings? You hear from them at all?"

Joel shook his head and replied sullenly. "They're all a bunch of fuck-ups."

Sofia was aware of his family background because she and Sanchez had been monitoring them for years. But this was an exercise in strengthening ties. Sofia grazed on a salad while Joel chewed on a turkey sandwich.

"How'd your parents meet?"

"Arranged marriage. By the church."

"Really? How interesting."

Joel relaxed and began to let his guard down. "Mom was 18. You can guess how difficult it was for her to meet guys with... so the church set her up on a date one day with my dad, Eugene. They got married four months later and my brother, Gord, came along nine months after that."

"She must have wanted a family very much."

"Her or the church. Seems she never made a move without their say-so." He frowned and spat out his next remark. "Newman was balls deep in our lives from day one."

"Is that something your parents fought about?"

"Mom was always going on about her family legacy, her relationship to the Order of Christ and all."

"And the robe?"

Joel gave the slightest of nods. "She never came out and said it, but after a while, Dad got the feeling she thought that she was better than him, destined for some higher purpose in life. The way I heard it; the church suggested a larger family might make them happier. So along came Colleen and then me. But that only made things worse. I was sixteen when Dad and my sibs left."

"Why not you?"

"I was sick, I told you that back in the car."

"Sick with what?" Again, Sofia and Sanchez were aware of this period, but the details were murky.

"Stomach problems. Anyways, after they left, I barely heard from them again."

"I can imagine you must have felt abandoned."

"Ya think? They didn't leave me with a mother. They left me with some religious fanatic, until I escaped to university."

"On one hand it sounds like you resent her. But on the other, you've dedicated yourself to finding a cure for her affliction."

Joel eyed her suspiciously. "Are you trying to analyze me?"

"Sorry, no. I was just trying to understand you a little better. What's that old saying, 'the unexamined life is not worth living'?"

"Socrates, but you already knew that. So, my turn. Married? Ever?"

Sofia smiled wistfully and shrugged.

"After all this time? Boyfriends? Ever been in love?"

Joel had such a penetrating look that she could feel his need to connect. "A few times." She took a sip of her drink and looked into space as her mind drifted back. "Antoine was a banker from a rich family in Brussels."

"Did he know you were 'special'?"

"After we got to know each other, yes, I told him."

Joel's eyes flickered with curiosity. "So how did you tell him, exactly?"

"I said I had a genetic condition, something that retards the aging process. He promised it wouldn't matter. But as he grew older and I remained the same, he worried it was inevitable that one day I'd take a younger man. Love turned to jealousy, jealousy into fear. Eventually I left him as he prophesized, but not for someone else."

"When was that?"

"1916. During the First World War."

"And then?"

Sofia paused and then a smile crossed her face. "Do you know what a beatnik is?"

"I've heard the term but... a kind of a hippy?"

Sofia nodded. "Daniel was a poet in New York in the Fifties. He was 22 years old, had nothing of consequence, no money, no material wealth. What he did have was the ability to squeeze the essence of life out of every moment. This time I made no mention of my gift. You try to learn from your mistakes, yes? We were together for eighteen years. As Daniel grew older, he just kind of accepted me for who I was without me having to articulate it." She stopped to take another bite and Joel watched the smile drift from her eyes. "One day, I came back to the apartment and two policemen were waiting for me. He'd been hit by a car. An undignified end to a magical romance."

"Sorry," Joel said with genuine compassion.

They ate in silence until Sofia wrapped up the scraps of her lunch in some paper. "Anyway, I'm not going to try to wring any kind of morality tale out of this. But what I've learned about life is, all we have to hold onto is each other. And second, time is not your friend. So, hang in there."

She stood up, threw her garbage into the waste bin, and trotted back to her work station. Natalie survived the next few weeks but her strength continued to ebb. Joel's conversation with Sofia softened his heart a little toward his mother and one night, after working hours, he came to her room. He knocked on her door and was granted entry. As usual Natalie was sitting in bed, reading. She didn't have energy for much more. Joel took a few steps closer, to 'test the waters.'

"So next holiday season, Ma, which is it, matzah or Easter eggs?"

"Next year? You're quite the optimist."

Joel smiled and gauged that she was in an approachable mood. He took a few more steps closer to her bed.

"Look, I know we haven't spoken much, but after what we've gone through these past few weeks, I understand better why you did some of the things you did."

"Thank you, dear."

Joel took a few steps closer and sat down on the edge of her bed. He lowered his voice and asked, "So, the robe, it's hidden somewhere safe, yes?"

"Yes."

"And you can get your hands on it if you need to?"

Joel's cell phone buzzed. He removed it from his pocket and looked at the face.

"Who is that?" asked Natalie.

"My professor," he replied.

"You're not going to..."

Joel shook his head, gesturing that he would never reveal their whereabouts. "Just let him know we're okay." Joel texted back saying he and Lisa were all right, not to worry. After shoving the phone back in his pocket, he returned to the conversation. "So?"

"What are you getting at, exactly?"

"I was just thinking, if the robe is supposed to grant immortality—"

Natalie shook her head, knowing where this conversation was leading.

"No."

"It did to Lisa."

"No!"

"But it could save you. Haven't you ever thought..."

Natalie reached out and took her son's hand. "Of course, I have. But I was afraid if I accepted the gift, I wouldn't be able to conceive. I know it's stupid and there was no proof but I wanted marriage and children, not immortality. Believe me, one life is enough. Death is just the punctuation mark."

"I hate it when you talk like that."

"What, practical?" She joked and then spoke a little more compassionately. "No child ever wants to think his parent won't be there one day."

Joel nodded his agreement and shifted his weight as if getting ready to ask a serious question. "Mom, with all the shit that's been thrown at you your whole life, don't you ever question your faith?"

Natalie took a moment to consider before she answered. "Do you remember that day a few weeks ago when you saw me get into a cab with that young woman?"

"You saw me? You knew I was there?" asked Joel. She nodded. "What was up with her?"

"She was from out of town and travelled to the city for an abortion. She came to the convent seeking guidance. You know the stand the church takes on that. Nothing I said could talk her out of it. But she was alone and afraid and, she asked me to go with her."

"To the clinic?"

"I could've refused, but the girl needed me. I made a choice, not to do what was right for me, but for her. When you saw us that day we were on our way to the clinic. I stayed with her during the procedure, and accompanied her back to her hotel. I wrestle with that decision every day, just as I wrestle with my faith every day."

Joel squeezed his mother's hand and they both smiled, grateful to be speaking again in civil, maybe even affectionate terms.

*　*　*

Life in the Biopharm labs was intense and exhausting. Constant demands by the executive for the formula put a strain on Joel and his entire entourage. On occasion they all needed a break. Knowing Newman and his people might be lurking anywhere, they only stepped out in pairs and for a short time. Joel and Lisa were barely talking, so one night, he and Sofia made a foray to the local market for food. Just as the sun was setting, they began their walk, scanning the street around them to make sure they were not being followed.

Joel turned his collar against the wind that was biting his neck and gestured to the building they'd been housed in for weeks. "That place is starting to get to me."

"Don't blame you. Fruits and vegetables do help compensate for the artificial light and lack of fresh air, though," Sofia said.

"Doesn't matter. At this point everything tastes the same."

"Maybe that has less to do with your taste buds and more about your emotional state. I mean your relationship with Lisa."

Joel replied with a whip-like retort. "You're giving *me* relationship advice? From someone whose last roll in the hay was in the Fifties?"

Sofia recognized that Joel wasn't angry with her so much as he was venting the frustration he'd been carrying around for weeks. She wanted to wrap her arms around him but instead, let him rant.

"You're never gonna have children or grow old with anyone. Who even cares if that robe proves there's a God? What good is a life without...?' The words and the emotions became stuck in his head and out of frustration, he kicked a garbage can next to him. "That thing has fucked up everything for me."

Joel noticed the blinking neon lights of a pub down the street and made a beeline for it.

Sofia called after him in protest, "Joel, wait, we can't..."

With no other choice, she followed him inside. The bar was a dimly lit watering hole with splashes of multi-colored neon everywhere. Country music blared from the speakers. Sofia adjusted her eyes and saw Joel heading to the bar.

"Molson, please," he called to the bartender.

The bartender nodded and went to pour the glass. Sofia sidled up to him a few seconds later and shouted, "The same for me." Then she turned to Joel. "People have been blaming God for centuries for crops failing, for innocent children dying, for the wrong people running the country. But even people diagnosed with cancer find hope and plan for the future."

"What kind of future is there for you, Sofia? What're your plans after all this?"

"God only knows," she said shrugging her shoulders.

"That's funny. You're funny."

The bartender came over with the two beers. Joel paid and waited for him to leave before he continued. "Know what I think? I think what's keeping you going is Newman or Promane or whatever he calls himself. We might believe in God but where would we be without our devils, eh?"

"Joel? Is that you?"

Joel recognized the voice immediately. It was not one he responded to with joy.

"Gord," he replied, turning to find his brother standing behind him.

Gordon Gardiner was a big bear of a man. Joel looked him over and shook his head at the man who virtually hadn't changed since the last time he saw him; tee shirt, varsity jacket and jeans fitted over a hefty frame, topped off with a baseball cap and his trademark scruffy beard. Gordon pulled his younger brother into a hug and laughed raucously. "Sonofabitch! How ya doin'?"

Joel pulled away uneasily and replied in a wary tone. "I'm good. You?"

"Great, great. Married with a kid. Another in the oven. I'm a district manager for a software company. Live maybe 20 minutes from here. What're the chances, eh?" Eying Sofia, he said, "And this is your girlfriend?"

"Just a friend," replied Joel in a clipped reply.

"Hi." Sophia offered her hand and Gordon shook it while he eyed the beautiful woman from head to toe. Then he turned back to his brother.

"How's Mom? Still bonkers?" Joel shrugged. "You know I called you a couple of weeks ago."

Sofia noted Joel's tacit acknowledgement.

"Yeah, I haven't had my phone on lately. Busy at work."

"So, catch me up, bro, what're you up to?"

"Come on, Gord," Joel replied. "You know exactly what I'm up to. This is no coincidence."

"Could be."

"But it's not."

"You're pissed at me, I get it. That's why I tried to reach out. It wasn't my call to leave you with Mom."

"I don't recall you reaching out after you left, or when I got sick."

"You got sick before we left. That's why you had to stay. The courts said you were better off with Mom until you got better. Dad had no choice."

"But he never came back for me. None of you did."

"We tried, believe me. But the bitch shut us out."

Joel gulped down his beer and took a moment to recollect. He hadn't examined the timeline of his illness in years. "Whatever," he said to his brother. "What can I do for you, Gord?"

"The old man is here." Gordon nodded to the sidewalk outside the bar. "Thought maybe he could have a word?"

"Fuck off."

"I know you're not gonna believe me, but he always felt bad about leaving you with the crazy lady. Anyway, will ya come outside for a minute?"

Joel considered the offer and answered. "Lemme use the can first. Sofia, why don't you keep my brother company 'till I get back?"

Joel manoeuvred his way through the crowd as he headed to the washroom. When he was beyond their line of vision, he peeked through the window to see his father, Eugene, and his sister, Colleen, standing by a van on the street.

At the bar, Sofia engaged Gordon in small talk. "You enjoy country music, Gordon?"

"Not my favorite, unless you wanna dance."

"Thanks anyway. Must be nice to finally connect with your brother. I have a sister I haven't been close to in years."

Gordon leaned in and took a drink from his brother's glass. "Oh yeah? She as hot as you?"

Sofia ignored the comment and continued. "Very painful. We grew up in an orphanage together."

"Hmmm," he said, turning around to look for his brother.

Sofia drew him back into conversation.

"My mother died after giving birth to her. My father left us soon after mother died."

"Shame."

"So, I know how much your brother means to you, especially now that your mother is dying."

Gordon looked surprised by the news, and then his face clouded over. "That whack job has been dead to us for years. I just wish we could've gotten Joel outa there sooner."

"You must have loved her very much to be so angry."

Gordon straightened his back and addressed her suspiciously, "Do I know you?"

"No, but it feels like we do, doesn't it? Like we have a few things in common. You're the oldest like me so you would have seen your mother at her best and her worst. When the family broke up, you took on the guilt."

"What the fuck do I have to feel guilty about?"

"Every child carries a certain amount of guilt because they feel powerless when the family breaks up. In their mind they reason that if it's their fault, then maybe they can fix it. It's a redundant response but sometimes it's all we have."

"What the fuck are you, lady, some kind 'o shrink?"

Sofia glanced through the window and noticed Joel speaking with his family out on the sidewalk. There were no hugs or kisses. In fact, everybody kept their distance. As they conversed, Sofia could see Joel's father relating a story to his son. Joel became more and more agitated until he shouted and stomped off. Sofia turned her attention back to Gordon.

"Tell my sister when you see her that I do miss her."

"What? How the hell am I going to..."

Sofia turned and walked out of the bar, leaving Gordon bewildered. Then he turned to the window to see what she was staring at outside; his father and sister arguing with each other. Gordon grimaced, finished his brother's drink, and left the bar. Sofia waited down the block, watching Gordon wade into his father and sister's argument. Then she turned and headed in the opposite direction.

* * *

Sofia checked her watch. It was ten minutes after nine in the evening. She'd been waiting almost an hour in an alleyway by the private door they used to enter and exit the Biopharm premises. When she saw Joel shuffle toward her with his hands full of groceries, she stepped out of the shadows.

"Thanks for doing the shopping."

Joel pretended not to be surprised and kept walking, his eyes focused on the door to avoid further discussion.

"What happened?" she asked when he got closer. She'd hoped that whatever ticked him off had blown over, but she could see he was still stewing.

"None of your business."

Joel handed one of the bags to Sofia. Awkwardly, he fished around in his pocket for the key card and then they walked over to a heavy steel door. While he concentrated on the keys, she glanced toward the front of the alley to make sure no one had followed him.

"I saw you outside the bar with your dad and sister," she said. "Looked to me like a set-up. Promane's people followed us and sent your family to meet you there."

"Ya think?"

Joel inserted his key-card into a reader and the lock on the door clicked. They both entered and marched down the narrow hall to the elevator.

"You were lucky to get away," she continued as she kept pace with him. "He could have held you hostage and blackmailed your mother into handing over the robe."

The elevator doors opened and the two entered. Joel used his key-card again, pressed a button, and the car descended. An awkward silence hung over them.

"Joel, if you keep that kind of anger bottled up it will kill you."

"You have no idea."

The elevator stopped and opened onto Sub Level Six. An anxious Father Sanchez was there waiting for them.

"Joel, where have you been? It's your mother."

***

The priest hot-footed it along the hallway leading the other two to the sleeping quarters. When all three entered, they found Natalie lying listlessly on her cot. Her complexion was ruddy and her breathing, laboured. A doctor hovered over her, administering a needle, a man Joel hadn't seen before.

"Hey!" shouted Joel. "What're you doing?"

The doctor withdrew the syringe and placed it on a tray. Joel rushed over to him but Lisa, who had been standing a few feet behind the physician, held him back.

"It's okay, Joel, he's a doctor."

"I don't know him," Joel said.

"Her regular physician was off," the physician replied in a measured voice. "I was the doctor on call." The M.D. waited for Joel to relax before he continued. "I've been briefed on her condition. What she's currently suffering from is hyperpyrexia. Elevated body temperature brought on by sepsis. Right now, it's hovering at 104 degrees."

"What was that?" asked Joel, pointing to the syringe.

"Anti-viral injection. When a fever like this takes hold," he explained, "other problems arise. Sometimes the body can fight off infection, sometimes not. But with your mother's ailments, well for now, keep her hydrated and give her cool compresses. The injection should help. Here's my number. Call me if you need me."

The doctor handed Joel his card and turned to leave.

"Doctor, I'm sorry. Thank you," Joel said. Then he asked, "By the way, who contacted you?"

"Marie Champlain was notified by the Father here and she called me."

"I'll show you out, doctor," said Sofia as she stepped over. "Again, thank you for coming."

Sofia escorted the doctor out of the quarters. After he exited Joel turned to Sanchez. "You know you might've compromised us by contacting that guy."

"And what was my alternative? Let your mother suffer? What about you? Where were you?"

"Out on a food run."

"All this time?"

Joel glanced at Sofia. Noticing the rising tension, she stepped in between the two men. "Gentlemen."

The priest collected himself and put a comforting arm on Joel's shoulder, then gestured to his mother. "She's looking a bit better. Why don't we give you two some time alone?"

Joel glanced at Lisa who turned away to avoid his gaze. Sanchez accompanied both her and Sofia out of the room. Joel approached the cot and gazed down at his mother who had never looked so small and frail. A lump caught in his throat and he swallowed.

"You were out shopping?" Natalie said weakly. "Did you bring back some fruit? I'd love some grapes."

The agitation in Joel's gut was still fueling his thoughts. "I saw Dad."

Natalie's eyes grew wide. "You did?"

"About an hour ago. Gord and Colleen were there too. They told me an interesting story." Joel's demeanor darkened and his voice trembled. "That time, when Dad and them left, I stayed behind because I was sick."

"No one else could take care of you. You needed me."

"And you knew exactly how to take care of me..." he leaned in accusingly, "...because you were the one making me sick."

Joel studied his mother's face, watching to see if she would avoid the accusation. But what he saw was firm resignation.

"I knew about your father's plans. He'd gone to Bishop Newman about a divorce."

"Did you ever tell dad about the robe?"

She shook her head. "Over the years I did tell your father about some of my family's history, The Order of Christ and such. Eugene thought I was hiding money from him. He said that he was owed something as part of the marriage contract. I denied there was any money time and time again. Bishop Newman even tried to talk him out of leaving me but he wouldn't listen. And he knew I wouldn't survive if you all left me."

Joel held his head in his hands to keep his brain from exploding. "The Bishop suggested you make me sick to keep me around?"

"I'm sorry. It was selfish but it was the only way. And just for a little while. Then after you recovered, you went off to university where you flourished, and I've been so proud of you."

"I can't believe my own mother poisoned me." Joel clenched his fists and paced to stop his entire body from shaking. "Do you know how fucked up that is?"

"Forgive me. I hope you'll never know what it is to lose everyone and everything dear to you."

Joel didn't wait to hear another word. He turned on his heel and left.

* * *

Over the next few days, Joel avoided conversation with everyone unless it had to do with the research. He stomped around the lab with a scowl on his face answering questions put to him with either a grunt or a monosyllabic answer. Father Sanchez approached him one afternoon in the lab to inform him that his mother's condition was stabilizing. Joel nodded but didn't ask any further questions.

"How long are you going to keep acting like a child?" Joel stared at him, biting his lip. "How long are you going to avoid your mother?"

"Well, she tried to kill me so, forever?"

Sanchez glowered at the young man. "So obstinate. She didn't try to kill you, she tried to keep you near her. But you don't want to see that. You're bound and determined to make her last days on earth a hell, aren't you?"

Joel shook his head and defended himself. "What about me? What if all of this is a hoax and I'm being played for a fool by both of you? I mean, your longevity deal, what if it's just some kind of freak of nature, a scientific anomaly? Plenty of superstitions and biblical prophesies have been disproven with science. Plus, the robe doesn't necessarily prove there's a God."

Sanchez relaxed his posture and replied like a teacher to a student. "Joel, this shirt you're wearing is blue, isn't it?"

"Yeah, so?"

"Your perception of blue and my perception of blue are inherently different because of the way our rods and cones interpret it, correct? That's the science."

"No argument there."

"What about the person who is color blind? He might say there is no such thing as blue because he can't see it. You could argue with him until you're 'blue in the face' and you'd never convince him. But even if you coerced someone into believing there is a color blue, so what? How would that change anything, besides serving your own ego? Which is why I always believed it folly to try to convert anyone, but that's another story. To be totally honest, I can't prove to you there is a blue or a God or what form he takes, or if my idea of him aligns with yours. Each man must answer that for himself. All I can say is, you need to accept that there might be a larger plan."

"My own mother poisoned me and I'm supposed to accept that was part of a larger plan?"

"Come on. Do you honestly think you were ever in mortal jeopardy?"

"Maybe." Joel thought a little more about it and murmured, "Maybe not."

"Joel, let me ask you, what would your choice have been otherwise? Leave her or stay?"

Joel didn't reply immediately so Sanchez continued. "More to the point, have you ever asked yourself why you're so obsessed with finding a cure to save a woman you claim to hate?"

Joel was about to reply, then changed the subject. "We need to get on with the work." He turned away and trotted off to another work station. Sanchez shrugged and said to himself, "You're a tough little nut, aren't you?"

CHAPTER 27

Eugene and his son, Gordon, stood in front of the prelate, hands akimbo, like altar boys who had been caught stealing.

"Bishop. I did everything exactly how you told me," Eugene said.

Bishop Newman sat at his desk, staring up at the two failures, and shook his head. Experience had taught him the best way to keep people in line was by reminding them how often they failed you.

"I have given your family everything, all the creature comforts of this life as well as a place in the hereafter."

Gordon said, "We tried, I swear, it's not our fault."

Eugene raised hand to stop his son from exacerbating the situation. "You've been more than generous to us, Bishop," Eugene said with genuine remorse. "We won't disappoint you again."

The bishop rocked back in his chair and dismissed them with a wave of his hand. "Go with God's grace."

Eugene and Gordon bowed and quit the room without turning their backs on the priest, which would have been ungracious. Disappointing the Bishop was tantamount to disappointing God himself and they half expected to be struck by a bolt of lightning as they exited his office. The bishop, however, was not disappointed. He never expected Joel to be persuaded by his father to turn against his mother. What he did want was to find their whereabouts because he knew the robe would be close by. After the two left, Newman turned to Belle.

"You're not going to disappoint me as well, are you?"

Belle smiled confidently, "Have I ever?"

She led the bishop out of his rectory, down the hallway, to a door. She withdrew a key from her pocket and unlocked the door. This room that was anything but sacred. It was dank and gray with dull brick walls and a hard cement floor. The only furniture was a table and a mattress. On the table sat two cell phones. On the mattress lay the owners of those phones, semi-conscious and bloodied. Their thumbs had been pulverized by a metal thumbscrew. Morphine quelled their pain for the moment, but after the drugs faded and consciousness returned, it would roar back.

During the attack on the university grounds, Professor Brown and Morgan were beaten, kidnapped, and forced to make phone calls from this room to both Lisa and Joel. A young I.T. wiz employed by the bishop monitored those calls in order to get a fix on their locations. Lisa did not answer the call from Morgan. But Joel did reply to the professor with a text message. The difficulty for the I.T wizard in honing in on their location was that the Biopharm labs were built deep underground, behind reinforced concrete and steel that blocked most electronic signals. But as soon as Sofia and Joel left the building to get supplies, their signals were detected. That's when Eugene and his two children were dispatched. The plan was not to persuade Joel to go with his father but simply to locate them.

"I followed the boy after he left the bar," said Belle. "They're all living together in the Biopharm labs."

The bishop permitted himself the slightest of smiles. If he was surprised by his own ignorance he wasn't going to let on. He swallowed his bile and caressed his paramour's cheek. Not only did she meet all his needs but quite often exceeded them. Although he'd never admit that to her.

* * *

Lisa sat in her makeshift bedroom staring blankly at the mirror in front of her. She was dressed in sweats that doubled as pyjamas. On the table in front of her lay a napkin, some makeup, a rosary, and a scalpel. More than once she'd found herself staring back at her image in the dim light, praying for answers. She recalled the wound she inflicted on Bishop Promane a few days prior and how it healed right in front of her eyes. A miracle. And then the day she wrapped the Judas Robe around her shoulders, feeling infused with a glorious, supernatural energy. Another miracle, she told herself, a gift from God.

From a young age Lisa had always dreamed of becoming a research scientist, someone dedicated to uncovering the secrets of the universe. But nothing she could have dreamed of could compare to what was now within her grasp. She envisioned herself standing at the precipice, ready to leap over the chasm of mortality and perhaps even looking God in the eye. *Unless the robe was a hoax.* If that was the case, she doubted that she could go back to her mundane existence. The fall would be too steep. She wouldn't survive it. There was only one way to know for sure. She put the scalpel to her wrist and willed herself the strength to slice her skin and prove her immortality. It wasn't the pain she feared but the disappointment.

At the end of another arduous day, Joel's team was only marginally further along. The path was clear enough; locate the exact enzyme made by bacteria in the human digestive tract to strip the sugars that determine blood type. That would effectively neutralize the blood type and allow it to become a match with any of the others. Sanchez had come upon it once and had given them a road map to follow, knowing the enzyme with that specific ability was hiding somewhere in the gut. The question was, how to identify it and isolate it. They were narrowing it down but it was like finding the proverbial needle in the haystack. Joel had asked Lisa for help on more than one occasion but she had become more detached than ever, either unable or unwilling to interact.

That night after dinner, little was said amongst the group, and all retired to their rooms separately, to put another frustrating day behind them. It was after 10:30 p.m. when Sofia heard a knock on her door. She put down the book on her cot, slipped on her robe, and answered. Joel stood there looking like he'd been dragged across a football field by a pack of dogs. He'd been walking the halls feeling agitated, unable to articulate his angst. Why he was standing here now was a mystery to even him. Sofia bore witness to Joel's struggle these past few weeks; stepping up, retreating, and focusing again. It would have exhausted the strongest of hearts. Without a word she opened the door and let him in. When she closed it again, she wrapped her arms around him. He nestled his head in the nook of her shoulder and held her. After a moment, the tension left his body. She kissed his ear and a different feeling infused him.

"Have you ever been with a 600-year-old woman?" she asked.

"No," he replied with a smile.

"Well if I can offer you anything, it's experience."

She slipped her hand down the front of his waistband and he groaned. Joel may have not known what he wanted, but Sofia knew what he needed.

* * *

Early the next morning, a business-like entourage led by Bishop Newman and Belle entered the Biopharm lobby. The priest offered a courteous nod to the security guard at the lobby desk.

"Morning, Bishop," said the guard.

"Good morning, Daniel. Did you see your doctor about that knee problem?"

Newman led his people toward the elevator.

"Not yet." The security guard watched the group march by and stood up. "Uh, these people here..."

"It's okay, they're with me."

Newman led his group to the elevator, and pressed the button.

"We have a meeting about the new charity for the children's hospital. Oh, and this year we're accepting donations personally as well as corporately. Hope we have your support."

Daniel offered an embarrassing smile. "I'll think about it, Bishop."

The elevator doors opened and Newman led his group inside.

"Thanks, Daniel," he said with a wave. "Take care."

The doors closed before the guard could get any further information from the bishop as to who these other people were and who they were meeting with. But the priest was such a familiar figure on the premises, Daniel didn't think much of it. The group rode the elevator to the executive offices. There, they exited and approached the secretary sitting at the large receptionist desk.

"Good morning, Nancy," said the Bishop. "I'd like a few minutes with Marie if she can spare them."

Nancy looked past the bishop at Belle and a few of their cohorts. She never understood the relationship between the elderly clergyman and the hot-looking cherub. Or maybe she did and she just didn't want to admit it.

"I'll ring her."

Nancy's dialed her boss's line. "Sorry to bother, Ms. Champlain, but Bishop Newman is here requesting a brief meeting?" She smiled at hopefully having conveyed his request politely because she not only disliked the bishop but feared him. The priest watched intently as a look of disappointment spread across Nancy's face as she hung up. "I'm sorry, bishop, but her schedule is full this morning." Nancy's fears were warranted. Newman turned to his entourage and instructed his followers to lock the outer door.

"Uh, bishop, what are you doing?" she asked with alarm.

The bishop then grabbed the phone out of Nancy's hand and hung it up before she could do anything about it. "Excuse me," she shouted. Belle swiftly crossed the room toward Nancy in such a threatening way that the secretary backed up. Having secured the room, Bishop Newman opened the door to the executive office and closed it behind him.

"I left instructions..." yelled Marie as the bishop entered. Marie's strident voice was generally enough to put the fear of God into anyone, but the bishop was not one to be intimidated.

"Forgive the intrusion, Marie," he said with a duplicitous smile, "I wouldn't have interrupted if it wasn't urgent. It has come to my attention that a possession of mine has been stolen by one of your 'guests.'"

"Guests? I don't have any guests. What do you think this is, a bed and breakfast?"

"As a matter of fact, that's exactly what I think. And the criminals I speak of are living somewhere here below ground."

"I have no idea what you're talking about."

Newman stepped around the executive's desk and pulled the seat right out from under Marie, making her stumble to her feet. Then he grabbed her by her shoulders and marched her forcefully to the door.

"What the hell do you think you're doing?"

When the priest opened the doors Marie found her secretary, Nancy, lying face down on the floor stripped to her underwear.

"What the fuck!?" said Marie.

Belle, who was similarly undressed, shoved a pill into Nancy's mouth, made her swallow, and then shimmied into the secretary's outfit. After which, she donned a wig and pinned her hair up to look as close to Nancy as possible. It wasn't perfect but it would do.

"I need access to the labs without drawing any attention," replied Newman curtly.

"I couldn't if I wanted to," replied Marie. "There are security protocols."

Newman withdrew a sharp knife and held it against her thumb. "I have protocols too. How would you prefer we do this?"

Belle broke an ampoule under Nancy's nose and she began to moan from the drug.

"Have a nice trip," Belle said.

One of the bishop's crew unlocked the outer door and they exited into the hallway, leaving Nancy in a stupor.

"What did you give her?" asked Marie.

"DMT, a psychedelic tryptamine compound with a kicker. It helps bring things into a sharper focus, colors, thoughts, ideas. She may even hear little elves singing. And it also has as a cool aphrodisiac effect. Should keep everyone amused for a while."

"I know it sounds like a cliché, but you'll never get away with this. There are cameras everywhere."

"Let me worry about that."

The Bishop escorted Marie out of her office, arm in arm, keeping the knife discreetly to her ribs. He and his people had been in the Biopharm offices on numerous occasions so their presence did not attract a lot of attention. In the foyer, the bishop pressed the button to the elevator. The door opened and the group entered. Newman looked upward in the direction of the camera fixed to the top corner of the car and smiled benignly. He was actually smiling at his I.T. wizard who had hacked into the Biopharm security camera system from a remote location and was tracking his movements.

The bishop turned to Marie. "Joel Gardiner and his mother."

Marie stared back with a venomousness look. Newman grabbed her hand and pricked it with the knife. "Owe!" she cried. Reluctantly, Marie fitted her pass card into a slot and placed her thumb onto the security pad. Then she pressed the button to the fifth floor and the elevator sprung to life.

* * *

It only took a minute or two but Nancy already felt the effects of a dizzying high. When she stood up to get her bearings, she found herself alone in the office dressed in her underwear, and started to giggle. For some unknown reason she found herself singing, "Rumplestiltskin had a farm Eee –I Eee-I-Oh." Amused with herself, she approached the outer door and opened it.

* * *

As Newman and his group descended in the elevator, Marie wondered what could be so important that the bishop would risk getting arrested. And how did he think he would ever escape after he got what he was after? Newman wasn't concerned with any legal repercussions. He knew that once he got his hands on the Judas Robe everything would change. This would be the turning point for him, his followers, and quite possibly, the entire religious world.

* * *

Father Sanchez was awake that morning, examining the previous night's lab work when his fingers twitched. It was a tell he'd developed over the years, an early warning system of sorts that alerted him to the fact that Bishop Promane was in the vicinity. He dropped everything and hurried to the sleeping quarters.

* * *

Nancy strolled through the offices in her panties and bra, humming to herself while she admired the walls, desks, and carpeting.

"So many shades of gray. That book was a revelation."

Everyone she passed stopped whatever they were doing and stared.

"Nancy? Nancy, dear, are you okay?" asked one of her colleagues.

Nancy spotted a young man she always fancied but was too shy to approach. She smiled as she sashayed over. "Hey, Reggie?" she said.

* * *

Sanchez knocked on Natalie's door first, knowing she would need the most time to get ready. Instead of waiting for an answer he entered the room to find the nun asleep in her bed.

"Sister Natalie, wake up. The bishop is on his way."

Natalie's eyes flickered open. She needed no more explanation than that. As weak as she was, she raised herself and edged her body out of bed.

Sanchez left the nun's room and hurried to the next one. "Lisa?" he shouted as he knocked. There was no response. He tried the handle on the door but it was locked so he knocked anxiously several more times. After that he had no choice but to rush to the next room.

"Sofia? Sofia!" he yelled. Sanchez heard a rustling inside and a moment later, she opened the door an inch.

"What is it?"

Before Sanchez could answer he noticed Joel rising from the bed behind her. Disappointment over their indiscretion was written all over his face. All the priest could manage to say was, "The bishop is here. I've already alerted Natalie. Lisa is not answering." Then he hurried away.

* * *

When the elevator door opened onto Sub Level Five, the bishop pushed Marie out of the car, toward the secured door.

"I have no quarrel with you. I simply want what was stolen from me."

"If you tell me what it is, maybe I can help you."

Newman snickered and gestured for her to use her key card and thumbprint to gain access to the next corridor. This time, the door did not open.

"Something you're not telling me?"

Newman pressed his knife into Marie's ribs. Reluctantly, she showed him her left hand. When he lifted it up to the light, he could see something embedded in the soft flesh between her thumb and first finger.

"A microchip. How devilish," he said.

The bishop gestured to Belle and one of her cohorts held Marie while Newman grabbed her hand. Before he could immobilize it, Marie struck him in the face with her elbow. Newman slammed Marie's hand against the wall and smashed his fist into it, making her gasp. Then he took his knife and cut into the flesh, digging out the chip. She screamed from the raw pain. Newman extracted the chip and placed it onto the security pad which triggered the door to open.

***

"Reggie," Nancy said. "I always thought your eyes were so amazing."

"Uh, thanks. What happened to your, uh, clothes?"

Nancy giggled. Unable to deny her lust any longer, she ripped Reggie's shirt open wide and fastened her lips onto his chest. All he could do was moan and fall back onto the carpet.

***

Joel, Sofia, and Sanchez raced back to Lisa's room and banged on the door.

"Lisa, it's Joel, open up. Hurry!"

Still, no answer. Sensing trouble, Joel started slamming his shoulder against the door until the lock finally broke. They all rushed in and found Lisa on her bed, folded up in the fetal position.

"Lisa, are you okay? Get up." Joel said.

When she didn't answer, Sanchez looked around the room and noticed the scalpel lying on the night table.

"Joel?" he said.

Joel followed the priest's eyes to the blade. "Oh, Jesus, no!"

Father Sanchez crossed over and shifted Lisa around to find blood on the sheets and cut marks on her wrists.

"Lisa, what'd you do?" Joel gasped. The first thought that came to mind was that she found out about his tryst with Sofia and harmed herself. He turned to Sofia and Sanchez with guilt-laden eyes.

"We need bandages or cloth or something!"

Sofia ripped some of the bed sheets and ties several strands around the cuts on Lisa's wrists to stem the blood flow.

Get her up!" Sanchez said.

The three of them helped Lisa to her feet and carried the half-conscious woman out of the room as her feet dragged on the floor. Outside they met Natalie.

"What happened to her?" she asked

"Not sure, exactly," replied Joel, "but we need to leave now. Do you have the robe?"

Natalie pulled a portion of the cloth out from under her blouse.

* * *

Newman and his entourage rushed down the Sub Level Five corridor. When he realized there were no other people around, he turned fiercely at Marie for an explanation.

"Joel said complete privacy so we moved everybody off this floor."

"Lead on. And there better be no more lies."

* * *

In the executive offices above, two burly security guards jogged down the hallway toward Nancy who had Reggie pinned to the floor, and was grinding on him. When she saw the guards, she giggled, "Oh boy, a threesome!"

* * *

Newman led his people to the next entrance. They used the security protocols to give them access and strode down the corridor to another sealed door. "Down there," said Marie.

"Open it," said Newman.

"No."

"I beg your pardon?"

"Listen, Bishop Newman or whatever horseshit name you go by, I didn't get to be C.E.O. of this company by letting con men like you push me around. You want something, we negotiate. Nothing happens on these premises without my consent. And just so you know, there are dozens of armed officers on their way as we speak, so...OWWE!"

Newman didn't wait for Marie to finish her threat before his knife dug deep into the flesh of her thumb and sliced off the digit. The executive's knees buckled and she howled with pain.

"The eyes and judgment of God are upon you," he yelled.

Belle plucked the security card from Marie's hand and ran it through the scanner. Bishop Newman pressed her detached thumb onto the security pad first and then the microchip while Marie sat on the floor, writhing in agony. When the doors opened, they were faced with a dark, empty lab. Infuriated, Newman grabbed Marie by the hair and brought his fearsome visage to hers.

"Next, I take an eye."

"This is the only access to the lab on Level Six. Another security measure," Marie said between sobs.

"Belle, take her through. If she's not telling the truth, do what you have to do and leave her there."

"You narcissistic psychopath," cried Marie, "What the hell can be so important?"

Belle and one of her cohorts pushed Marie through the next entrance. She hoped somehow that her stalling would give Joel and his crew enough time to escape, if in fact, they knew they were being besieged. Newman remained where he was and watched the group proceed.

* * *

Sanchez, Joel, Lisa, Natalie, and Sofia hurried down the corridor toward the elevator.

"Where are we going to go?" asked Natalie.

"We'll deal with that later," answered Sanchez. "First thing is to get out..."

The stairwell door behind them creaked open. Sanchez turned around to see Belle and her cohorts appear at the far end of the corridor with Marie who looked bloodied and bedraggled.

"Hurry!" said Sanchez to his people.

Sofia reached the elevator first and pressed the button. Belle and her crew advanced threateningly toward them. When the door finally opened, Bishop Newman and one of his thugs were standing there inside the car. He'd anticipated their escape and had effectively blocked it at both ends.

"Sofia, it's been ages," said Newman in mock surprise. He looked past the girl to see the other four and asked calmly, "The robe?"

"We were just on our way to get it," Natalie said.

Belle pressed Marie's bloody hand, making her shriek. Natalie knew there would be more torture unless she did something. Reluctantly, she pulled the robe out from under her blouse. Newman gestured for one of his minions to fetch it. When he handed the cloth over to the bishop, the priest took his knife and tried to cut it. To his chagrin the knife tore right through the fabric.

No one was more surprised than Lisa who let out a pitiful cry. She had cut herself to prove her immortality. When she began to bleed, she assumed the wound would heal as it did on the Bishop. But there was no healing. She kept cutting herself, hoping the miracle would happen. Now it was painfully clear that the robe she'd had in her possession was a phoney and she felt like a fool.

"Oh, shut up, child," said the bishop. "No one is more disappointed than me."

Without another word Newman grabbed Natalie and dragged her inside the elevator car. Joel lunged forward to rescue his mother, but Belle drop-kicked him from behind and sent him crashing into a wall. Sofia attacked her sister and the two began pummeling each other. Sanchez attempted to intervene but the bishop's comrades kept him at bay until the elevator doors closed and Newman could escape.

"I don't have it," Natalie said when she and the priest were alone in the cab.

"I know you don't care much for your own life," said Newman, "but if you don't give me the genuine article, I will end the lives of Joel, Eugene, Gordon and Colleen, every member of your family."

"You're despicable!"

"It's all a matter of perspective, my dear." he replied.

The elevator came to a stop on the main floor and the doors opened. The bishop called for assistance. "Somebody, help! There's been an attack on Sub Level Six! Marie Champlain is down there, wounded. Somebody!"

Newman held Natalie so close to him that she could neither speak nor resist. When Security officers ran to investigate Newman's claim, he and the nun walked past them and out of the building.

The Security team arrived on Sub Level Six to witness a full-fledged melee. Upon their arrival, Belle and her people broke off the attack and simply gave up. They knew the bishop would have them released from jail soon enough. Joel, Sofia and Sanchez had all suffered serious beatings. Marie Champlain was folded over on the floor, holding her bloody hand. Lisa was standing nearby in a catatonic stupor. The Security team put Belle and her crew in handcuffs. As they led her out, Sofia sneered, "I can no longer call you, sister."

Bishop Newman stood on a street corner outside the Biopharm offices, hailing a cab. Natalie stood next to him, too weak to put up any kind of fight. When the car pulled up, he warned the nun, "I have given Belle orders to murder your entire family within the hour unless she hears from me. Their lives are in your hands."

Natalie knew there was no point in resisting. "The convent," she muttered with sad resignation. The bishop helped Natalie into the back seat and turned to the cabbie. "Saint James Convent at Porter and Dupont, my good man."

***

The main floor of the Biopharm building was in chaos. Alarm bells rang throughout the building, employees ran in every direction asking for information while police tried to establish order. A security team emerged from the elevator with Belle and her cohorts in handcuffs and handed them off to waiting officers. Bleeding profusely, Marie was ushered by first responders to an ambulance that waited outside the front doors. Joel, Lisa, Sofia and Father Sanchez emerged from the second elevator, escorted by a separate security detail.

Joel whispered to Sanchez. "I'm not going to sit in some police station while that maniac has my mother."

Sanchez nodded and turned to Sofia, "A small distraction, Sofia?"

Sofia acknowledged the request with a wink and strode over to Belle.

"You call me your sister? You traitorous bitch!"

Sofia slapped Belle across the face. Belle struggled to fight back as police attempted to subdue them both. Sanchez and Joel took the opportunity to sneak out of the building while everyone's attention was on the two women. When they hit the street, Joel's stomach was churning. "Where do we find him?"

"You know her better than anyone else. Where would your mother have hidden it?"

Joel pondered the possibilities for a moment but shrugged. No idea.

Twenty minutes later Newman's cab pulled up to the convent. The cab driver turned back to see Natalie slumped over.

"She gonna be all right?" asked the cab driver.

"Just a case of dehydration. The convent has hospital facilities, my son. She'll be fine as soon as I get her inside."

"Need any help?"

"Thanks anyway."

Natalie tried to object but the bishop discreetly pressed his fingers to her throat.

"Don't try to speak, dear. Just rest."

The bishop went into his pocket to pay the cab driver.

"Forget it, Father. On the house."

"Nice to know there are still some God-fearing people in the world."

Newman clapped the cabbie on the shoulder. Then he helped Natalie out of the cab and escorted her to the front door.

***

"What about Lisa?" asked Joel.

The group was standing on the sidewalk in the frosty night air outside the Biopharm offices. Sanchez hailed a cab. When a taxi pulled over to the curb he said, "Sofia, I'll drop you and Lisa off at our house. Make her comfortable and wait for my call."

Sofia escorted Lisa by the arm into the cab. The girl obeyed like a placid child. When they climbed inside Sanchez turned to Joel. "I can think of only one place that your mother would keep the relic."

* * *

"You know this is the first time I've been inside this convent," said Bishop Newman. "I never wanted to intrude upon your privacy. And just so you know, I never bore you or your family any ill will."

"You never cared about anyone but yourself."

"As you wish."

The bishop knocked on the front door and waited until one of the sisters answered.

"Mother Natalie...and Bishop Newman?" said Sister Gabriel with surprise.

Though he had never been within the convent walls the Bishop was well known in the city's ecclesiastical circles. Having him in the house was like having a rock star come to visit, and the bishop took full advantage.

"Sorry for the intrusion at such a late hour, sister, but Mother Natalie isn't feeling too well."

The bishop helped Natalie inside. The elder sister gave the younger one a few furtive glances, but the nun remained oblivious to the warnings.

"You heard about the intrusion the other night, Bishop?" said Sister Gabrielle to the priest as they made their way down the hall. "Hooligans."

"And I heard how brave you all were. Natalie?"

Natalie knew his threats against her family were serious and didn't challenge him. Perhaps an opportunity would arise. "This way, bishop," she said weakly.

"Mother Natalie, Bishop," said the sister with a twinkle in her eye. "I could make you some tea?"

"That would be lovely," replied the priest, smiling gratefully.

Natalie led the bishop to the library at which point the nun scurried off to prepare the refreshments and tell the others about the late-night visitor. Entering the room, Natalie went to turn on the lights but he stopped her.

"No need," he said in an intimidating tone, "And no more delays."

Natalie hesitated, hoping someone would interrupt them.

"If you're expecting God to intervene," he said, "Think of all the prayers that have wafted up to the heavens, from the innocent children stricken with cancer to the starving poor. If he didn't answer them, why would he answer you?"

"I know who you really are."

"I doubt it."

Natalie straightened herself up to her tallest height. "Bishop Promane, inquisitor from the royal court of Queen Isabella," she replied. "Torturer. Murderer. Blasphemer!"

"Oh, that's the least of it. The robe, please?" he said.

Natalie paused as if waiting for a miracle. The bishop leaned in menacingly. She relented and gestured to a painting that hung on the wall. It was a portrait of two bearded in robes men sitting under the moonlight in biblical times. The one dressed in the turban looked like a student listening intently to his teacher. When the bishop cast his eyes upon it, he faltered. There was something about the portrait that disturbed him. Regardless, the bishop moved a chair to the wall, then stood up and gingerly brought the painting down. Natalie watched him as he stared at the figures on the canvas.

"Why this one?" he asked, his lips pursed and scowling.

Natalie looked flummoxed. "I, I don't know."

Natalie shrugged her shoulders in a bewildered fashion and sat on the nearest chair. The bishop turned back to the painting and stared at it with a deep reverence as his fingers caressed the images of the men.

"Hello, old friend," he whispered.

"What?" asked Natalie.

Newman ignored her and reached behind the frame to find a ragged cloth with faded crimson stains that was pasted onto the backboard. He ripped the cloth from the board, confident that if this were the genuine article, the fabric would remain unharmed. As he predicted the frame splintered and dropped to the ground and the cloth remained intact. He held the fabric to his nose, invigorated by its musty fragrance. Natalie leaned against a wall and wept. All these years she had devoted herself to a relic, an idea, a familial responsibility. She had no idea what the robe meant to the world at large but she was willing to die for it. And now it was torn from her grasp.

The gravity of the moment was interrupted by the shocking gasps of the curious nuns who were standing at the library doorway, staring wide-eyed at the incredulous sight. The prelate stepped down off the chair and marched toward them with the robe in hand. Mother Natalie reached out to stop him, but he wrenched her hands from his clothing and she fell to the floor, splaying her body across the portrait of the two ancients. Sister Gabriel dropped the tray of tea cups on the floor with a loud clang as the priest strutted past the women as if they weren't even there.

CHAPTER 28

By the time Joel and Father Sanchez arrived at St. James convent the ambulance and police had already shown up. The officers were reluctant to let the two in until Joel convinced them his mother was inside and needed medical assistance. When he entered, he saw Sister a few of the distressed nuns huddled in a clutch.

"Sister Beatrice?" he called.

The sister turned and recognized Natalie's son. Her hand flew to her mouth as she tried to suppress her anguish. With world-weary eyes, she shuffled over to Joel and Father Sanchez.

"You mother—"

"Where is she?"

"In the library."

Joel and Sanchez marched down the hall. When they arrived, they found the door closed and guarded by police.

"Officer," said Father Sanchez, "We understand Mother Natalie is inside. This is her son."

"Her son?" replied the cop.

"May I see her?"

It wasn't so much a question as a demand.

"Wait here."

He opened the door and entered the room, closing it quickly behind him. Joel and Sanchez looked at each other, their anxiety ratcheting higher with each moment. A moment later the officer peeked out and allowed Joel inside but held Sanchez back. That is until Joel objected, "This is my priest. He comes too."

The officer nodded and allowed both to enter. Inside, the room was abuzz with police officers and forensic specialists. The glaring lights and all the worker bees made the atmosphere seem like some surreal movie set. One of the officers was bent over, taking pictures of the evidence on the floor. Others were busy interviewing witnesses. At the center of the action lay a body with a sheet over it. Joel's stomach turned when he recognized his mother's frail wrist hanging out from under the sheet.

"Mom? Oh God, no!"

He rushed to her side but the police held him back. "Sorry, son, this is a crime scene."

"Crime scene?" His brain made some quick mental calculations and reluctantly came to its inevitable conclusion. "He killed her!"

"Who?" asked one of the detectives.

"Bishop Newman or Promane or whatever he calls himself," replied Joel, as his stomach heaved and heartache engulfed him.

"How do you know that?" the detective asked.

"Because he kidnapped my mother an hour ago and brought her here."

"Kidnapped her from where?"

Father Sanchez gave Joel a discreet look as if to say, *'It might not be in our interests to answer that right now.'*

But Joel was too overcome with grief and rage to stop. "We were at the Biopharm building downtown. He broke in and kidnapped my mother."

"Why?" asked the detective.

Sanchez discreetly tapped Joel on the hip. "Joel, take a breath. It might help you think more clearly."

The priest's advice was more a warning than a calming effect, but it succeeded in getting his message across. Joel gathered his wits and settled down. "I dunno, exactly."

The detective scowled at both men. The priest's advice was meant to encourage a more succinct answer not muddy it. Joel overheard another cop interviewing a few nuns off to the side, all of whom looked distraught.

"Sister Beatrice told us that Bishop Newman brought Mother Natalie home," replied one of the sisters. "because she was ill. We came to the library to give her some assistance. When we arrived, Bishop Newman was standing on a chair."

"On a chair? Doing what?" asked the officer.

"I'm not sure. The painting was on the floor with the broken frame...the Bishop stepped down and walked right past us...and Sister Natalie...she fell onto the canvas over there."

"Did any of you see the bishop put his hands on her in any way, in an aggressive style?" asked the officer.

"No. She reached out to him but..." continued Sister Boniface.

"Did the bishop have anything he was carrying? Something he might've come here for?" asked Sanchez.

"Maybe, I don't know, we were all down the hall," said the nun.

"It couldn't be the painting because it's right there."

"It doesn't matter," Joel yelled at the police. "He killed her."

Everyone in the room stopped what they were doing and stared at Joel. The detective took both him and Father Sanchez to the opposite end of the room to allow his people to continue their work. The paramedics lifted Natalie's lifeless body onto a gurney, strapped it in, making sure her face was properly covered.

"Where are you taking her?" said Joel.

"An autopsy will be have to be done to determine cause of death," replied the detective.

"Hasn't she been through enough?" argued Joel.

"It's procedure, sorry."

Joel approached the gurney but one of the cops kept his hands away. A second later they wheeled the body out of the room.

"The look on his face," murmured one nun to another.

Sanchez overheard and responded. "The boy just lost his mother."

"Not him," replied the nun, "The Bishop."

The nun's comment piqued Sanchez's curiosity and he asked, "Did you see if he had anything in his hands?"

"I'm not sure. Uh, maybe something bunched up," she replied.

"A cloth, perhaps?"

"Could have been."

"Sonofabitch!" Joel said.

Sanchez cautioned the boy to keep quiet and then looked around the room. With the body gone, the portrait was now in plain sight and curiously, Sanchez edged closer to look at it.

"Familiar?" asked Joel quiet enough so that he wouldn't be overheard.

"It's a well-known drawing of our lord and Nicodemus."

"Who's Nicodemus?"

"Nicodemus was a member of the Sanhedrin, the Jewish high court of the time."

"So, an enemy of Jesus?"

"On the contrary. He was both a friend and follower. This is a portrait of their meeting as written in the Gospel of John."

"Meeting for what, for why?"

One of the nuns who'd overheard the conversation, began to recite, "Rabbi, we know that you are a teacher who has come from God. For no one could perform the signs you are doing if God were not with him. For God so loved the world that he gave his one and only Son, that whoever believes in him shall not perish but have eternal life."

Gripped with vengeance, Joel turned to Sanchez and whispered, "Where do we find the bastard?"

The interviewing detective picked up on the conversation and suggested, "I'd like you both to come back to the precinct to give us a statement."

"As you can see, detective," replied Sanchez, "The boy is distraught. Would it be alright if we dropped in tomorrow when his head is clearer?"

The detective clearly did not like the question. "I'd prefer to do this now while things are fresh in his mind."

"I understand, but as his religious leader, my concern is for his spiritual well being."

"Tomorrow, first thing," replied the officer, handing him his card.

"Thank you, officer. Come Joel."

As Sanchez led the boy out of the library he whispered, "Why don't you announce to the whole world that we're going to assassinate the bishop next time we see him?"

"I thought I just did."

Sanchez cuffed the boy as they walked down the hallway.

* * *

After leaving the convent, Joel and Father Sanchez took a walk to cool off.

"Your mother was a true soldier of God," Sanchez said.

"Is that how God rewards his followers, treats them shitty and then slaughters them like cattle?"

"The world mourns countless people of faith. Some suffer more than others. I know that makes no sense and it's no consolation. We need to gather the troops and devise a plan. Get some rest and book a room in your school library tomorrow morning at 10:00."

"I'll text you." Joel left the priest on the sidewalk, wandered around for another half hour, and took a room in a motel. The next day he showed up at the university library reading room to find Father Sanchez, Sofia and Lisa waiting for him. Lisa stood up immediately and put her arms around him.

"I'm sorry, Joel."

"Me too," added Sofia. "Your mother was a—"

"...a true soldier of God. I know," he said with a hint of sarcasm.

They all took seats around the worktable. Sofia brought Joel up to speed on the Biopharm incident. "Your boss is not pressing charges against Bishop Promane—"

"You mean, Newman."

"In any case, your boss fears losing her job above losing more digits."

"What the fuck does that mean?"

"It means that Promane is a stock holder in the company with a seat on the board. Ms. Champlain is on shaky ground as it is with the slow pace of our work. He's blackmailing her to keep her mouth shut and he has the power to do it."

Joel countered, "There were witnesses, there had to be evidence on security tapes."

Sofia shook her head. "Our sources in the police department say no. They must have been wiped."

"And as far as your mother's death is concerned," added Sanchez, "You heard the nuns last night, the Bishop did not lay a finger on her."

Sofia added, "As of now the police are treating her death as a misadventure."

"Misadventure?" Overcome with anger and fatigue, rubbing his face with his fists. Sofia watched the boy, acutely aware of the anguish churning inside him.

"I liked and respected your mother," she said soothingly. "I'm sorry. But it won't do any good to—"

"What I need is some good old-time biblical vengeance!" he shouted.

Sanchez took a seat next to Joel. "Up to this point, all our efforts have concentrated on keeping the robe from Promane. Now we must take it back from him. I'm not a military strategist. I've never plotted murder against a man."

"He's got the robe. We know he's going to use it for something, and it's not going to be for the good of anyone but himself."

Lisa suddenly came to life. "His church."

"What do you mean, his church?" asked Sanchez.

Her explanation came out in drips and drabs like someone who had just come out of a coma. "I went there, to interview him, to get proof of who he really was. They were getting the church ready for something, something big."

"She's right. I was there too," Sofia said.

"Then that's where we need to go," said Joel.

He stood up as if he was going to race out of the library and run straight to the church, seeking revenge.

"Joel, wait," Sanchez said. "We can't put the interests of one before the needs of the many. It's safe to assume he has the robe. The mind boggles at how he may use it. We'll only get one chance to stop him. We cannot waste it."

* * *

The sunlight streamed through the stained-glass windows flooding every corner of the sanctuary with the image of the Bishop's omniscience. Hundreds of the faithful along with an invited press were present to record the event. The excitement in the air was akin to an old-time revival meeting. At the appointed hour, rapturous music poured through the speakers, announcing the event was about to start. The Bishop entered, adorned in a tall white cap and black and gold vestments. The crowd hushed as Belle and five other officers of the church followed in the procession. The prelate ascended the steps to the altar in the center of the room. The taped music halted and the priest addressed his adoring flock.

"Children, members of the press, faithful, and skeptics alike, thank you for coming. Our church has been preparing for this moment for months, but it has been in the making for over two thousand years. My friends, we all want to believe there is a God, but to be honest, in our heart of hearts, we have our misgivings. I am here today to give you absolute confirmation of God in the material world."

The Bishop placed his hands under the altar. He opened a drawer and withdrew the robe, holding it up for all to see.

"Behold the one and only physical proof of God, the Judas Robe."

Murmurs reverberated throughout the church, but no one was particularly awed. They were waiting for proof. The Bishop knew it and would not disappoint. Belle approached the altar with a tiki torch and a barbeque lighter. Some of the members of the press began to giggle. This 'ceremony' certainly bore no resemblance to anything they'd ever seen in a traditional Church.

"BBQ in the church? Pass the beer and hot dogs," someone shouted.

Belle lit the flame and placed the torch upon the cloth. The cloth did not burn. Someone in the crowd shouted, "Flame-retardant material. Gotta do better than that, preacher."

Giggles turned into outright laughter. Sanchez, Joel, and Sofia discreetly entered through the back of the church and edged their way up. At the sight of the Bishop standing proudly on the altar, Joel clenched his fists and readied himself for an assault. But Sanchez held him back, pointing to the press who were videotaping everything.

"Sir, please come up," said the Bishop to the heckler.

The man smiled at the people next to him and made his way through the crowd to the altar. Belle pulled a seriously long knife from her belt and handed it to him. Four of the Bishop's acolytes stretched the cloth by its ends, making the material taut.

"Strike me," said the priest.

"What?" asked the heckler.

"Thrust the blade through the cloth and stab me with all your might."

"I, I can't."

"I can!" yelled Joel. Several of the Bishop's followers grabbed the student by the arms to subdue him, but the priest waved them off.

"I know this fellow, let him be."

Joel shook off the men and pushed his way to the altar. He marched up the steps and stared murderously at his nemesis.

"Joel," said the Bishop calmly, "Contrary to what you think, I did not harm your mother in any way. She died, unfortunately, because her heart gave out. But I understand your sorrow and anger. If it is God's will, strike me."

Belle, who was standing next to the priest, handed him the knife. The Bishop stretched out his arms, inviting the attack. Without hesitation, Joel thrust the blade at the cloth so that it would pierce the robe and Promane square in the chest. The cloth bowed in the centre but did not tear. The crowd emitted a chorus of oohs and ahhs. There were even gasps from the gallery of reporters. The priest cast his eyes up at the ceiling as if giving thanks to the Lord. Joel cocked his arm and thrust, harder this time. The crowd yelped in surprise, having been caught off-guard. Still, the cloth remained intact. The entire audience was astounded.

"Thank you, son," the Bishop said.

The crowd began to cheer over the miracle.

Undaunted, Joel tried to grab the robe but Belle and her cohorts pushed his hands away.

"The robe does not belong to you!" he shouted.

"Nor does it belong to you. Your family kept it from the world for years."

"Because they knew you'll use it—"

"I'll use it to bring glory to God."

Bishop Promane's confidence played against Joel's erratic behavior, making the priest look like the more rational of the two.

"What is that robe made of, Bishop," someone called.

"Ordinary cloth fibres...touched by God himself."

"You called it the Judas Robe?" asked a reporter.

A chorus of jeers rang out at the mention of Judas's name.

"Why would God bless the robe of the man who betrayed his son?" shouted someone.

"There is a theory among the cognoscenti, that Judas was not the villain he was portrayed to be. Yes, he betrayed Jesus and that betrayal led to our lord's crucifixion. But consider for a moment a world in which Jesus was not betrayed and did not die on the cross. He would most probably have lived his life and guided his people for years. But he would not have died a martyr for our sins. God would not have ended up sacrificing his son for humanity, and Jesus' resurrection would not have occurred. Might it be possible that Judas was doing God's will by setting the wheels in motion? That he was part of a grand scheme to create the greatest religion known to mankind?"

Promane's little sermon was so effective that it created a considerable buzz of comments throughout the sanctuary. It also made Father Sanchez wonder what the Bishop's ultimate objective was.

Belle said, "To answer your earlier question, the robe was taken from the body of Judas after he was buried in Potter's Field."

"What proof do you have it actually belonged to Judas or anyone of that time for that matter?" asked another reporter.

Promane addressed the skeptic in a sobering tone. "The demonstration of its invulnerability should be proof enough. But in these modern times I can understand your need for absolute certainty. We are currently in the process of authenticating the garment using the most sophisticated, independent scientific methods available to man. And sir, when it's proven, you might want to ask God for his forgiveness."

As the volume of chatter rose in the room, the Bishop placed the robe in a small ornate box.

"You and I, we're not done," Joel said.

Promane smiled benignly and left the podium. With hundreds of people watching, Joel had no alternative other than to let him go. Belle gestured for the knife back and reluctantly, Joel returned it.

CHAPTER 29

The event closed with the Bishop promising to publish any and all proofs of the robe's authenticity as soon as they became available. After that, he said the robe would be put on display in his church for the faithful to worship. The robe promised to confirm many of the grandiose claims of the bible and satisfy hungry souls. The crowd dispersed infused with a sense of euphoria and wonder rivalling the most fervent evangelical revivals.

"It's time we had an old time miracle," enthused one follower.

"Gonna be like the Rapture or the Second Coming," said another.

"Praise be to God," said a third.

The skeptics still laughed but the faithful were primed and ready.

Sanchez, Joel, Sofia, and Lisa left through the back entrance of the church and escorted out by a phalanx of security guards to avoid any further skirmishes. The group followed the paved steps that led to the garden. Father Sanchez put his arm around Joel.

"I warned you, Joel."

"I don't care," he said. "Right is right and wrong is wrong."

"I know you want vengeance, son, but this is not the way to get it."

"What's his endgame, you think?" asked Joel. "What's his deal with the robe?"

Sofia looked at Father Sanchez. "The ossuary?" she asked. Sanchez nodded.

"What's an ossuary?" asked Joel.

"The world is filled with false idols. Every time someone sees an image of Christ in a piece of toast, or witnesses a religious statue oozing blood, or an archeologist presents a sliver of wood he claims came from the cross, it's a miracle and the people flock to it. Obvious fakes, easily disproven," said Sanchez.

"But then there was the discovery of the Jonah Ossuary," Sofia said, "An ossuary is a box that held human remains, part of ancient burial traditions. This was a genuine relic. The markings on the Jonah box looked like a fish with a stick figure in its mouth. People interpreted it to mean that the stick figure was Jonah, the old testament character who was swallowed by a whale. Experts concluded the drawings were not of an upside-down whale swallowing a man but a funerary monument of the time. The skeptics call that Rorschach test archeology, where you see what you want to see."

Sanchez carried on. "After that came the discovery of the ossuary in Talpiot with the names 'James, son of Joseph, brother of Jesus' inscribed on it. A chemical analysis of the box actually dated it to the correct period. But it couldn't be that of Jesus, because that would have undermined one of the central tenets of Christianity, that Christ was resurrected and rose bodily to heaven after his crucifixion."

"If Promane confirms the robe belonged to Judas, then what?"

Sanchez looked around at the extensive garden with its areas of quiet reflection.

"He's put a lot of effort into these grounds. My feeling is he is going to start a new sect."

"And if he authenticates the robe, he'll have what he needs to do it," said Sofia.

They wandered past the garden and when they reached the cemetery, it triggered another matter.

"Joel," Sanchez said, "We need to talk about your mother's funeral."

Lisa suddenly stopped and stared at the shards of glass that resembled tiny tombstones. "Not here. Please."

"What's wrong?" Joel said.

Lisa's eyes grew large, hollow and fearful. Something about the glass shards filled her with dread and she couldn't explain it. Father Sanchez read the apprehension in her eyes and took her arm.

"Why don't we get out of here?" he said gently.

The group continued walking in silence toward the street. But a host of questions troubled them about what Lisa saw in the yard that shook her so badly. And what brought her to cut herself when she was at Biopharm? Joel feared that it still might have to do with his tryst with Sofia.

* * *

Natalie's funeral was held two days later in a cemetery owned by the sisters of her convent. Father Sanchez officiated over the intimate gathering which included Joel, Sofia and Lisa and some of the members of Natalie's order. Lisa hadn't said much more since her vague pronouncement at the graveyard. Nevertheless, she stood next to Joel, holding his hand and lending him support.

The group was unaware of a separate contingent watching them from a nearby hilltop. After Father Sanchez invoked his final prayers, the caretakers of the cemetery lowered the casket into the ground and began to shovel dirt into the grave. Attendees stepped up to console Joel.

"What will comfort you the most," Sofia whispered, "is that your mother loved you. Believe me, that's more than some of us ever get."

The nuns took turns offering their condolences. Then another voice spoke up. It was familiar yet startling. "Sorry about your mother, Joel."

Joel turned to find his father and siblings, who had been watching the service from a distance, standing next to him.

"You mean your wife?" Joel said, swallowing the bile in his throat.

"Let's be honest, bro,'" said Gordon, "First, she poisoned you physically and then she poisoned you mentally."

"What asshole coached you to say that?"

To avoid coming to blows, Gordon smiled and put his arm around his brother.

"We're family. We should all be on the same side."

Colleen sidled up to her brother. "That robe never belonged to Bishop Newman, Joel. It belongs to us. There's a reason why Mom kept it hidden all those years. She knew Newman would use it to make himself rich."

"But if *we* managed it, like," said Gordon, "then we'd all benefit."

"Including you, right?" Joel said.

"It was your ma's wish," added Eugene. "to have us all reunited and protect the robe from people like the bishop."

"Waddya think?" asked Colleen.

"I think that you should all go fuck yourselves."

Eugene's eyes clouded over, a look Joel had come to know and fear since he was a child. But that look no longer had the same intimidating effect. In fact, Joel stared back at his father, defying him. Gordon discreetly rapped his father's elbow to remind him of their mission.

"Think about it, bro, just think about it," Gordon said.

With that the family left Joel and the cemetery.

* * *

There was no further communication from Joel's family after that. He and Lisa returned to their apartment, living as friends more out of convenience more than anything else. They resumed classes and whenever asked about their absences, they claimed they were traumatized by the recent murders and the death of Joel's mother. None of that was far from the truth. The university was not known to be lenient because so many other candidates were waiting to take their slots. But the couple pleaded their case eloquently and even offered to repeat the year if they had to at their own cost. In the meantime, they waited for word from Father Sanchez and monitored the ever-growing chatter online about the Judas Robe, of which there was plenty.

Bishop Newman availed himself of every opportunity to publicize it. The priest requested every qualifying test including carbon dating, accelerators, chemicals, and genome analysis. Those, in turn, were cross-referenced with historical records and accounts. No one was yet prepared to claim the garment did in fact belong to Judas, but it hadn't failed any tests either. The one thing experts did agree on was that the fabric was indeed a product of that age.

Marie Champlain was on a campaign of her own, to woo Joel and his crew back to the project. She knew she was dangerously close to losing her job. Her future with the company lay in the breakthrough of the universal blood formula and her amputated thumb would garner her only so much sympathy before she was turfed. After much cajoling, Joel agreed to Marie's offer only if he could pursue his research to find and isolate the gene for ectodermal dysplasia, a pledge he'd made to his dead mother.

Joel prevailed upon Lisa to join the team and she agreed because, truthfully, she had nowhere else to go. She'd been numbed by the experiences of the past few weeks and felt like a ship without a rudder. Joel hoped she'd eventually come around but until then, she needed to be watched for her own safety. Any conversation they had together was limited to the work at hand and he accepted their emotional distance as penance for spending the night with Sofia, even though neither had brought it up. By keeping her close, he hoped to find a way to mend their relationship. One day in the lab, Joel came over and offered Lisa a cup of tea.

"You know I didn't get the chance to thank you for being there for me at my mom's funeral. You didn't have to."

"Sure." Her answers were generally curt and to the point.

"Look, Lis,' I know it's been difficult, especially after that day when we found you in your...condition. And then, when you got spooked in the church yard... Listen, I'm not sure I know what's going on with you a hundred percent but if you ever wanna talk or anything..."

Lisa considered whether she could express in words what was on her mind. And then she blurted said, "The cemetery is where all the sins are buried."

"Whose sins?"

Lisa stared off into the distance, unwilling to look Joel in the eye. "Bishop Promane's followers. He explained...when I went to see him a few weeks ago...he's big on having people confess their sins...then he transfers the sins to this piece of glass...and buries them in the cemetery. Hundreds of them... and then his people are reborn."

This was more than Lisa had spoken in three weeks. He took a seat next to her, encouraging her to continue.

"Yes?" he said, encouragingly.

"I lost my faith years ago...and he could see that, I don't know how. That night when I followed you to the convent and the wine cellar, I watched you and your mother. She showed you the robe, and after I got locked inside, I had to know for sure. I searched around and found it... and then I wrapped it around my shoulders and I felt, I dunno, something miraculous."

"It wasn't the real robe, you know."

"I know, but in that moment it felt like it."

"I should never have involved you," Joel said, taking her hand.

Her eyes flickered into focus and she turned to him.

"You took up medicine to help find a cure for your mother's condition. For me, my passion was always to find a way to help people. When I found the robe, I thought, maybe this was chance to unlock some of the secrets of the universe. I had it in my hands. I wanted to believe. I did believe."

She reached out her hands in a supplicating gesture and he took them in his.

"Then, that day," she continued, "when the bishop and I were talking in the garden about immortality...I cut him."

"You what?"

"I needed to know if he was immortal. If he was, it would prove everything. It would restore my faith. Who wouldn't take that chance?"

"What happened? What did you see?"

She withdrew her hands and looked at them. "His wound healed - right in front of my eyes."

"So that's why you cut yourself."

"Yes, but then after I realized the robe was a fake....do you know what it's like to stand on the peak of Mount Olympus and fall all the way back to earth?"

"I'm sorry, Lis.' I never meant to...Look, I don't know where we are, you and I."

"Me either. Maybe friends is enough for now?"

"Sounds good."

Lisa had been so open about herself that Joel wanted to confess his discretion with Sofia. But he didn't want to risk the fragile connection they'd just made, so he kept quiet and resumed his work.

* * *

In the days that followed Joel kept his distance from Sofia and she didn't question it. But when the news that Bishop Promane was going to hold a news conference he knew they both had to be at the event. Sanchez agreed to stay behind to watch over Lisa as long as Joel informed him of every facet.

They rented a car that morning and drove to Promane's church. On their way, conversation was stilted. "Lisa seems better these days," Sofia said.

"Yeah," he replied, "Listen, Sofia—"

"Joel, you don't have to worry. We shared a moment, that's all. You needed me and I needed you. It doesn't have to be more complicated than that."

"Thanks."

They arrived at Promane's church a half hour later to find the sidewalks lined with hundreds of people and numerous television units parked across the street. Joel called Father Sanchez on speaker phone so they could all converse. Sofia opened a laptop to monitor the news feeds.

"It's a circus out here, Father," Joel said. "People, news vans, reporters everywhere."

"And it's going to get worse. The Vatican just dispatched three emissaries who will arrive on Saturday to determine its authenticity."

"Maybe it's better this way, that the world knows. I mean what's the worst that could happen?"

Sofia began surfing various internet sites on her laptop. "This," she replied by reading some of the headlines.

"Everyone is equal under One God."

"Jesus rules."

"What's so bad about that?" asked Joel.

Sofia continued, 'One religion, one God, one people.' Where does that leave the Jews, the Muslims, the Buddhists and every other faith? Father, you and I both remember a time when one religion tried to dominate an entire country. 'Convert or die', the law of the land. It created monsters who sent countless innocent people to their deaths. With the robe in the wrong hands, it could be worse, a lot worse."

"That's one of the reasons it's been kept hidden all these years. If the Vatican makes a declaration even remotely close to that, I'm afraid one of the worst chapters in history may be repeated."

After further discussion there seemed to be no choice. Joel hung up on Sanchez and called his father to meet. Later that day, he and Sofia waited in a coffee shop near the church. Eugene entered, accompanied by Joel's siblings. They saw Joel and Sofia sitting at a booth and joined them.

"How ya doin,' son?" Eugene said.

A waitress came by and they asked for coffees all round. After she left Joel began the conversation.

"We thought it over, Eugene—"

"Dad."

Joel swallowed hard and continued. "'Dad, some of what you said wasn't wrong. Bishop Newman's interest in the robe is selfish, no question. But I never wanted to be in the religion business. I've always wanted medicine and I still do. So maybe by joining forces—"

"Good thinking, son. What's your plan?"

"Simple. After Newman authenticates the robe and it's back in his hands, we steal it."

Colleen's eyes danced with anticipation. "Yeah, but how?"

"I've known the bishop since I was a girl," said Sofia. "My sister, Belle, is his second. I can get us inside, then Joel secures the robe."

"Where do we come in?" asked Gordon.

"When I take my shot, I'm going to need a distraction. That's where you'll come in. Then after I give it back to the church and get a reward—"

"Wait a minute. Why would you do that?" asked Eugene.

"Because that way it would end up where it belongs. I mean, who better than the church to keep something like this?"

Colleen glared at her brother, "Us, that's who. I don't trust the church for a minute. With all the diddling that went on with those choirboys for years and no one said a thing. And what about all the land they own and the treasures they keep?"

Sofia said, "You have a better idea?"

"You set up a meeting with Newman," Eugene said. "While you're keeping him busy, we'll shuffle on in with the faithful and grab the robe ourselves."

"So, *we're* the distraction?" asked Joel. "What happens after that? We never see you again?"

"Listen to me. I know people, rich Catholics who'd pay millions for something like this."

"But—"

"Look, son, I'm older than the both of ya put together and way more experienced."

Joel and Sofia gave each other a discreet glance and let Eugene continue.

"You don't wanna be sittin' on this until someone comes along one day and proves it's just another Shroud of Turban."

"Turin," said Sofia. "Shroud of Turin."

"Whatever. Anyways, the robe is already back at the church."

"How do you know that?" asked Joel.

"I have my spies. The testing has been done and Newman's just waiting for the results before he makes his big announcement."

"Okay. But the thing is, it's gotta be done before Saturday."

"Why?" asked Gordon.

"Guess you don't know everything, big brother. Because that's when the three wise men from the Vatican arrive to verify it as a holy relic."

"After that, we'll never get another chance."

"See how good we work together?" Eugene, said. Then he reached across the table and clapped his hand around Joel's head. "I'm gonna make it all up to you, Joel. Trust me."

An hour later, Joel and Sofia returned to Biopharm and filled Father Sanchez in on the details.

"All right then," said Sanchez. "Friday, we go to Promane's church and when Joel's family steals the robe—"

"You know they're going to double-cross you," Lisa said.

"I'm counting on it," Sanchez replied with a sly grin.

For the next two days, Joel and his crew continued their work on the blood formula. Lisa was still fragile but wanted to help. She'd heard Father Sanchez and Joel referencing a biblical character named Nicodemus on the night Natalie died, so she did some research.

Marie Champlain dropped in on the labs on occasion unannounced. Since the attack she had become increasingly anxious to the point of being paranoid. She'd struggled all her adult life to reach the pinnacle of her profession and even sacrificed her marriage and the opportunity to have children for it. If the board fired her, she'd have nothing.

"Where are we on this, Joel?"

Joel rubbed his eyes from fatigue. "Every day, a step closer."

Marie held up her hand with the missing digit. "Are you trying to take advantage of a poor cripple?"

Father Sanchez interrupted. "If I may say, Ms. Champlain, there are only one or two steps left."

"Give me a date. I need a date."

"What might really help is a good, long bath," Father Sanchez said.

Joel sensed Marie was about to explode and jumped in, "What Father Sanchez means is, let us work up a report for your board. It'll be enough to keep them off your back until we reach the finish line. As he said, there are only a few small hurdles."

Marie stared daggers at Father Sanchez. "If you need me, I'll be in my bath," she said and stormed off.

"You can't talk to her like that," said Joel. "These days that would get you fired, or sued, your name would be blackballed."

"In my day we'd haul her off to the baths and drown her." Sanchez walked away.

Lisa read the agitation in Joel's face and took him aside. "It'll be all right. Anyway, I've been doing some digging on that guy, Nicodemus."

"Who?"

"You mentioned him the night your mother died."

"The dude in the portrait with Jesus?"

She nodded. "In those days the Romans ruled with an iron fist but they did allow the local Jewish council to settle minor disputes."

"The Sanhedrin, I know."

"Nicodemus was a member of that council."

"Okay, so?"

"Well it seems Nicodemus didn't just know Jesus. According to the Gospel of John he was one of the people who buried him after he was crucified. Him and another man named Joseph of Arimathea."

"I don't know what that has to do with anything."

I'm not sure either, except that was the portrait that your mother chose to hide the robe behind. Anyway, I just wanted to help."

Lisa turned away looking dejected. Joel shook his head at his indifference and called after her.

"Lisa, thank you. Maybe it will help."

* * *

Eugene and his children had been part of Promane's flock for years. When his marriage grew rocky it was the Bishop who helped engineer his divorce. Eugene always felt the church gave him a raw deal over the arranged marriage. There was the expectation of a payoff for his loyalty but it never materialized. When things between him and Natalie began to sour, the bishop assured Eugene that one day he'd be rewarded. It looked like the time had finally come.

The article about the Judas Robe began as a curiosity on the local news. But when the bishop started giving interviews and posting them on the internet, interest went viral. Pressure was applied and forensic testing was completed in ten days which confirmed the cloth had been scientifically verified as being at least 2,000 years old. Its fibres were created from plants that flourished in the mountainous region of Galilee, and the red streaks were blood stains. As to the nature of its tensile strength, no one could account for it. It was impervious to fire and puncturing. Some of the scientists jokingly compared it to Superman's cape. They asked for more time to study the artifact but the bishop demanded that it be returned for spiritual assessment. When he leaked to the media that Vatican officials were coming to authenticate it as a religious relic, the story exploded. By the end of the week, the streets in and around the church were lined with Christians, agnostics and atheists.

Father Sanchez, Joel and Sofia gathered in the lab to discuss the results of the testing and their next move.

"What's your father's plan?" Father Sanchez asked Joel. "How will we know when they've made their attempt?"

"Eugene wouldn't tell me. He just said our job is to keep Promane busy and when the time came, we'd know."

"Nonsense. We need to know now," said Sofia. "How are we supposed to keep Promane and Belle occupied all day long and distract them?"

"Clearly, he wants to keep us in the dark," replied Sanchez. "This is going to make things much more difficult. How is Lisa about this, Joel? We're going to need every available person."

"She wants to help. She'll be okay."

On Friday morning, the church was scheduled to open at noon to allow people inside for a viewing. Joel, Sanchez, Sofia, and Lisa arrived two hours earlier. Security guards were posted at all entrances and exits. Visitors were to be funneled through the front door and into the sanctuary to view the robe. They would have a minute or so and then they'd be ushered out the back through the garden and out onto the street.

Sanchez and Sofia stationed themselves near the front of the line while Joel and Lisa made their way around the back of the church.

"How do we distract Promane?" Lisa said.

"The bishop and his people already know we're here. That should be all the distraction we'll need." Looking around, he admired the landscaping. "Quite the garden."

At the mention of the garden, Lisa stopped and stared at a patch of ground. He followed her gaze past the vegetable patch to the cemetery and the glass shards that stuck out of the earth.

"Come on," he said, trying to both sooth and distract her.

At twelve noon the doors of the church opened. Security guards checked all bags and allowed people to enter single file. Sanchez and Sofia spotted Joel's family dressed in wigs and baggy, nondescript clothes. Eugene, Gordon, and Colleen inserted themselves into line, carrying bibles and bouquets. The guards gave them cursory looks as they approached the front door.

"You can't leave those flowers inside." said one of the guards to Colleen. "Can't leave anything inside."

Colleen nodded and continued. The interior foyer of the church was dimly lit. The single line of worshippers snaked through into the sanctuary where soft, liturgical music played. The guests circled around the pews so that everyone could get a glimpse of the robe which sat atop the altar in the center of the room. The robe sat inside a clear plexiglass case under spotlights that shone from the ceiling making the viewing a theatrical spectacle.

Colleen was first of the family in line. She followed the person in front of her from the foyer to the sanctuary. Her father, Eugene, entered further behind and stepped out of line to go to the washroom. He shut the door and placed his bible in the bottom of the waste bin. Then he exited. At approximately the same time, Colleen reached the altar and laid her bouquet down on the floor in front of it.

"Hey!" shouted another security guard. "You can't leave that there. Pick it up and take it with you on your way out."

"Sorry."

Colleen picked up the bouquet. While the attention was on her, Gordon, who was also in line, discreetly slipped his bible under a bench behind a pew. Then he advanced in line, and after viewing the relic, exited through the back entrance along with everyone else.

Joel waited in the garden studying the faces of all the visitors who exited. When he recognized his sister, Colleen, he turned away to avoid eye contact. At the edge of his sightline Joel watched his sister leave the grounds and stroll down the sidewalk with all the other visitors. A minute later Joel's father and brother exited the church and left in the same direction. Sensing something was about to happen, Joel tensed up. He turned toward the church expecting something, anything, but nothing occurred. Then he spent the next twenty minutes scanning the grounds for any sign that might reveal or betray his family's plan. When he found nothing, he gestured to Lisa.

"Come on."

"You don't think anything is going to happen?" she asked.

"I dunno. Maybe they just came to scout the church one more time before they pulled whatever stunt they were planning."

Joel and Lisa returned to the front of the church to inform Father Sanchez and Sofia. By then it was almost 1:30. They ambled down the street away from the crowds, to confer.

"They came out of the back about thirty minutes ago and walked away," Joel said.

"Did they say anything to you?" asked Sanchez "Give you any indication of their plan?"

"Nothing."

"Maybe things didn't go according to plan," Lisa said.

"Or maybe they did and this is right where they wanted us, in a state of confusion."

All Joel and his comrades could do was to wait. They took shifts circling the block hour after hour, waiting for something to happen. It was 5:30 and the church was scheduled to close in a half hour. Father Sanchez wondered whether Eugene might be waiting for nightfall to make his move. There would be less security visible but there would be other measures. Promane wasn't stupid. As the four stood across the street on the sidewalk debating what to do, Joel noticed his brother, Gordon, dressed in an entirely different disguise this time, stepping into line. A moment later, his father and sister joined in behind.

"Whatever they're up to, it's going down now," Joel whispered to Sanchez.

The priest gestured for everyone to take their positions. Joel and Lisa hurried to the back of the church while Sanchez and Sofia got into line behind the Gardiners. Two minutes later, security guards approached. Father Sanchez steeled himself for an altercation. Had they been ratted out? The guards walked right past him only to cut the line off for the day. Slowly, the remaining faithful edged their way to the entrance. Sanchez kept an eye on Eugene, Gordon and Colleen who were about a dozen people ahead of him. As soon as they went inside, Sanchez put on his clerical collar and escorted Sofia to cut into the front of the line.

"Hey, buddy, you can't do that," said one of the followers.

Sanchez showed his credentials to both the follower and the security guards. "I'm a priest. This woman is ill and I need to get her to a washroom."

The security guard gazed at the beautiful Sofia and waved both of them in.

"That's not very Christian of you, letting someone butt in like that," said the follower to the security guard.

"May God strike me down for my sins," replied the guard, gesturing at the evening sky.

Sanchez and Sofia strode through the hallway and approached the sanctuary. Both were on alert, looking for any clue, but the room looked no different than earlier. Liturgical music continued to play as the line of faithful made its way toward the altar. The worshippers at the front took a moment to gaze at the robe. Those who carried bibles touched them to the glass and kissed them before moving on. Among them was Colleen, again, carrying another bouquet. Sanchez looked around the room with a puzzled look on his face.

What?" asked Sofia.

"Not many security guards here for a relic so valuable. Knowing we were coming, knowing anyone at any time could steal the robe." Sanchez stopped speaking to think. "You've been in this church before. Where would the rectory be?"

Sofia turned and left the sanctuary with Sanchez following her. As she hurried along, she made a cell phone call.

"Rectory downstairs."

At that moment several things happened: a finger pressed a button on a small, hand-held electronic unit. A small incendiary device hidden in a floral bouquet that Colleen managed to leave at the foot of the altar, ignited a flame.

Sofia showed Sanchez the stairway leading to the basement. She opened the door and listened for movement. Hearing nothing, they crept stealthily down the stairs. When they reached the bottom, they saw several doors off to the side of the long hallway. A male and female exited one of the rooms and locked it behind them. When the couple turned to the staircase they ran into Sanchez and Sofia and froze. Both looked as guilty as hell.

"What's in that room you just left?" asked Sanchez.

"Who are you?" asked the male.

"A truth seeker," Sanchez said. Fast as a striking cobra, he grabbed the man by the throat. "Keys."

The female tried to run past the priest but Sofia punched her in the stomach. The woman doubled over, gasping for air. The man handed the keys to Sanchez.

"Stay where you are," he said.

He and Sofia proceeded down the hall to the room the couple had just left. Sanchez unlocked the door, opened it, and held his nose against an awful stench. As soon as he and Sofia entered the room the male and female fled upstairs.

Two unconscious bodies lay on a filthy mattress, a male and female. Their digits were blackened and bruised. On a table next to them sat a thumb screw and two cell phones. Two sets of feet came padding down the stairs and a moment later Joel and Lisa entered.

"Morgan!" Lisa cried, putting her hand to her nose.

Sanchez bent down to take a pulse from the bodies but there was none. He made the sign of the cross and said a quick prayer. Then all four left the room for the hallway.

The button on the electronic unit was pressed again. This time it ignited a small flame in the bible that Eugene had placed in the waste bin of the men's' room.

In the basement, Sofia gestured to the room that sat at the end of the hallway, the rectory.

"You should leave now," said Father Sanchez to Lisa and Joel.

"Not gonna happen, Father," Joel said.

Sanchez shrugged, "I hope you're prepared for whatever's behind that door."

He led his group warily down the hall toward the rectory, each one of them covered in sweat and fear. Seconds later, Sanchez tried the door knob and found it unlocked. That could only mean that they were expected. The four steeled themselves and entered to find the room dimly lit. At the far end, sitting behind his desk in the half-light, was Bishop Promane. He smiled as if he'd been waiting for his guests.

"How did you know?" asked the Bishop.

Upstairs in the sanctuary, a woman with her child sniffed the air. "What's that?" she yelled. Everyone turned to find smoke rising from behind the pews. Someone also ran out of the men's washroom, screaming. "Fire!" Security guards ran for the nearest fire extinguishers. Alarms rang throughout the building. Overhead sprinklers sprayed water throughout the church. Panic-stricken worshippers surged in every direction, trying to escape the sanctuary which was quickly filling with smoke. Security guards had their hands full trying to douse the fire and guide people to safety at the same time. Eugene, Gordon and Colleen slipped on portable oxygen masks they'd hidden in their pockets. Eugene raced to the altar and cracked open the plexiglass case with a crow bar he'd hidden in his pants. He slipped the robe out and stuffed it under his shirt. Then he made his way out the back door along with all the other panicked parishioners.

The racket upstairs filtered down to the basement and everyone in the rectory stared up, alarmed by the chaos.

"What the hell?" said Joel.

"Your family, no doubt," Promane said, looking calm and cool. "But don't worry, the robe is safe. You know me well enough to know that I would never be so foolish as to leave such a precious relic out in the open. The bishop reached into a small wooden chest that sat on the table in front of him and revealed the real robe.

"Magnificent, no?" said a female voice from behind them.

Sofia turned around to find her sister, Belle, standing at the door's entrance.

"I have no quarrel with you, Belle."

"Nor I with you, sister. All I ever wanted was to help you back to the righteous path."

"Me?" Sofia pointed at the man sitting across from her. "That man is a monster who destroys everything he sees to get what he wants!"

"My bishop only wants to prove to the world that God exists. You and your people have kept that evidence from everyone through your own arrogance."

"Children, please," said Promane in his most conciliatory voice. "I thought we were past this."

Belle was not about to relent and continued to lambast her sister. "You make decisions for the rest of the world when you fail to control your own life."

"My choices are my own to make."

"You mean like Antoine, the mama's boy who couldn't live with his own jealousy? Or pathetic Daniel who literally couldn't afford to put food on the table? What was your last shared meal, a few sticks of celery, bread and soup?"

"You spied on us?"

"He didn't deserve you. He kept you in poverty when you should have been living like a queen. Believe me, I did you a favor."

"You did me a what?" Sophia searched her memory of that fateful day and came to a startling conclusion. "You ran him over! You killed him!"

"My only crime was I wanted more for my sister."

Sofia screamed like a banshee, bared her claws, and charged at her sister. Bishop Promane stood up and threw a knife he had hidden in his palm.

The garden in the back of the church looked like a war zone. Smoke and fire hovered over the building as first responders tried to assist victims and push back onlookers to make room for arriving emergency vehicles. Gordon and Colleen stood amid the throng waiting for Eugene. A moment later he appeared. Because he'd used an oxygen mask, he seemed suspiciously unaffected by the smoke. One of the security guards approached him.

"You! Stay where you are!" yelled the guard.

Colleen collapsed on the ground to distract the security guard. When the officer turned to her, Eugene melted into the crowd.

Promane's knife landed firmly in the door frame, inches from Sofia's jaw. It was enough to stall her attack. Smoke was beginning to seep into the rectory.

"We need to leave," Father Sanchez said.

"By all means. Save yourself and your friends. He shifted in his chair to get a more comfortable position, but made no attempt to get up. Sanchez saw the panic in Joel and Lisa's eyes.

"I blame myself," said Sanchez to Promane. "If you had never found that scroll in my rooms, we wouldn't be here."

"Oh, I knew about the robe long before I saw the scroll. I'd been searching for it for years."

"How? The scroll is not mentioned in the bible or in any text."

The sound of burning wood crackled around them yet Bishop Promane and Belle did not look afraid.

"Only two men in history ever knew about the relic," continued Promane. "And when I reveal the truth, one of them will be the most hated man in Christendom."

"What?" said Joel.

The sound of chaos upstairs was growing louder and the situation becoming more dire. Still, Promane did not appear to be alarmed.

"This room," said Joel, "It's protected, isn't it? Flame retardant paint, wood, steel reinforced, something like that?"

Promane nodded but Sanchez said, "What do you mean?" he asked, "About the truth?"

"The final events of Christ's life are well documented," explained Promane. "The last supper, Judas's betrayal, Jesus' crucifixion, and his burial."

"And?"

"As you know, upon his death, a man named Joseph of Arimathea came to Pilote to plead for the body."

"Joseph, a member of the Sanhedrin?" said Lisa.

Promane turned to Lisa to acknowledge her. "Very good. Joseph was an admirer of Jesus and a man wealthy enough to give the master a proper burial. But he couldn't do it alone."

"He enlisted the guy in the painting with Jesus," said Joel, "Nicodemus."

Promane nodded and recited from memory, "John writes of the discussion between Nicodemus and Jesus one night, 'Rabbi, we know that you are a teacher who has come from God. For no one could perform the signs you are doing if God were not with him. For God so loved the world that he gave his one and only Son, that whoever believes in him shall not perish but have eternal life.'"

Promane sighed. "Pure fiction."

***

Eugene was sipping a beer in a downtown pub when Gordon and Colleen entered.

"Have a seat kids, beer's on me."

"You have it, right?" asked Colleen as she and her brother sat opposite their dad.

Eugene grinned and pulled out a fist full of cloth from under his jacket. "I just made you rich beyond your wildest dreams, baby girl," he whispered.

"Lemme see, dad," she said, gesturing for him to pass it to her.

Eugene slid the robe under the table to his daughter. "Waitress? Two more beers," he shouted. Then he took another pull of his drink, leaned in, and whispered, "This robe is going to fetch so much money that 'stinking rich' won't even come close to it."

After another guzzle, he got up. "Need to see a man about a horse."

After Eugene left, Gordon leaned into his sister.

"My turn," he said. "Lemme see."

Colleen handed the robe to her brother under the table.

"Hey," he said drunkenly, "Remember that thing the bishop did?"

Gordon spread the robe across his lap. Then he pulled out a pistol and handed the gun under the table to his sister.

"Where'd you get this?"

"Bought it. For protection."

* * *

"What do you mean, fiction?" Father Sanchez said.

Promane stretched his arms out in a way that indicated he was about to impart some enormous knowledge.

"It's widely acknowledged that the Gospel of John was not written by either John or any one man. The author or authors, in fact, are anonymous. If Jesus and Nicodemus were the only ones there that night, who else would have known what was said?"

"Are you going to dispute the text of the entire Bible? Any atheist can do that."

Promane shrugged. "And any clergyman or atheist knows that most of the Bible was authored by anonymous writers. If you want to accept it as parable, all well and good, go right ahead. It can teach you some very valuable life lessons. But if you want to treat it as an historical document then you'll have to dig a little deeper." The bishop shifted his weight. You must understand it was a dark age for humanity, slavery, pestilence, famine. Jesus' ideas to overcome those kinds of problems were so revolutionary that it would take brave and drastic measures to succeed."

* * *

"Are you crazy?" Colleen said.

"Don't you remember when Joel tried to stab the bishop and the cloth protected him?" Gordon said. "C'mon."

Colleen loved her brother and hated her father who had bullied and belittled them both for most of their lives. It was she and Gordon who devised the plan to steal the robe, not him. Yet Eugene was taking all the credit. Music was blaring, people were carousing. A gunshot from a small calibre pistol would hardly be noticed.

"Come on. We did it, you and I," Gordon urged.

Colleen put her drunken finger on the trigger and aimed the gun at the robe draped across Gordon's stomach. Gordon poured another shot of whisky in each of their glasses. They toasted and downed their drinks.

"Do it, Colleen. Show him."

"You stupid bastard." She laughed and pulled the trigger.

* * *

"What measures are you talking about?" asked Sanchez.

"That Jesus was willing to sacrifice himself for his beliefs was not in question. He and his disciples were all in agreement over that. After the crucifixion, Joseph supplied the tomb and Nicodemus supplied the spices required to give Jesus' body a proper burial. The prophesy, as you know, stated that on the third day Christ would be resurrected from the dead and Jesus would be declared the son of God."

"What measures?"

"The day after the entombment, Joseph asked Pilote to place a boulder in front of the entrance to prevent grave robbers from stealing Christ's body. On the third day, as you know, they removed the boulder to find the body had vanished."

"Get to the point, damn you."

"It was imperative that the prophesy come to pass. So that night when Nicodemus met with Jesus, the two made a pact to ensure that outcome. The night before the tomb was sealed, the evening of the second day, Joseph and Nicodemus removed the body."

"Blasphemy!" yelled Father Sanchez. "If that was so, what did they do with it?"

"Buried it in Potter's field."

"Potter's Field?" asked Lisa. "Where Judas was buried?"

"There were two reasons for that. First, it was common in those days for grave robbers to dig up bodies and steal whatever they could for profit. They wanted to protect Christ's body at all costs so the best place to bury a body was in an unmarked grave."

"And second?" Sanchez asked.

"As I said before, if not for Judas, Jesus would not have been betrayed and sentenced to death. Following that, Christ would not have been crucified and would not have become the spiritual head of Christianity – our hope for the future. Ergo, Jesus owed his legacy to Judas."

"They were brothers in arms?" asked Sofia.

Sanchez shook his head vehemently. "But according to you that makes the story of Jesus' resurrection false."

"The story survives as it was meant to," replied Promane. "Sometimes we need God's help, and sometimes he needs ours."

"Preposterous!" Sanchez said. "You said so yourself, only two people were at the meeting that night, Nicodemus and Jesus. So how could you know what was said?"

"Because that night the master told me that when his death came to pass as was preordained, that Joseph and I were to commit to the plan in order to ensure the prophesy realized."

It felt like the air had been sucked out of the room. When the group took its collective breath, Joel was compelled to ask, "You're saying that *you* are Nicodemus?"

"You cannot possibly offer a single shred of proof," shouted Sanchez.

"You are the proof! I am the proof! They are the proof!" Promane declared, pointing to Sofia and Belle. "You stand in a room among four people who have lived for over 500 years. Is it so hard to believe I have surpassed them by a few more?"

"By a few, you mean, fifteen hundred?" Joel asked.

"Methuselah lived for almost a thousand years. If you believe that, then how much more of a stretch is it to believe that a man could live for two thousand?"

"There is absolutely no scientific evidence that any person could live beyond one hundred and twenty years let alone two thousand," said Lisa.

"And yet you and millions of people like you believe a man dies and three days later, rises from the dead. You can't have it both ways." Promane paused to let his point sink in and continued in a calmer tone. "But your original question to me was, how did I come to know about the relic known as Judas' Robe? Because that is somewhat of a misnomer."

"You mean all this time you were lying?" asked Joel.

A small, knowing smile crept across Promane's face as he made his confession. "When Joseph and I buried Christ, we switched robes on the bodies to protect our lord from grave robbers."

"Your logic does not hold water," said Sanchez. "If a grave robber wanted Christ's body he certainly would not be fooled by the cloth. One died of strangulation, the other died of crucifixion."

Promane lowered his gaze as if revealing a shameful secret. "When we were finished, Judas looked the same as...his brother."

Everyone in attendance stared at Promane slack jawed, imagining the barbarism of the act.

"Considering Judas's role, wouldn't you have done the same to protect your lord?" Again, he waited for the group to consider his theory before he continued. "Yet I confess, in time, I came to regret it. Years later I even wrote an apology of sorts. I told the master's story as it actually happened, and my hand in it."

"The Gospel of Nicodemus," said Sanchez.

"It's a thing, as the kids say today. After it was transcribed, I tried to end my life but I could not. Then I realized why; God wanted me to atone for the transgression I committed. I swore to him that I would find Christ's robe and offer it back to him one day."

"Are you telling me...that the robe here in front of us did not belong to Judas, it belonged to Jesus?" Father Sanchez said.

Promane nodded. The revelations piling one on top of the other, were becoming so incredible that no one had any words.

Promane continued, "When I returned to my home, the apology was gone, missing. I learned that one of my servants found it. Reading it, he would have also discovered my crime and the true nature of the robe. I believe he took them both and left the city, not to sell it to the highest bidder, but to preserve the myth of our Lord's ascension. Then and there I made a vow to find and reclaim the robe. I became a thief, horse trader, an antique dealer, in order to avail my eyes and ears of any word of the relic. I searched for years. I followed up every rumor about the Gospel I'd written and the secret it held. Over time I became a Christian myself, hoping to offer penance for my transgression. I travelled across Europe and across time, ingratiating myself in the highest circles of the church until, in the 1400s, it finally happened. Pope Sixtus summoned me. He'd heard of someone who had news of the missing gospel and something called the Judas Robe. I asked the holy father to send me to Spain to investigate."

"Someone in my village told you about the scroll the Garcia family gave me?" asked Sanchez.

Promane nodded. "Unfortunately, there are always those who would put profit above conscience. My sins extend far beyond anything you could imagine." Promane stood up and stretched his arms wide. "Judas may be the most vilified character in the Bible but behold the real criminal. With the best of intentions, I robbed God of the opportunity to resurrect his son."

Every person in the room looked gobsmacked. Belle stared at the bishop like a woman betrayed.

* * *

The shot rang out louder than expected, causing the entire room to fall silent. A second later people ducked, screamed, and dropped to the floor in sheer terror. At that same moment Eugene exited the bathroom and saw his son slumped over the table.

"Noooo!" he cried.

Patrons raced to the exits, trampling everyone ahead of them in their effort to escape. Colleen sat frozen to her seat, watching the life blood slowly drain out of her brother.

***

Bishop Promane turned to Father Sanchez. "And now you're wondering why, Father, I disclose all this to you. Because now that you have heard my confession, I ask for your absolution."

"If what you say is true, there can be none."

The man who just confessed that he was Nicodemus rounded his desk to face Sanchez. Then he dropped to his knee in front of him. "Say the words, Father."

The priest could not utter a sound. It was all too much. Nicodemus grabbed the priest's hand and spoke the words in his stead.

"God, the Father of mercies, through the death and resurrection of his Son has reconciled the world to himself and sent the Holy Spirit among us for the forgiveness of sins; through the ministry of the Church may God give you pardon and peace, and I absolve you from your sins in the name of the Father, and of the Son and of the Holy Spirit. Amen."

Father Sanchez pulled his hand away in revulsion.

"Give me my penance, Father," said Nicodemus. "Only you can do this for me. Please, I would take on the sins of the entire world if I had to."

"Stop this abomination. I cannot absolve you. I wouldn't even know how, where to begin."

A wood beam suddenly cracked and fell through the ceiling, narrowly missing everyone in the room. Plumes of smoke seeped in and began to billow.

"We have to leave. Now!" Sofia said.

Joel grabbed the robe and rushed out the door, taking Lisa with him. Sofia stayed at the entrance to ensure their escape. The air in the basement hallway filled with smoke. Joel and Lisa fought their way up the stairs, their lungs burning with each labored breath. They made it to the main floor only to be confronted with a wall of flames. Each took a breath and raced right into them, bursting through the back door of the church and stumbling into the garden. Firefighters and police ushered them over to paramedics who put oxygen masks on their faces and tended to their burns. Moments later, Sofia emerged followed by Belle and the man who called himself Nicodemus. They too, were surrounded by paramedics. Sofia reached out to her sister but Belle was inconsolable. The man she worshipped as a God had failed her.

The building began to convulse and implode under its own charred weight. Police forcibly pushed back the throngs of onlookers into the cemetery grounds for their own safety. Belle noticed the bishop standing there and traipsed over.

"You swore to use the robe to unite the world under the one true religion," Belle cried to the bishop.

With a mixture of love and remorse he looked into her hate-filled eyes and asked, "Are you my Judas?"

Then he opened his arms to embrace her. Belle took two steps forward and shoved him with such force that he fell back onto the hundreds of sharp glass fragments. His body twitched and twisted. He stared at Belle with a mixture of pain, joy and relief. Until at last he closed his eyes. Paramedics ran to his aid but it was too late. The man who had lived for over two millennia had at last gone to meet his God.

* * *

Two hours later, firemen were still dousing the last of the flames in the church grounds, but the worst of the carnage was over. The death toll from the fire stood at twelve with dozens more injured. Witnesses said Bishop Newman was one of the last people to escape the building, probably ensure that no one was left inside. The word 'saint' was used over and over. Rumors spread that he suffered a fatal heart attack while trying to save his followers and died in the very cemetery he'd built for them. A new myth was born. Five blocks, away three survivors sat in a coffee shop.

"I don't know," said Lisa. "There was too much confusion, I lost track of him after we got out of the church."

"He escaped," Sofia said.

"Yeah? Where to?" asked Joel.

"Father Sanchez left to seek peace in his own way. It's no longer his battle. It's yours."

Joel took a sip of coffee and wondered out loud, "My mother's gone, he's gone. What do I do now?"

"Well, on the bright side," Lisa said, "the Bishop's also gone."

Sofia put her coffee cup down and levelled her eyes at Joel. "But not my sister, Belle. And there is no telling what her state of mind is."

Joel shook his head and slapped the table with his hand. "I never wanted any of this."

"Neither did your mother, neither did I," replied Sofia.

Joel turned to a Walmart bag that sat next to him. He reached inside and ran his fingers over the ancient cloth to confirm that, in fact, it did exist.

"The question is," Joel said, "do we tell the world or do we keep it a secret?"

EPILOGUE

Nine days later Joel returned to the Biopharm labs. He'd made two promises to his mother, finding the gene that caused her condition, and guarding the robe. And then there was his obligation to Marie Champlain, a lot for a young man who once had no one to worry about except himself.

Joel crossed over to Father Sanchez's work station. It had only been a matter of days but he missed the man terribly. Looking over his things, Joel felt his presence. He opened the drawers and pulled out the priest's notes. Leafing through them he found a blood slide taped to one of the sheets with a handwritten note. He read the words, took the slide, and inserted it under a microscope. Something was different. He rushed back to the notes and opened another drawer that sat beneath the first one. Inside lay a vial of blood marked 'Sanchez.' He looked from the blood slide to the vial, to the notes and back again. Incredible! The gene they'd been looking for was present in the priest's blood sample and identified in his notes.

A smile crept over Joel's face as he picked up the phone.

"Marie Champlain, please. Tell her it's Joel Gardiner." 'One miracle at a time,' he said to himself.